THE SPINWARD FRINGE SERIES

Spinward Fringe Broadcast 0: Origins
Spinward Fringe Broadcast 1 and 2: Resurrection and Awakening
Spinward Fringe Broadcast 3: Triton
Spinward Fringe Broadcast 4: Frontline
Spinward Fringe Broadcast 5: Fracture
Spinward Fringe Broadcast 6: Fragments
The Expendable Few: A Spinward Fringe Novel
Spinward Fringe Broadcast 7: Framework
Spinward Fringe Broadcast 8: Renegades
Spinward Fringe Broadcast 9: Warpath

Fantasy
Brightwill

Horror Adventure
Dark Arts

For other books by Randolph Lalonde visit:
www.RandolphLalonde.com

Spinward Fringe Broadcast 6.5

THE EXPENDABLE
FEW

Randolph Lalonde

Print ISBN: 978-0-99373989-7
EBook ISBN: 978-0-9865942-6-7

Special notes to the reader:

The author would like to thank you. Your support and appetite for stories set in the Spinward Fringe universe made this experimental book viable. Without you, the ideas driving this novel would only exist in a pile of notes in a trunk. The characters, story and ideas here are better now that they've been brought out to breathe.

This novel takes place between Spinward Fringe Broadcast six and seven. If you haven't read the series, please look for Spinward Fringe Broadcast 0: Origins, available for free from Smashwords, Amazon, the iBookstore, Barnes & Noble, Kobo and many other eBook retailers.

**FREEGROUND INTELLIGENCE
PERSONNEL ONLY**

This is a dramatised record of events surrounding Clark Patterson based on recordings made by his Command and Control Unit's auto-logger, security records, neural captures, military files, and action reports. For educational purposes only.

**FREEGROUND INTELLIGENCE
PERSONNEL ONLY**

CHAPTER 1
OLDEST OF FRIENDS

"You've got to get rid of this contraband before they do a random inspection," Mary tells me as she looks through three data chips that she knows are as dirty as they come. The small, light gold bits fit in the palm of her hand - easily hidden from anyone but a Freeground scanning crew.

I ship out in sixteen days. That's why she's worried; they always scan commanders' quarters before you ship out. "Can't believe that's contraband now," I tell her. "Especially at my pay grade."

"Let's see if I remember," she says, holding the first of the chips up between us. She's sitting cross legged on the floor, I'm stretched out on the sofa. "This one is your collection of Valance's security footage."

"You learned a few things," I remind her.

"Sure, after nine hours of watching a bounty hunter do his job, I'd better learn a few things. It's the twenty hours of him walking around with his crew that I don't understand."

"There's only five hours," I say.

"Okay, only five." She holds up the second data chip. "This one, with the notch on the side, has the outlawed First Light documentary, and Jacob Valance's public speeches. That last bit is enough for them to dock you a month's pay and put you under active watch for a whole tour."

"Not the worst that could happen," I tell her. Yeah, what she's telling me is true. I'll pass those data chips along to someone else, maybe Kevin. Nothing I have is enough to get me drummed out of the service, but I could end up being passed over for promotions for a few years. At least until the political climate changes.

She shakes her head, tsking at my indifference. "This last one, with a big divot on the top side..." She sighs, drawing her playful scolding out. "All the service records of the First Light Crew, recordings of Ayan Rice, and Ayan Rice the Second. I mean, I'd shag her in a heartbeat, too, but if Freeground Fleet found this with the other two chips you wouldn't just have Intelligence on your ass, you'd be calling down Admiral Rice, her mother. That's like naming your executioner."

"I know, I know." I laugh at the mental image of one of the most well known admirals in the Fleet sitting down across from me in an interrogation room. I've never met the woman, but if she's as severe as she looks in the Fleet News Casts, then it would be an experience I'd never forget. "Last time they scanned my place two days before I shipped out. I'll get rid of that stuff five days ahead."

"Why don't I just take them tomorrow?" Mary asks, holding them up like tiny playing cards. "I mean, what's the real difference between five days and two weeks?"

"You just want my Ayan collection."

She blushes a little, caught. "Ayan the Second, but only because she stood up in front of the highest court-"

"You like the curves," I tease.

"Hey, she fought for reincarnate rights. I applied for that program, remember? If I get slagged in combat I'd like to know that my parents can grow another me and copy my scans into her, and that Mary two-point-oh will be able to continue where I left off."

I didn't press. Practically everyone in Fleet and the Infantry applied for the reincarnation program, myself included. The possibility of getting killed was becoming more real every time one of us shipped out, and the galaxy was becoming a more violent place all the time.

"And because I like the curvier version of Ayan," Mary admits after a long pause. "I like a natural figure."

We have a laugh. It's good to have her back. She had been gone for two years, not the longest stretch, but it wasn't always easy to keep in touch. Mary is like my second sister. We grew up together in Pod 1414, or what they call 'B Pod Two' because it's the second pod the British from the outer core worlds settled in. My parents returned to Edinburgh after my second tour. Mary's dad stayed in Freeground station when her mother left. Her mom couldn't stand the embarrassment of Mary coming out as a non-breeder: a lesbian. That's a massive taboo in a breeder culture. The social drive tells people to have families, to fill the empty habitation pods with children who will grow up in this isolated space station and never know what's out there.

The breeder culture really took hold six years ago, when people started leaving Freeground in droves. The tactic was to encourage heterosexual coupling and marriage. Big emphasis on marriage and keeping the most honest part of the breeder culture behind closed doors. They want families, not a few million over-sexed youths taxing the social system, after all.

It hasn't worked. People are already sick of their entertainment being saturated by sappy love stories and family adventures. Everyone who's smart enough to realise that the approved entertainment and social activities on Freeground are really a form of social programming protests in his or her own way.

Mary works out to the point of obsession. She's a one point eight metre tall soldier who wears tight fitting vacsuits just so she can show off.

I keep contraband about a group of patriots who went out into the galaxy to help the Freeground Nation only to find out that their sheltered lives didn't prepare them for what they found. I'm sure I don't know everything about their journey, but from what I can piece together, they managed the ship Freeground Fleet gave them very well, developing technology that was rushed into service later. But they couldn't deal with the culture they met out there, and in the end they didn't see betrayal coming. A former Freeground Fleet Intelligence officer named Wheeler was supposed to work with them on a critical mission and burned them in the end. He made a deal with the enemy, Vindyne Corporation, and sold out the First Light crew.

That crew, led by Jonas Valent and Ayan Rice, was celebrated for a long time. I had been in the service for eight years when the First Light returned with some of the heaviest combat damage I'd ever seen. Jonas Valent had sacrificed himself so his crew could get back home.

Years later, recordings of someone who looked a lot like him started turning up on the Stellarnet, the unregulated galactic data network. Surveillance videos of this bounty hunter going under the name of Jacob Valance added a new chapter to the First Light story, and only a short time later Ayan Rice stole a prototype ship to go after him. She died before long, and Ayan Rice the Second was born on Freeground, a genetically pure woman who was given all of her predecessor's memories. She was the beginning of the Resurrection Program. When Freeground refused to grant her the identity and rights of the first Ayan Rice, she left.

That's when all footage of Jacob Valance, the First Light, and her crew became contraband. As if that wasn't bad enough, other former crew members of the First Light abandoned their posts, including Captain Terry Ozark McPatrick, who had just been given command of the refitted version of the First Light carrier. They renamed it the Sunspire, and that became its own special kind of disaster.

"Lost in thought?" Mary asks.

"Just thinking about the First Light crew. They changed everything. I don't see it when I'm out there on a starship," I point to the star field outside the transparent steel window in my quarters, "but whenever I get back home it's like the Puritan Party is desperately trying to stuff the genie back in the bottle."

"It's not working," Mary says, dropping into an arm chair and stretching out. "Especially since the Puritans contradict themselves all the time." She yawns. "Find a partner, start a family, but don't show skin in public, don't quit your job if you manage to spawn six kids, and don't ask for public money if your marriage doesn't work out."

"You're the poster child for resistance, with two citations for public affection under your belt. Well, I'm glad we get a pass in the military, that's something."

"Oh, that's another thing. Random arrests at public protests, and us military folk get officially reprimanded for appearing. No wonder a few thousand people were leaving every week before the transit ban," she says.

"That's lifted. More people are leaving than ever," I tell her. She just got back, so she's not all caught up on recent events.

"Wow, big win for the Nationalists," she replies. "Hey, mind if I bunk here for a while? There are promotions coming up, and my chances might be a bit better if I pretend I'm hetero for once."

"As long as you don't mind my alarm going off early. I have to send my sister off tomorrow, she's leaving for Edinburgh Colony."

"Connie's leaving?" Mary said.

"Yup. She's changed in the last two years," I reply. "We barely talk now unless it's on Status Comm, through the network. I think it's because of the new behaviour guidelines."

"If I weren't in Fleet, I'd go with her."

Edinburgh, light years away from Freeground, part of the extended British Colonies. It's not perfect, but it's centuries old, and if what my parents say is even half true, there's a job for everyone and a whole world with hundreds of cities to live in, to make a life. It makes my four room quarters and the habitation pod we live in seem stifling.

As Mary and I are huddled together in bed a little later, I can't help but think about my parents, and maybe following them after my next tour. In my dreams, the bare sunshine warms my face and I don't feel like the eyes of the Puritan Party are on me every second of every day.

CHAPTER 2
GATE 2807

Freeground station has fantastic space ports. There are five major ones in use by the general public, and numerous other commercial ports. Military ports are separate and secure. I put my Freeground Fleet uniform on that morning by mistake. It's just a habit, and when you're stumbling around, concentrating on trying not to wake someone up, habits can take over.

Mary snores through me taking a shower, having coffee, and getting dressed twice. Most of my adult life has been spent on starships, properly dressed for duty; the loose fitting civilian vacsuit doesn't feel right. My long black trench coat is part of my commander's uniform. It's worth a minor citation if I wear it with civilian dress, but I wear it anyway. No one I know has been cited for mixing and matching their weather gear in the time I've been serving. It's an ignored regulation these days.

The boots I'm wearing are almost exactly the same as the ones I wore when I led a burster shuttle against the Courageous. That was the last mission Mary and I had together, a fantastic conclusion to that chapter of my career, and to the time we had on the same crew. There's nothing like having a squad leader who knows you so well that you swear you're communicating telepathically.

My heavy kickers echo in the subdued environment of the departure deck. The black metal deck is like a stark canvass where hundreds of travellers slowly creep up the lines to the boarding gates. Through the transparent hull above I can see hundreds of ships making their way around the East Port Pod. This is my fifth visit to a departure gate since the end of my last tour. I've sent off more friends since I've been back than I have in years.

"So, I'm all clear," my sister says with a forced smile.

I embrace her for a good long time and end it with a squeeze. "You tell Mom and Dad that I'm only a couple of years behind. I'm doing one more tour and then I'm out of this can." She's twenty four, five years younger than me. I still remember when she was a toddler, following me around endlessly. It was annoying back then, but now it's one of those memories that makes you laugh, adds weight to love.

"You've said that before," Connie reminds me. She's on the verge of tears. "I'm not going to tell them unless you're sure."

"Oh, I'm sure," I tell her in a whisper. "No doubt in my mind this time. I'll even try to take Mary with me."

"All right, I'll tell them. You stay safe, though," she says, a tear escaping and rolling down her right cheek. "Make it through the tour, it's dangerous out there."

"You haven't heard? I'm the great Commander Patterson; another tour on a starship is like vacation."

The boarding light paints the people around us green. "That's the last call. Give us another hug," she tells me.

I oblige and kiss the top of her blonde head. "You know, I saw this coming. How long can a botanist live in a space station? Forests in an oversized can can't be like jungles in the wild."

That brings on the short laugh that I was looking for. Even with our differences we always manage to cheer each other up when it's important. "Okay," she pulls away, wiping away tears. "I'll see you after your next tour. Promise me, Clark."

"I promise." I say it, I mean it.

There are quiet, quick goodbyes happening all around us. I shouldn't feel alone when she walks off with luggage in tow. We've parted ways more times than I can count, playing this scene in a mirrored stance over and over again. Maybe that's it. This is the first time I'm sending her off.

When I shipped out I always hated the short stretch of time while I stood in line after we'd said our goodbyes. I knew she was looking, that I was being watched as I slowly made my way through the queue. I never knew whether to look back and acknowledge her or just stare straight ahead, providing a last, stoic image of myself before disappearing into space. I stare at her. It could be years before we see each other again, and unlike many officers I've known, I tell my sister everything when we get together.

She turns towards me after a while as though suddenly realising that I'm watching from behind the blue line and makes a shooing motion. I laugh silently, something that probably looks pretty strange to a few people around me, but I don't care. I don't care about being late for work, either; it's only report overview. I'm one of those poor sods who checks over other officers' work if they're on probation. It pays well, and I get to keep in touch with Fleet from the dockside instead of getting rusty while I wait for my tour in the field to begin.

Connie gets to the gate and smiles at the guard to the right. They are in full plated, dark green combat armour and stand a head taller. She's nervous. The guard on her left steps behind Connie, expertly gathering her wrists behind her back.

Connie struggles, and the guard snaps a quick restraint band closed around her midsection, pinning her forearms to her back at awkward angles. I realise I'm running towards her when I burst through the front of the line.

"Hold there," the remaining guard says, putting his hand out.

I finish crossing the space between us in a few more steps and my training kicks in. It doesn't matter whether or not he's wearing combat armour - leverage is leverage. I kick the back of his knee as I plant my hand against his shoulder. He hits the ground and I keep running towards Connie. Alarms go off, the whole area is painted red.

"Stop! I can clear this up! I'm a commander with Fleet!" I call after the other guard as he shoves my sister to the ground and turns on me, drawing his sidearm.

Other guards are rushing towards the scene, and I'm suddenly aware of how badly I've handled the situation. I put my hands above my head slowly and get on my knees. "I'm Commander Clark Patterson with Freeground Fleet. That's my sister, Connie Patterson. I can clear up whatever's going on."

Connie twists towards me and our eyes meet. From where she's laying on the deck she mouths, "I'm sorry," and everything gets worse.

"I'm sorry, Commander," the guard tells me. "You'll have to take this up with Fleet Intelligence."

Then he blasts me in the face with his stunner.

CHAPTER 3
TRUST

What's the first thing I realise? My Command and Control Unit, the cornerstone to communication and a device that's been on my forearm for ninety-nine percent of every day of my life for years, is gone. I'm laying down on a firm cot. When I open my eyes the rest of the picture comes clear.

This is my first stay in the stockade. Cheap metal walls, moulded plastic floors and ceilings. Old fashioned bars keep me in. A metal toilet and sink are there to keep me clean.

"Good morning," says someone from beyond the bars. It's a woman with black pin-prick eyes and a too wide jaw. It's like genetics dealt her a bum hand. Why people like that don't get modifications when they come of age, I'll never know. "Call me Shannon."

Just like that I realise I'm talking to Fleet Intelligence. No rank, no presentation of docket number or charges, and she's wearing a dark green and grey military vacsuit without insignia. She doesn't even have a Command and Control Unit. "So, how are you folks going to disappear me? Airlock? Matter recycler with the safeties disabled?"

"You have a dark impression of us, Commander Patterson," she says, a little too slowly. I already want to rattle her by the shoulders until answers start falling out.

"Why did you detain my sister?"

"She's a traitor, what the Order of Eden calls a West Keeper," Shannon says, leisurely crossing her legs and straightening a crease in the sleeve of her vacsuit.

"Bullshit," I reply, stretching the word out, weighing it down with my disbelief and outrage.

"All the evidence is there, Commander. Two months and three days ago, she sent her hundred thousand credits in from our planet-side colony and received an encoded transmission. A few days after you returned from your last tour she started relaying everything you said to the Order of Eden. You really should watch those family status taps. Anyone related to you can track everything you do."

I stare at her as these ridiculous words come falling out of her little mouth. It feels like my skull is shrinking. There is no worse enemy to humanity than the Order of Eden. They released a virus that infected artificial intelligences everywhere so they would attack anyone who didn't send one hundred thousand Regent Galactic credits in. West Keepers are their spies, and, to my knowledge, no one I know has ever met one. "Bullshit," I repeat.

"Tell me," Shannon starts, completely unaffected by the situation. "Has your sister had more interest in your job than usual? Especially through Status Comm? You're in a sensitive position, overseeing probationers. They're located across the fleet, and you're qualified to monitor infantry as well as fleet officers. I see your general aptitude tests scores are relatively high. You're an intelligent man, think about it."

I don't want to think about it. There's a better reason behind any evidence she's presenting here.

"She was taking that transport to Icarus. From there she would travel to Aphrodite, an Order of Eden world where followers are rewarded for service." Shannon leaned forward in her chair, her beady dark eyes peering into mine. "Do you know what she traded to reach that kind of status in the Order? It's like leaping from Ensign to Captain in a week."

I search through memories of conversations I had with Connie over the network since I've been back and catch myself. There's no way she's guilty, why am I even entertaining the idea? "She doesn't have the access." The officer in me takes over for a moment. "Let me see the evidence. You have the wrong woman and I can prove it."

"She gave them the location of the Sunspire," Shannon whispers. "That ship that you've been checking in on because you're such a fan of her former crew. The crew that ran her when the ship was called the First Light - Jonas Valent, Ayan Rice, Terry McPatrick, and so on - your obsession with that dark spot of history led her straight to it. Now the Order of Eden are sending ships into the Sunspire's hunting ground."

"I was researching the Paladin incident," I explain. I don't know why, something about this bitch makes me want to talk.

She smiles at me, obviously satisfied. "And you happen to have the clearance to see exactly how the Sunspire destroyed a super-carrier while under the influence of the Holocaust Virus. Where were you when you looked up that information? Think for a moment."

I was in my sister's living room, waiting for her to return from the store. "Let me see the evidence," I repeat. "Please. I have to clear her."

"Fleet Legal, Intelligence, and a Parliament representative have reviewed your sister's case. She'll be executed in twelve hours," Shannon says as she stands and starts walking towards the outer door in one motion.

"She's innocent!"

The outer door opens.

I rush to the bars and collide with them so hard that I'm sure I crack a rib or two. "Please! Give her a reprieve so I can look at the evidence, speak with her representative!"

"Her lawyer has already applied for a stay, it was denied. We're reviewing your case next," Shannon says over her shoulder as she passes through the thick outer door. It slams shut behind her. Grief thickens time, stretching minutes into what feels like hours and days.

At first I'm frantic, trying to find a way to get my sister free of this situation. "Let me see her!" I shout at the walls, knowing that surveillance is picking it up. "She's innocent!" And finally, in my desperation I add, "It was me! I'm the West Keeper!"

I'm dealing with Fleet Intelligence. I know none of it will work. They act on evidence. I could tell them I'm a spy representing every organisation that's ever stood against the Freeground Nation but without proof they'll just leave me alone. Taking the blame for whatever Connie's done won't save her.

Whatever she's done. Just like that, I believe it. Connie has been interested in my history of service, in the supervisor work I've been doing whenever we talk on Status Comm. She even put up with me gabbing on about my fanboy fascination with the First Light crew. I believe it all and collapse onto the cot. "Let me see her," I say to whoever's watching, hoping they haven't forgotten their sympathy. "Please."

CHAPTER 4
POWERLESS

Hours pass. Enough hours for me to start thinking that I'll never see my sister again. I can't handle it. I've seen people fall apart in the service before. I admit that I've never sympathised. I thrive in the command structure, love travelling beyond the invisible boarders of the Freeground Nation, and I consider myself a die hard patriot. Just like Jonas Valent when he set out. He lost his parents in a terrorist attack, and it broke him. He didn't commit to another tour of duty until they cornered him into it.

When I woke up this morning, I loved Freeground Fleet, even with the complications that it brought into the lives of my friends and family. Right now there's nothing I hate more, and I've never hated so hard in my life. You can't sit idly while that kind of inferno burns you alive from the inside, so I start doing pushups.

The cell is only just wide enough for me to go all out, and I welcome the burn when it comes. I'm pumping the deck away from me so hard that I'm getting thirty centimetres of air by the time I hear Connie's voice. "I'm so sorry, Clark," she says.

I slip and scrape my hand, then roll onto my side. The hologram is so perfect that it's like she's standing over me in the cell. I know she's somewhere else, but every instinct drives me to take my baby sister in my arms. "The representative they gave me tried everything, but when you're guilty..." She sighs, tears rolling down her cheeks. "God, I told myself I wouldn't fall apart." She shakes her head.

"They won't show me the records." My lame way of trying to tell her that I'm doing everything I can. "I can't even pull rank." An idiotic way of saying I want to stop what's happening, but can't. Her holographic image kneels down and looks me in the eye. I've never felt so small and powerless.

"Mom and Dad are already on Icarus," she tells me. "It was my idea." She starts sobbing so hard that she has to heave breath in. "They're safe, happy. There's no safer place-" she used to hyperventilate when she was young, and for the first time in a decade she can't breathe.

"It's all right," I reassure her. I'm up on my knees, wishing I could take care of her one last time. "Just breathe, everything will be fine." It won't be.

Someone injects her with something; I only see a white gloved hand. Just like that, she can breathe again, and she looks me right in the eyes. "I'm guilty. I was approached on the Freeground colony before the riots," she explains in a rush. "I've been spying for the Order ever since so I could move to Icarus. Nowhere is safe if you're not with the Order of Eden, not even Freeground, and I wanted to leave, to see forests and live in a real colony."

I find a hidden reserve of strength and smile at her. "It's all right, I don't blame you. You're a botanist trapped on a space station," I explain for her. I even start convincing myself.

"It was so stupid," she warbles. "I love you Clark, I'm so sorry."

"I love you, Sis." I reach out and pretend to touch her holographic cheek. The tears flow under my fingers unswept.

"I have to say goodbye now," she says, uncharacteristically resigned. The little sister I know is a brawler, a fighter when things get tough.

"I love you," I repeat.

Like a phantom the hologram fades. Desperation and grief take over.

I picture her being gassed to death in a hollow room. I'm on my feet screaming, hurling myself at the bars so hard that before long, I'm bleeding from somewhere. The pain doesn't matter. Visions of my little sister and the partnership we had for as long as I can remember stoke the inferno in my head.

My vision narrows, and the last rational shred of me realises that they're filling my room with odourless, invisible gas. The difference between the gas I'm getting and what my sister is breathing is that I'll wake up. The world spins one last time.

CHAPTER 5
PART 1 - TIME

Mad gas. I can't smell it, I can't see it, but something is holding me down on my cot. High school wrestling with Sarah Piper comes to mind. A girl with two first names, who was twice my scrawny weight back then. Damn girl took to the mat with me in co-ed phys-ed, and the class laughed as she flipped me down and smothered me to the floor with her soft-yet-crushing bulk. Through one eye I could see the class laughing as I was mashed into the mat. They're laughing now, as my body feels so heavy on the cot that I try to tap out, and manage to flick my index finger instead. Tap-tap - little tap out. Can the ref see this through the circle of laughing students? My laughter joins in, and the echo reminds me of where I am.

The cell. I'm sinking into my cot and remembering that my sister is gone forever. I feel guilty for taking a break under Sarah Piper, about spending even a moment without thinking about Connie. My face feels hot, a tear pools in my eye and grows as I refuse to roll my upturned face. Moving is out of the question while pressed under a girl with two first names. Laughter bubbles up through my lips and it turns into a short wail as I regret the strange, amusing mental image. My vision is blurry, like I'm sinking into a shallow pool, then I feel a tear break free of my eye and roll down the side of my face.

My chest expands and rattles, filling with air. It doesn't feel natural. It's as if someone flipped a switch and my body is rebelling against my grief by taking deep, slow breaths. I don't want to calm down, I want to remember my sister and wonder if she was forced to perform in some elaborate scenario, in some kind of ruse. Maybe I'm a candidate for Freeground Intelligence, and it's all a test. Holograms can be faked. My sister is smarter than that. The alternative explanations cloud my pain but before I know it I'm remembering sitting at her table after dinner, arguing about censorship and the transit ban. She was never much of a patriot.

I don't know how long I had my eyes closed, or what I was doing under those heavy lids, but when I open them, Shannon from Fleet Intelligence is standing over me with some squat-headed doctor. I can tell he's a doctor because he has a long white coat and those searching eyes. I chortle, surprised by the man with the too-short head. It gives his face an unnatural roundedness. "Commander Patterson, can you hear me?" His head splits in the middle with each word like some kind of pre-school puppet. It's at the same time horrifying and the most amusing thing I've ever seen.

"Flip top head," I whisper as I tap my fingers on the mattress - tap-tap, little tap out.

"What did he say?" Shannon says. The way she speaks, the way she looks is completely normal.

"It's the ichni," says the doctor, his head flapping open and closed with each syllable. "He's under such a heavy dose that he's hallucinating."

"Will he remember everything we're saying?" asks Shannon, taking no notice of the Doctor's unusual physiology.

"What good would this treatment be if he didn't? Be careful, his subconscious is wide open."

I check the top of my head and, to my relief, find no new orifices through which they can access my subconscious. Then I remember how heavy my hand is and it flops onto the mattress.

"Do I ask the questions now?" Shannon the Fleet Intelligence officer asks the Doctor in a whisper.

"Yes, but do not deviate," Doctor flip-top head replies.

"Commander Patterson," says Shannon, raising her voice slightly as if there was something wrong with my hearing. "You are undergoing an expedited trauma treatment so we can get you back onto your feet as soon as possible. Is there anything I can get you?"

"New doctor," I manage even though my tongue suddenly seems too big for my mouth. "This one's too..." I hesitate to finish the thought.

"Doctor Marlin is the best we have," Shannon tells me. "You're in good hands."

"Marlin is a fish," I comment aloud. Just like that, everything made sense. I blink a few times and they're both gone. The passage of air across my teeth, tongue, down my throat and into my lungs becomes a conscious thing. Thoughts of better days, and a time of innocence begin flowing in and out of my thoughts. At best it feels like my life is being rolled out onto an examination table, at worst it's as though it's being repackaged so it can be placed in an overhead bin. Save it all for later, it does this soldier little good spread all over the floor, tripping him up.

PART 2 - PATIENCE

I don't know how I got here, but all that matters is the exercise table on my lap. Put the block in the square cutout. Put the ball in the circle cut out. Punch the octagon button when the red light flashes, the square when the yellow flashes, and when the table beeps I've done it all correctly and fast enough. I feel like I've been doing it for hours from the edge of my bed. Why is this hard?

Just as the thought occurs to me, Doctor Marlin - I've started calling him Fish - stands up from his fold up chair and fixes me with a grin. "Very good. You beat your best time from Academy training," he tells me.

I look back down at the table balanced across my knees and realise that the simple puzzle I was doing is gone. Maybe it never existed. Instead I'm looking at a VX-77, or Vex, as we used to call them. It's the nastiest handgun anyone in the Freeground Fleet is allowed to carry. My hands remember what I was actually doing: disassembling and reassembling the deadly double barrelled death dealer.

A pair of hands takes it and the padded lap table away. I look up and the Doctor is leading the way out of the cell. "You have a visitor," he says.

I'm still stunned, feeling as though I have been asleep for days. The ache that sat in my belly like a stone doesn't seem as important or overwhelming as it once did. My sister was a traitor, and now she's a dead traitor. Images of her appearing in my cell, or of our past together, don't come up at the recollection of recent events this time. It's as if the connective tissue between the fact of her death and those memories has been weakened.

Mary Reed enters. Her eyes nearly boggle at the sight of me. Still, she doesn't rush over. Instead she pretends there's nothing wrong and sits down beside me. "They've got you pretty heavily medicated," she says as she wipes the corner of my mouth with her long sleeve. She's in loose red and black striped prisoner's clothing. For the first time I realize I'm dressed the same way. "I'm probably pretty heavily medicated," I admit slowly.

She laughs and puts her arm around my shoulders. I didn't mean to say that last bit aloud, but hearing her laugh feels good. I always enjoyed that, making her laugh. I lean towards her and my head lands in her lap. I close my eyes and see myself picking up that Vex hand cannon, raising it to my temple and pulling the trigger. I don't know where that ultra-clear image comes from, it's just there until I feel her hand stroke my face. Life gets easier, everything feels softer.

"They're running you through accelerated rehabilitation," she explains. "A lot like Minh-Chu Buu started when he got back, only with a real kick."

"Got you, too," I tell her.

"Yup. I thought I'd come in here and break your nose since you got me locked up. I was holding your contraband when they took me in for questioning," she tells me. "But I'm not one for preying on the defenceless."

"Sorry," I say. "So sorry."

"It'll be okay," she replies. I've never seen her take care of anyone before, but she's doing a pretty good job. "A little time in the stockade never did me any harm, especially in isolation. Besides, no point in pretending I'm anything other than who I am anymore."

"Wonder where you'll get stationed?" I ask. My speech is still slow.

"Well, I'm not getting busted down to private, but there are a lot of new restrictions on my file, so it'll be interesting."

"Wonder when they'll fire me," I ask, picturing a military policeman entering my cell and announcing my discharge. It's so clear in my mind's eye that I'm sure he'll be standing right there if I open my eyes.

"They don't work this hard on commanders who are about to get drummed out of the service," she chuckles.

That leads me to a far darker thought. "Will I be me?" I ask.

"What's that?" she asks as though prompting a child.

I don't mind. A little soft condescension goes a long way in my soft-headed state. "Will I still be me at the end of therapy?" I ask, chortling at the ring of the rhyme.

"I'll make sure," she promises. "I'll tell you all about yourself." They let us stay together for a long time, even though I can't think of anything to talk about while she's cradling my head in her lap.

PART 3 – PRUDENCE

"Open your eyes, Clark," says the big voice from above.

I'm struggling to stay on my feet in the middle of an arid plain. The sand swirls around my feet, the sun summons beads of sweat from my pores. Everything feels heavy again, but I remain on my feet. "Where am I?"

"What do you want to do, Clark?"

What a ridiculous question. In all directions there's nothing but sand, scrub bush, and sky. I meet the question head on with a worthy answer. "Dig a hole." It ceases to make sense the moment I speak it aloud. "For water," I add, trying to sound a little more intelligent. My mouth is dry. I check for the emergency water tube in the collar of my vacsuit and, to my surprise, find it. I stick the tube in my mouth and bury it in my cheek, sucking precious moisture.

"You're hydrating, very good," congratulates the voice from above. "Now find your way out."

I want to lay down, but find myself looking in each direction. The heads-up display from my comm unit appears before my eyes. My fingers feel my left wrist for my command and control unit but find nothing but bare vacsuit. I ignore that discrepancy and glance towards the scanner icons in my peripheral view. Within a few seconds I locate a map of the area - I'm in the Scacha Valley, the nearest town is called Christine. It should be surrounded by a landing field.

Without a second thought, I seal my vacsuit. It begins cooling my skin, lowering my body temperature back down to normal, and I start walking. Despite weariness and leaden limbs, I place one foot in front of the other, sometimes having to steady myself by extending my arms, but one step follows another.

My lids begin closing on their own, as heavy as emergency bulkheads. I force them back up every time, eventually gnashing my teeth and grunting forth. This is a battle for survival. There are no medical scans available from my vacsuit, I keep trying to scan myself, but the system isn't working. I could be injured, drugged, there's no way for me to know. I have to use any time I have to get to civilisation, it's my best shot at surviving.

My eyes close again, and I hit the ground as limp as a training dummy. I try to press against the ground, to get myself back up on my feet but fail. The sounds of running feet come towards me, the sun goes down in an instant, and then I see something that can't be real.

On the First Light, that ship I once studied, there was a Doctor named Carl Anderson. He was at once the advisor and the overseer of the First Light crew. He allowed them to make their own decisions, but reported their actions back to Freeground Intelligence. He's running towards me now, in a black vacsuit with red pinstripes down the arms, legs and shoulders. The official Freeground Intelligence uniform that I've only ever seen in training manuals.

Doctor Anderson turns me over onto my back and disables the hood of my vacsuit. "Just breathe, son. The air is cool, you're in your cell."

A few blinks later, I realise that he's right. I'm in my cell. He's kneeling over me. Doctor Marlin is standing behind the bars. I'm still in my prisoner's uniform. My limbs still feel like they're weighted down, however. It's difficult to move.

"What the hell are you doing to him?" Doctor Anderson asks, appalled. "He's a few cc's away from overdosing."

"He's becoming more difficult to manipulate," explains Doctor Marlin. "We have to perform this series of tests now, before it's too late."

"This series of tests? What kind of testing is this?"

"We're trying to find out how ingrained his training really is. The order came down from Fleet Command; he's not to be released until we are absolutely certain he can perform."

Doctor Anderson picks me up and puts me down on the bed. I'm like a child in his arms. He has more grey hair than he did in his profile. Other than that, he's exactly as I would have expected. "He finished the grief therapy, what else are you going to take away from him?"

"Take away?" asked Doctor Marlin irritably. "We're making sure he's ready to reenter service. This deep psychological character and skill building could save his life, and the lives of those under his command."

"This stops here," Doctor Anderson says. I'm watching, my mind a complete blank. "You're going to let the ichni and everything else in his system wear off, give him a chance to sleep for a day or two, then you'll call me and I'll give him his choices."

"You should take a look at the regimen I have scheduled, maybe you'll understand what it is I'm trying to accomplish, Sir."

Doctor Anderson shakes his head slowly. "I don't care. As of today, you're on vacation. Don't come back to this facility for a week."

Doctor Marlin wordlessly retreats, walking down the small hallway through the secondary security door.

Doctor Anderson looks at me and smiles warmly. "Three weeks with him dosing you up and pushing your buttons. I hope there's enough of you left after you've made your way back through the looking glass."

CHAPTER 6
THE ART OF BEING CONCIOUS

For the first time in I don't know how long, I wake up. I'm not feeling like I'm seeing through a fog, my limbs feel as light as they should, and my head feels like it's the proper size. I'm not in a cell anymore. Instead, I'm in a small bedroom overlooking the docking operations of a port I've never seen. This looks like Freeground.

I keep looking and realize the construction is slightly different. This is a super-carrier. I'm on the Amazon, the quarantine section, by my best guess. It makes sense; I'm a criminal, and the quarantine section of a super-carrier is just as isolated and secure as a prison. The difference? Comfort, and the promise that I may be free to visit other parts of the ship.

Through the floor to ceiling transparent metal window, I see half a dozen patrol carriers - four hundred twenty metre ships with launch bays stretched across the front, giving them the look of snakes grinning with slightly parted teeth - all docked a few levels below. My room is simple. A fairly comfortable bed, small lockable dresser, narrow closet, and a door that will lead to a toilet and sink.

Before I know it I'm basically washed up, wearing a basic spray-on black vacsuit and sealing my combat boots. This room is in a barracks somewhere, and they're officer's quarters, so I haven't been demoted too far. The memory of my last conversation with my sister comes back and I feel absolutely nothing. I know that's strange, but don't care enough to dwell. It's time to figure out where I've ended up.

I leave my room and enter a common lounge. There are several older-looking armchairs arranged to view the port through a transparent section of hull and a couple of tables with metal chairs around them. The room is octagonal, four stories high; three walls are transparent while the rest feature three levels of quarters. Each lets out onto a walkway with stairs regularly spaced around. It doesn't look like any barrack configuration I've seen before.

It's dead in here. At a glance I count four people in the seats, all with their backs facing me, looking out at a carrier that's almost centred in view, its engines flaring as though it's trying to keep up.

One of the people stand and look at me. It's Mary Reed. It feels like everything happens in the wrong order. I smile, then I feel like smiling at her. I wonder why I'm smiling when I see this woman, then realize that we've been friends since we were toddlers. It's all backwards, but by the time the muscular, expectant woman is standing in front of me, it feels like everything's back where it should be - emotionally speaking.

"How bad is it? Did they completely reprogram you, or did Doctor Anderson catch you in time?" she asks, stroking my cheek with her palm.

I have a flash of her taking care of me in a dark cell, my head on her lap, and I catch a hint of what that forlorn moment felt like. Before I realize it, my smile is gone. "There's enough left," I tell her. "I think.",A slim faced, gum chewing soldier spins his chair dramatically and asks; "Soldier! What's your name? Your serial number? Rank? Which pod did you hatch in?"

I answer before thinking. "I'm called Clark Patterson, oh twenty eight nine seventy dash thirty five, Freeground Fleet Commander-"

"Ignore him," Mary says with a look that tells me that my young inquisitor is someone she tolerates more than likes. "That little wanker has a strange sense of humour."

"Where are we?" I ask.

"You are aboard the Amazon," replies Doctor Anderson as he stands. He's looking at me with the reassuring smile I've seen in videos. "As of two days ago, you all separated with dishonour from the Freeground Fleet and were pressed into the Grey Section of Freeground Intelligence."

"He's going to tell you that you serve with them or spend the rest of your good breeding years in prison," the copper topped soldier says from his seat.

"Ensign Sands is right," Doctor Anderson confirms. "How are you feeling, Commander?"

The question is more important than it should be. Normally I'd mechanically answer with 'I'm fine,' or offer some bravado bullshit like 'ready for anything' but this moment is slow. I look from Doctor Anderson, who I still half-believe to be an illusion, to Mary, who stares back with expectation, to the new guy who's watching me like I'm the eight AM show, then back to the doctor. It feels like Sarah Piper is pinning all my emotional extremes to the mat, muffling my peaks and valleys leaving only the boring, middle range of feeling. Before I realise it, I tap my leg twice. I don't think anyone else notices. "I feel numb."

"Let's sit down," Doctor Anderson tells Mary and me. We take seats in a semi-circle in front of that big window. For the first time, I see the last person enjoying the lounge. She's curled up in an arm chair, her long dark hair half obscuring her face as she sleeps. I recognise her, but can't remember where from.

Sands claps and folds his arms as if to hide the act.

The woman, who looks younger than me by five, maybe even ten years opens her brown eyes and they focus right on me. I can't look away as she slowly smiles. On a station with millions of pasty white citizens, she's blessed with features that are every shade of human brown. Beautiful.

I manage to tear my eyes away as she stretches into a yawn.

"All right, everyone, let's welcome the commander properly," slim-faced Sands says. "Name, rank, and tell him a little about how you earned your spot here."

Doctor Anderson settles into the last seat in the semi-circle and watches us.

The dark young woman answers first. "I'm Lieutenant Isabel Fonte, pilot with all vessel class qualifications and a small ship combat specialisation." She looks at Sands. "How we earned our spot, Remmy?"

"Your offence. I think we're all here because we've been bad little citizens, so spill."

"Oh," Isabel says, straightening up. "I organised a protest in the parliamentary pod against the travel ban. After it turned into a riot they tossed me into the stockade." As soon as she says protest I remember the various news broadcasts depicting her as a terrorist, a villain to social order.

"That riot was over a year ago," Mary says.

"Yup. Thought they forgot about me until Doctor Anderson turned up."

"You mean they didn't actually put you on trial?"

"Nope. They kept rescheduling me. I was never even arraigned." She looked to Remmy. "Your turn."

"Me? I was caught red handed with enough digital contraband to properly entertain half of Freeground for the rest of their lives. As if that wasn't enough, a little Order of Eden propaganda got mixed in by mistake. Well, maybe not always by mistake, no one knows how to capture a holographic tour of a nature preserve like those Order weirdos. There was this holo of a hawk gliding over the mountains on Eden Prime... I'm telling you it was like you could smell the pine trees. There was another-"

Isabel clears her throat.

"Right, Order of Eden propaganda bad, Puritan Party propaganda good," he says, correcting himself. "But, yeah, they sentenced me to fifteen years. When Doctor Anderson came for me I was working on month three. I don't think they managed to completely reprogram me while I was in there, I almost feel like myself again." He leans forward in his chair, looking at me. "It gets better. In a few days you'll feel almost normal."

"Good," is all I say.

"What did you do to get the worst case of brain burn I've ever seen, anyway?" he asks.

"My sister tried to defect to the Order of Eden," I tell him mechanically. "They executed her."

"Wow," Remmy says, leaning back. "Family turning to the enemy. That's a career ender."

Mary takes my hand and squeezes it. "Commander Patterson was also charged with gross social misrepresentation and dissemination of contraband. I was charged with gross social misrepresentation, possession of contraband, and assaulting an officer of the court."

I stare at her, wondering how the last charge came about.

She must see the question on my face, because she smiles back. "My lawyer called me a stupid dyke so I broke her nose and called her a puritan breeder drone. I think the harsh language hurt more."

"I think I'm in love." Remmy swooned exaggeratedly. "Why do I always fall for unavailable women?"

"Anyway, I'm an infantry sergeant, specialist in ship to ship incursion."

Mary glances at me and answers Remmy's questions. "The commander here was in line to become first officer on the Dimitri."

"Wow," Isabel says, straightening in her seat.

"The Dimitri's right on the front line with twelve thousand aboard," Remmy says. "That's a seriously high-end commission. I think I've only met two or three officers who have ever had that much pull."

"That's not going to happen now," I tell him passively. I actually wanted to sound irritated, peevish at least, but it just comes out like everything else: flat.

"Yeah," Remmy says. "Sorry."

"I hope you don't mind me speaking for you, Clark," Doctor Anderson says.

I shake my head.

"The commander was undergoing deep reprogramming so he wouldn't turn on Freeground Fleet until I managed to get through the red tape and take him into my chain of command. He finished the first course of treatment, so he'll need about a week to come all the way back to us."

"Personality revision?" asks Isabel quietly, sympathy written all over her face.

"Do you mind if I tell them?" Doctor Anderson asks me.

I don't see withholding anything I've been through as important. In fact, as I give him my consent with a nod, I start feeling that I want people to know. Like a revelation, it strikes me that I might not have deserved anything that was done to me.

"Doctor Marlin and his team finished administering deep grief treatment, re-prioritisation, and they were just starting on combat fitness reinforcement."

"They were trying to turn you into a drone," Remmy says. "Brutal."

"I got there in time," Doctor Anderson tells them. "Clark," he says as he turns to me. "You were sedated for a day after you were placed in my custody, so some of the re-prioritisation programming could be rolled back. As for the grief treatment, that's something you'll eventually have to break through, but I doubt you'll ever completely overcome it. The combat fitness reinforcement wasn't a factor, they were only in the early stages of assessing your readiness so there wasn't much of an impression made. You should feel mostly like yourself soon, just like Remmy here said."

"Sedated for a day," I say. Everyone is hanging on my every word. "No wonder I had to piss so bad when I woke up." I deliver the punch line slowly, but they're laughing before I finish.

"What about us?" asks Isabel. "They had me dosed for at least a few days."

"Most of the modifications to Remmy's personality didn't actually take," Doctor Anderson tells them. "He was about to go under for another round of intensive treatment. As for you, Isabel, well, they were drugging you for passive interrogation, getting you to relive the last few months of your life aloud so they could record the names of your co-conspirators and other anti-Puritan Party citizens. Mary here was just starting a round of sexual reorientation. I was able to get the backing of a few New Liberal Party representatives in securing her release."

"Thank you," Mary tells him. "Thank you very, very much."

"Don't thank me yet," Doctor Anderson says. "There are conditions." He pauses and stands, pacing into the space between us and the window. "First, let me tell you about myself. For over thirty years I've been indirectly involved with the politics of Freeground. Not intentionally, mind you, I hate politics. The first time I got involved was when my partner and her daughter were exiled from the British Colonies for violating the limitations placed on genetic engineering. As an Intelligence Officer, I assisted the British exiles in securing asylum, then citizenship on Freeground. When the question of military service came up, I was one of the official supporters of British exiles with military experience serving in the Freeground Fleet, a move that the Puritan Party opposed then and won't let me forget now.

"After the British exiles were settled, I was allowed to retire from Freeground Intelligence and pursue my medical career, putting as much distance between me and the political arena as possible. However, I often served as a watcher for Intelligence while serving as a medical officer, which made me perfect for an assignment on the First Light. As some of you already know, I was the intelligence oversight officer for the duration of that short tour. I retired again to pursue research in genetic restoration and advanced maturation. After completing my first human trial with Ayan Rice, she decided to leave for various reasons. The Puritan Party began calling her departure a defection when they secured a parliamentary majority, and she's been branded a traitor along with most of the surviving First Light crew.

"The New Liberals don't see things the same way. Most of them believe that the First Light mission never ended. They look at Ayan Rice, Minh-Chu Buu, Oz, or Terry Ozark McPatrick as you know him, Jason Everin, Laura Everin, as well as Jacob Valance and see a group of people who are gathering an incredible amount of information about the galaxy beyond our borders. They also acknowledge that they may be forming relationships and gathering technical knowledge that could be crucial to the survival of Freeground in the future. Saying so in public forums is beyond taboo, however. Captain McPatrick and Jason Everin are deserters. If they returned, they would face charges of treason, desertion, terrorism and sedition. They're guilty of two charges on that list, and would be executed."

"So, how do we fit into this huge mess?" asks Remmy. I can't help but agree that it's about time we were told, not that I'm ungrateful for Doctor Anderson's timely save.

"I'll get to that in a minute," Doctor Anderson says with one of his gentle smiles. "With the help of several representatives in the New Liberal Party, a few active and retired friends in the military and other people in power, I've been reactivated with my former rank in Freeground Intelligence. Colonel Gregor McPatrick has been reactivated as well, and we've been gathering people into teams so we can recapture the Sunspire before the Order of Eden finds her."

"Okay, so we're going to join one of those teams," Remmy says, his eyes as round as saucers. "And by Sunspire you mean the former First Light, the ship that took out the Paladin."

"That's right. The Sunspire was renamed the First Light when it was assigned to Jonas Valent and his crew."

"But when their mission failed," I start mechanically. The story of that crew, the ship and the events since are like gospel in my mind. I recite. "The ship was refitted with technology the First Light crew brought back and renamed the Sunspire. Eventually Terry Ozark McPatrick was put in command in name, but it's well known that there was so much oversight that every decision he made was scrutinised and criticised. He and Jason Everin left to find out if Jonas Valent was still alive, because a man who looked a lot like him, Jacob Valance, was running around the galaxy, cashing in as a bounty hunter. The Puritan Party and the Order of Eden call him a terrorist, but if you watch his speeches, you'll realise that he's a freedom fighter." I look from one face to another before going on. They're all paying attention, mildly surprised that this information is coming from me, but all intensely interested. "Then the Holocaust Virus started infecting artificial intelligences, forcing machines to kill anyone who wasn't a member of the Order of Eden cult. The Sunspire was infected, killed everyone aboard and began patrolling the Blue Belt, destroying targets of opportunity and any ship it couldn't infect. The biggest kill was the Paladin - a mobile space station twelve times her size."

"Thank you, Commander Patterson," Doctor Anderson tells me. "Colonel McPatrick and I are almost finished recruiting crew members to take the Sunspire back. When she's under our control, he'll assume the commission of captain while I'll lead the Intelligence unit. You are one of five groups I'm recruiting specifically for my operations. You all have infantry training, great overall ratings, and specialisations that will be critical in the very near future." He takes a moment to check our reactions. Mary leans back in her seat, cool and quiet. Remmy's mouth is hanging open. Isabel actually looks equal parts excited and shocked. I'm a spectator. This is a holomovie and I'm just hoping I'll like the ending. Doctor Anderson goes on. "You can sign up with me or go back to prison. The current government won't allow you to return to Freeground station proper unless it's in chains, so after your service with me is finished, you'll all be free to leave Freeground space."

"But not to return," Isabel says. "We're exiles."

"Exactly. The political environment could change given time, maybe in your lifetime," Doctor Anderson tells us. "But the Freeground you return to won't be the same as the one you left."

"What's the mission after we retake the ghost ship?" asks Remmy.

Isabel smacks him in the shoulder. "Don't call it that."

"Why? That's what the Sunspire is - no crew, all automation, killing everything it sees."

"All you have to concern yourself with is retaking the Sunspire," Doctor Anderson tells us. "We'll be in range of the Blue Belt and her hunting ground in about two weeks. You have that long for recovery, to learn everything there is to know about the ship, and to get some coordination going in group sims. We plan on taking the Sunspire with a few hundred soldiers, so every group will have to be sharp. By the time we arrive, I need the four of you to be a command crew."

Hundreds he says. Hundreds against a ship that wrecked a carrier twelve times her size and has the soul of a serial killer, stalking its victims in the Blue Belt. I'm almost glad my mind is still a little hazy. I let my idle eyes drift towards Isabel, who sends me a warm smile that almost cuts through.

CHAPTER 7
RANDOM TESTING

The revived necrotic veins of the reanimated crew of the Sunspire are shambling towards us. The moaning, cracking, and scraping sounds are a result of flesh forced into service after its time.

The four of us, Mary, Remmy, Isabel, and I, made it all the way to the transit control system before getting cornered. Now there are hundreds of them in our area, and, who knows how, but most of them remember how to use weapons. I step behind a reinforced service door and fire my Vex without looking. There are so many of them stumbling and jerking towards us that I know I have a good chance at hitting *something*.

"How the hell did this happen?" asks Isabel.

"Nano-medicine," Remmy replies. "The Sunspire managed to take direct control of the crew by infecting their brains, or maybe their nervous systems with nanobots. Those nanobots must have built cybernetic nerve controllers, so this crew are pretty much deadly puppets."

"But some of them look..." Isabel hesitates, taking a moment to fire her Vex sidearm several times. She plugs one squarely in the forehead, burning through the protective layer of the slack faced crewman's vacsuit. She follows up with a second shot, misses, then burns through the upper half of his head with the third. "Well, some of them look dead."

"The nanobots are obviously building life support systems into some of these people," Remmy says as he desperately tries to hack into the onboard transit system using his communication unit.

"This is ridiculous," Mary says as she takes cover to reload her rifle. "Why the hell would the Sunspire go to all the trouble of reanimating the whole crew? It would be less complicated and more reliable to build defence drones. That, and they wouldn't have a habit of slipping in their own drool."

"I don't think that's drool," Remmy says from where he's taking cover across the hall.

"I've chosen to believe it's drool," shouts Mary, slapping a fresh clip into her rifle.

"But it's not. Observe the colour and lumpy-"

"Don't fuck with my comfortable ignorance!" Mary replies as she pulls the trigger, sending particle bolts through the next wave of mindless crew.

"Hey! I think I got it!" Remmy shouts, finally. "Get ready to get on the main tram! It's straight to the control column from there!"

As promised, the tram behind us lights up, and the doors open.

We rush in, me in the lead and Mary at the rear, firing at the mob to keep them at bay just long enough. The doors close and the tram car starts to move down the length of the ship.

The simulation ends; we completed the primary objectives. Our eyes open and we are back in the lounge.

"Well, that was bullshit," Mary says, removing the little input node from between her eyes. "Zombies? Really?"

"I know," a tall, grey haired man says from where he is sitting closest to the window. "It was thrown in as a half-joke by Doctor Anderson. You've finished all the sims we wanted to test you with, and I'm more than a little surprised."

I look him over in the dim light and recognise from the red slashes up his arm that he's a colonel. He also bears a remarkable resemblance to the last commander of the Sunspire, Terry Ozark McPatrick.

"I didn't mean any disrespect, Sir," Mary says peevishly. It's something she does: offering an apology with enough attitude to cancel it out.

"You were ordered to enter the simulation and complete the tasks assigned. You did so without letting your opinion get in the way. You have nothing to apologise for, Soldier," replies the Colonel. "It doesn't matter that it was the Doctor's idea of a joke."

"I thought it was hilarious," Remmy says, grinning.

"What did you think of the simulation, Commander?" asks Colonel McPatrick.

"I thought it was unlikely. I doubt that's happened anywhere, and I couldn't imagine an artificial intelligence would see that as the most efficient way to crew their ship."

"It has happened, technically. The science is based on the work of a researcher who lived a couple of centuries ago. Don't tell Anderson this, but I find the similarities between that researcher, a fellow named Doctor Shawn Gray, and our Doctor Anderson a little too clear. Their kind might have brought us the vacsuit and artificial gravity, but genius is unpredictable, especially behind closed doors."

"I'm of the same mind, Sir," I tell him. It's true. The Holocaust Virus is the first example that comes to mind. "It's an honour to meet you."

"I wish I could say the same," Colonel McPatrick says as he stands and straightens the top of his black and red uniform. "I don't like the idea that the best people Doctor Anderson could find for our mission are also the most disobedient and least trustworthy citizens. You're the last of the five teams aboard. Visiting the other four has twisted my stomach in knots. If my nephew wasn't out there, making Freeground Fleet look like a ragtag, do-as-you-please drifter colony with guns, I would have stayed in retirement."

I did not expect that from someone like him. He's fit for his age, and seems as sharp as any commander I've ever served under. Hearing his opinion is insult piled on top of injury. I do my best to disregard his attitude.

In the two weeks since I was released from therapy by Doctor Anderson, we haven't been told what the specifics of our mission will be, only that we're in a mobile station and are on our way to the Blue Belt. We're to retake the Sunspire and remain aboard after, but the question of why has never been answered. "So we're going to be tracking down your nephew after we take the Sunspire back," I say.

"Bullshit mission," Mary says, barely under her breath. She's the only one who would dare do so. Isabel and Remmy have fallen into the habit of letting me take the lead when speaking to superior officers.

"Secure that shit!" Colonel McPatrick barks. "I won't take mouth from officers who can't follow simple rules while they're in civilian dress."

Everyone recoils in their seats. The colonel has a voice that could crack bulkheads.

He takes a breath and lets it out slowly. "The Sunspire will eventually make her way to a location near Captain McPatrick, and an attempt to retrieve him may be necessary. The Sunspire is a carrier, and as such, we can run several missions at a time. Yours will be made clear after the ship is recaptured and her fitness is determined. I'm here to congratulate you on your performances in the simulation testing. The four of you scored second highest out of the five command crews Doctor Anderson recruited, so you'll be leading a full boarding contingent onto the Sunspire. You'll receive the mission details in thirty hours, brief your unit in thirty two, then you'll depart this station in thirty four."

"Is there any way we can get the details sooner?" I ask. It's always better to know earlier rather than later; knowledge is essential to preparation.

"No. You'll get the details when you get them."

"Colonel," Mary addresses, sitting rod straight in her seat. "Why didn't you get officers with spotless service and civilian records for this?"

"You're too smart for that question, Sergeant," Colonel McPatrick replies. "If this mission were in line with the political alignment of Freeground right now, then I would have the people I want. The Puritan Party doesn't want us operating out here at all, but we managed to get this mission going thanks to some political manoeuvring and a willingness to work with the trash of Fleet. They don't expect us to succeed, and if we do it'll be a big win for the New Liberal Party."

"Big deal," Mary replies.

"Permission to speak freely," I whisper to her.

"Oh, fine," she spits. "Permission to speak freely, Sir?" she asks Colonel McPatrick.

"Out with it," he replies.

"Why do we care? We could cut and run at the first sight of an unguarded hyperdrive equipped shuttle."

"You care because a short term of service is the path of least resistance to real freedom. The galaxy isn't what you think it is. There's chaos out there, and it'll eat you pod-born children up like chum. At least when Fleet Intelligence is done with you we'll make sure you've got what you need to make a go of it.

"Besides, If you run, you'll be found. I'll hunt you down myself if I have to. Then you'll be executed. If you serve for a couple of months, and we get a few key objectives taken care of, then you'll be freed into exile and when the New Liberals come into power, we'll see about allowing you back. No prison sentence, no executions, you'll be bloody heroes to the opposing party. It's better than you deserve."

"Thank you, Sir," Isabel says. Her soft voice and smallish appearance seems to momentarily disarm the colonel, who turns on his heel and starts for the door.

"Orders in thirty hours. Be rested, be ready," he says without looking back at us.

"Sorry about all this," I say to Mary. I know Isabel and Remmy earned their way into the situation with their actions as civilians, but Mary is another story. She was caught with my contraband, and I can't stop feeling guilty.

"What? For helping me keep my career mostly trouble-free by pretending to be my boyfriend for years?" Mary asks. "If it weren't for you, I'd still be a private, or I would have been shifted into the Fleet re-training program as a low-grade tech."

"You were caught with my contraband," I remind her.

"Yeah, that's nothing compared to evidence of years of gross misrepresentation. Bet you didn't know there was a scanner in your bedroom. They knew something was up when there was no record of us having sex in the six years we've been faking it."

"Oh," I reply, feeling deeply stupid. Freeground Fleet specifically stated that their staff's bedrooms and bathrooms were safe from surveillance, but that was before the Puritan Party took power. "I should have known better."

"You're not the only one," Mary says. "I'm gonna go clear my head and get some shuteye. See you in ten hours."

"You never even threw him a freebie?" Remmy asks. "I know you're a lezzie, but not once in six years?"

Isabel smacks him in the back of the head, not for the first time either. "You really don't get people at all, do you?" she asks. "Mary's like his sister."

"Oh, right. That could be nasty," Remmy admits. "Sorry, Clark."

"No worries." I sit there, looking out at the glittering line stretching across the transparent section of hull. It looks like a tightly grouped parade of stars, but I know it's the Blue Belt, the Sunspire's hunting ground. The mobile station is decelerating towards it.

"Need snacks," Remmy says, rising from his seat. "You guys want anything?"

"No thanks," I reply.

Isabel shakes her head.

My comm sends a tingle up my arm and I look at it, summoning the message. HEAD'S UP! ISABEL ASKED FOR THE ALL-CLEAR AT LUNCH.

I delete Mary's message, wishing she'd given me more notice. The 'all-clear' is something that women ask Mary for when they want to make sure she wouldn't mind if things got intimate with me. Even though Mary tries not to stand in the way of my relationships by giving the wrong impression, women who are interested - and there haven't been many - always feel they have to have a talk with her on the side, as if she's my coital guardian.

Isabel and I have shared plenty of time since I woke up on the Amazon, sometimes alone, just talking. She likes to talk about home, and her huge family. I heard the few latino communities are busy, with children everywhere and a rich culture that hails back to old Earth days. In all my years on Freeground, I have never set foot in one of their pods. I even visited several of the primarily Oriental pods, but never the Latinos. After talking to Isabel over the last two weeks, I wish I had.

All I have to offer in return are war stories. She asked about my family, but nothing could interest me less. I thought I was the most boring sod on the ship.

There are times when I can't stop looking at her. Isabel's got this smile that makes you feel warm inside; you forget about everyone else in the room. When that moment ends, I start thinking that she just has this great way of looking at people, and that it's how she looks at everyone.

I think about that message, combine the fact that Mary has never been wrong, and it dawns on me that Isabel probably doesn't regard everyone with that special smile. Our long talks may lead to something, and for the first time since grief therapy, bona-fide emotions start taking hold. That excitement is like being born again.

Everyone but her and I are gone. She slides from her seat to her feet and steps up to the expansive window. Her feminine silhouette is tiny against the alien constellations outside. She wears a loose, long sleeved over-shirt cut at the midriff. I stare at her a moment, admiring how the black, form fitting vacsuit seems to disappear in the low light. Her delicate form cuts a dark shape out of the star field. It took millions of years of evolution to create something small and perfect to stand between me and an ancient universe.

Not a thought passes through my mind as I quietly find my feet and cross the space between us. My arms are around her and her shoulders shrug into my chest, making my body a home. "I used to sit in front of the windows and stare at the stars. As soon as I could walk, I'd get as close as I could and watch them as they drifted by." She sighs, unfolds her arms and pulls mine around her more tightly, resting her hands on mine. "I don't remember how old I was when my father showed me that we were the ones who were turning, the stars were staying still. I think I started realising how big the galaxy was then. He was a mechanic, but turned me into a pilot before I knew how to say navigation."

"He sounds like a great man," I tell her.

"No, not a great man. He's a good man. Gave us everything we needed, was so proud of me," Isabel says. "Until I got myself locked up."

"I'm sorry," I say.

"All my life I wanted to be out here. Now I can't wait to finish whatever they have planned for us and find a safe place to wait until they'll let me go back home."

"We'll get there," I tell her. The reassurance feels hollow. I hope it rings true in her ears.

She stares out at the stars, slowly caressing the backs of my hands with her warm palms. "They're so much brighter out here."

"You've never been this far out?" I ask.

Isabel shakes her head.

We stand there for a long time, her back leaning into me, before she breaks the silence. "You and Mary have gone on boarding missions before. How are our chances?"

I want to reassure her, but it doesn't feel like there's enough room in the moment for a lie. "I heard someone from the Paladin call it a demon ship. They tried to board the Sunspire before it was too late. Only a couple survived out of a thousand marines. It's not going to be easy, but I don't think people like Anderson and McPatrick would try it if it were impossible."

"You could have lied," Isabel says, turning her face to the side so she can read my expression. "Make me feel better."

"Sorry."

"Remmy would have lied," she says, a hair away from touching my lips. "But that's why I'm with you, I think. You don't back away from hard answers."

"A lie is a rock waiting to be overturned. The truth is a stone you can build on." They're better words than I usually find in intimate moments. I don't know if it's the conditioning or an effect she has on me, but I've never had so much confidence.

"I like that," she says with a smile. "Yours?"

"Minh-Chu," I smile back.

"One of my favourite pilots." She's a tease whose nearness is telling me what she wants, but refuses to do the taking. That millimetre between our lips may as well be a mile filled with the rules I'll be breaking as her senior officer. I cross the distance and she reciprocates, kissing me as if she's been looking forward to it for weeks. She reaches back over her head and runs her hands across the back of my neck. I'm wrapped in the sensations of the moment: the faint smell of lilac in her hair, the sounds of us breathing, parting lips and, most of all, her body leaning into me. It's only when it's happening that I realise I've wanted to be with her since I first saw her. Everything I sense from Isabel tells me I'm welcome.

My hands flatten against her, pressing as they cross over her stomach, around her waist. Isabel's nails trace up and down the back of my neck as I caress her. It's a rare collision of chemistry and unrestrained sensation. I've found my way out of the haze I've been in for weeks and she feels incredible. We're locked together, wordlessly living in a timeless moment.

It goes on in a trade of warm caresses and long kisses. The past, the future, and all of creation cease to matter as we enjoy each other without restraint. She's summoning a gale of emotion where for too long I've felt muted gusts.

Isabel turns towards me on tip-toes so we're chest to chest. I run a hand across and down her back, over her hips, and lift her off her toes. Isabel squeals and lets a little laugh slip between our locked lips. Her hands grip my vacsuit beneath the back of my neck, as if I'm still not close enough.

The rustling of a snack bag opening behind us fractures the warm cocoon.

"Don't mind me," says Remmy before popping a cherry-flavoured rice puff into his mouth. "This beats anything on holo."

Momentary embarrassment gets crushed by irritation as I fix him with a look that would make an Order of Eden platoon take a step back.

Isabel kisses me on the cheek, whispers, "I'll see you tomorrow," and sets off to her quarters. I watch the sway of her hips as she goes, wishing more than anything that I was following. She spares me a glance and a smile before the door slides closed behind her.

I'm about to throw my hands up in exasperation when a bag of rice puffs hit me in the side of the face. I glower at Remmy, who shrugs. "Sorry, thought you were ready."

I snatch the bag of tomato and vinegar flavoured rice puffs from the floor and walk over to Remmy, who eyes me warily. He flinches as I take his bag of rice puffs out of his hands, up-end it over top of him, and shake the contents out in a shower of snack food. I let the empty bag fall and take a seat in an arm chair.

He watches me open my bag of puffs in silence. Then he snickers.

I look at him out of the corner of my eye; he has rice puffs in his hair, his lap, a couple balanced on his shoulder, and he's suppressing a grin.

He plucks one from his hair and pops it into his mouth.

I suppress a chortle that comes out of nowhere.

As casually as I could imagine, Remmy takes the bag in his hand and starts putting the rice puffs back inside, one by one.

I burst out laughing as though it's the funniest thing I've ever seen, and Remmy joins me. For a good long time the sound of us cracking up fills the common area. When it subsides I ask; "What are you watching tonight?"

"From my extensive collection of early colonial dramas," Remmy starts with a flourish, "I'll be playing For the Love of Water."

Colonial dramas aren't normally my thing, but I stick around. There's no point in trying to go to bed, I'd just lay there trying to get to sleep.

There was no forgetting Isabel, but I have to admit that I enjoyed the holographic movie. There's something very simple and enjoyable about hanging out with Remmy. If he has any expectations of the people around him when he's off-duty, they're completely hidden. Being yourself is almost too easy. Truth be told, while I'd rather be with Isabel as the show starts, I don't mind spending time with the youngest of my team members after the frustration subsides.

CHAPTER 8
ADRIFT

Our shuttle rotates slowly amongst the drifting asteroids. The dwarf star illuminating that section of the Blue Belt comes into view. My helmet compensates for the naked light.

I watch the light colour the lazily drifting stone and ice around us. Another plane of stellar leftovers orbit the star, glittering blue-silver. The movement of the distant ring looks slow, but anything caught in it would be mulched in seconds. Like so many things in space, it's beautiful from afar, but deadly at close range.

A gargantuan ship emerges from a wormhole above the asteroid rings. "There she is," says Mary from the deck below me. Four squads of marines surround her, half of what I'd like for this mission. "Wake up and check your gear. We didn't get all dressed up for nothing." She's in command, and no one dares question it. It's a worthy position. I've seen her command troops during an incursion before, and I can't think of anyone else I'd like to see in charge.

We are not the only shuttle adrift, waiting for the show to start. If we fail, they'll ask, "what do you expect from traitors and law breakers?" If we succeeded there will be no celebration, only quiet acknowledgement in the back rooms of the New Liberal Party offices.

I don't know whether it's the programming they crammed into my head during grief therapy or if it's my upbringing, but I still want to show Freeground Fleet, or Freeground Intelligence, that I can still get the job done. I want Mary to show them that they've underestimated her value, as well.

The shuttle continues its rotation, giving us a better view of the Amazon, the twelve kilometre long command carrier that brought us to the Blue Belt. The light of the star falls on the technical crew around me. We're on the upper deck, overlooking the soldiers below. Isabel stands in front of me at the controls of the shuttle, waiting to initiate the thrusters. Remmy and three other communications techs are behind me. A group of nine other tactical and mechanical specialists make up the rest of our team. Most of us are watching in anticipation, hoping everything goes as predicted.

Even though the Amazon rivals most space stations in size, it still looks like nothing more than a dot against the backdrop of the blue star. I zoom in on it with my heads-up display, examining her hull. Outrigged engines turn to fight the force of gravity, long B-90 rail guns and shield emitter arrays extend along her length, mixed in with with long stretched equipment booms. Obvious, and showy - perfect bait.

I look up her length, over the Amazon's thickly armoured skin to the forward-most section. There are three sections fanning out from the front of the ship. Each is as large as the average modern Freeground Cruiser, and just as heavily armed. Repair bots, called scurriers and scrubbers, are already launching to perform a quick inspection of the area. "There are people aboard that ship that will probably only leave for vacation," says Isabel. "Could you imagine calling that thing home?"

"The Paladin was home to four generations," Remmy says. "Until she was jumped by the Sunspire a couple of light years from here."

"I'm surprised they're risking the Amazon for this," I say.

"The New Liberals are the majority government aboard the Amazon," Remmy says. He'd know. Despite his generally flippant attitude, he's a good communications and intelligence officer. It only took me two weeks to realise it.

"No more chatter. We should get a bite soon," I say. My memory of the Sunspire tearing into the Paladin and finishing her off is enough to put me well on edge. When the combat footage was made available yesterday, I made sure to watch it three times.

The Amazon is the last of her kind; Freeground won't build another super carrier even half her size. The Sunspire demonstrated to everyone how vulnerable the largest of our ships can be when they are caught by surprise. That, and the fact that the Puritan Party are big advocates for hoarding raw materials, prevents the construction of another mobile base.

A wormhole opens, lensing the light from the blue star into a furiously intense point. Then, within six kilometres of the Amazon's port side, the Sunspire emerges.

The kilometre long ship is propelled by three main tilting thrusters at the rear. One flares out at the top, the other two spread out side by side, set behind the main mass of the ship. Her smoothly shaped, silver-blue hull broadens at the mid-point, stretching out into thick, close curved wings that have two more tilting thrusters near the ends, and ram scoops across the front. The ship's fore is extra heavily armoured with a reinforced vertical beam running down the front. It is something the Sunspire installed herself, and it served as a ram in the battle with the Paladin. It's how the Sunspire broke that great ship's back after nuking her shields down. Atop of the Sunspire's dorsal side is the bridge. At the bottom I can see the sealed hangars and launch decks.

It heads for the Amazon the instant it clears the mouth of the wormhole, launching a barrage of anti-shield and anti-missile rounds from rows of rapid-firing rail guns. "Why does it look meaner than it did in the brief?" asks one of the marines surrounding Mary below.

"What I don't get is why we have to bust in from these tin cans when the Amazon could launch marines of her own," comments another.

"Launching boarding shuttles would leave openings in her shields long enough for something to get through to the hull, moron," replies one of the electrical techs.

"Can it!" orders Mary.

I watch the Amazon's broadcasted reports. The Sunspire is trying to hack every system aboard. The sight of the Sunspire focusing fire on one of the Amazon's shield emitter arrays is mesmerising. The ship rolls so all her rail guns can fire in turn, streams of white hot projectiles raking the larger ship's energy shield. There's no one aboard the Sunspire, and most of the civilians left the Amazon. Several families refused to leave, which is normal for a super-carrier of the Amazon's type. Depending on how the next few minutes go, they might regret their decision.

The protective barrier surrounding one of the port emitter arrays fail, and then there's a flash. The communications stream coming from the Amazon stops for the better part of a minute. My comm line is so quiet that all I can hear is the sound of my own breath. I take a moment to look over the four squads of marines accompanying us. They're as still as can be. When I hear a squawk from the Amazon's comms I'm relieved, but I check the report and find that the nukes opened a few compartments. At best the Sunspire killed a few dozen people. I don't consider the worst case scenario. There's a bright side, however; the reserve shields are up in time to block the second nuclear detonation. The Sunspire is winning, her shields are deflecting whatever she can't outmanoeuvre.

A warning is transmitted from the Amazon. The Sunspire has managed to hack several systems. It is part of the plan, but it's risky. I wait to see if the counter virus works. Long seconds pass. Reports of weapons systems shutting down on the Amazon start coming in. The Sunspire is disarming the grand old ship.

Then, to my relief, the Sunspire's engines go out, and her shields begin to fade. "Alpha team, Beta team, you're a go," I hear Captain McPatrick order.

"Aim and fire, Lieutenant Fonte," I command.

The manoeuvring thrusters on our shuttles fire. Inertial dampers built into our armour activate. We manoeuvre away from the nearest asteroids and the high-thrust, low-duration rockets mounted on the rear of our ships blast. We're riding a controlled explosion, just like the astronauts of yore.

A counter appears on my visor, marking distance and time to impact. Isabel manages to aim at the Sunspire perfectly. We're lined up to hit exactly where we want, right behind the starboard wing.

"This is gonna suck," says Remmy.

"All right!" says Mary. Her voice is more authoritative and intimidating than most drill instructors when she wants it to be. There are marines who regard her as more of a machine than a woman. "This is the Sunspire! We will break through her hull using a directed disintegration bomb. If it misfires, I'll see you all in hell in about eighty four seconds. If it doesn't, we will have a great big white hot ring of metal three metres deep to jump through." I watch as we get closer and closer to the Sunspire. Mary's instructions are the perfect accompaniment for our approach. "Our suits may not completely protect us from that kind of heat, so measure twice, jump once, and don't fall backwards when you land. Check your weapons now, you will not have a chance when you're inside. You watched the same briefing I did, so you know we have no intelligence on what resistance we'll face inside. Anything that moves is a viable target. We have the honour of conducting Commander Clark Patterson and his command team to the main data port, and I promised we'd get him there first. Do not let him down."

I like the last touch. Even though we've all been marked as traitors, Mary still puts me on a pedestal. Every one of the people around me have some kind of violation on record, which is why they're under our command. The timer says she finished her speech with forty seconds to spare. It counts down to impact as the Sunspire looms closer. I watch the Amazon disappear into a wormhole. Only a few compartments are busted open, and secondary systems are covering for the damage. The bureaucrats and politicians will bitch about it, but she got off light considering the Sunspire's kill record.

The Sunspire may be momentarily dormant, but she put defences out. I silently pray we'll make it through as a shuttle beside us strikes a pacer mine and explodes. Hull fragments and soldiers - some partial, some whole - batter our port side. We drift off-course for a second but get back in line before long. Another shuttle bursts apart above.

My prayer is answered. With a collision that reverberates through the hull, we connect with the Sunspire. The disintegration bomb stretching across the front of the shuttle goes off. The vacuum in the shuttle doesn't allow for sound outside our vacsuits, but even in our armour we can feel the vibrations. I would have been knocked on my ass if it weren't for my stabilisers. The ambient temperature read normal for vacuum before the explosion, twenty eight hundred degrees after, and that's with the heat shield in place. The plate protecting us from the blast drops and starts to turn red as soon as it touches the white-hot metal of the Sunspire's violated hull. Marines pour out into the exposed hallway.

"Drone!" one shouts. That's the beginning of a hell I'm sure I won't forget any time soon. Two marines get split open from stomach to spine by drone cutting lasers before anyone has a chance to open fire. The lower half of the shuttle and the hallway beyond flashes with the strobe of firing rifles as marines flood into the Sunspire. My turn comes up. Instead of holding back and waiting for my subordinates to enter, I take the lead of the second wave. "Let's take the beast back," I say as I stride towards the breach and leap across. The marines have the hallway choked in both directions and they're making room for me and my specialists.

I pick up a rifle from an eviscerated soldier. Nothing alive is made to survive this heat without protection. The incredible heat incinerates anything bare and organic within moments of exposure. The first wave of marines are laying down cover fire, burning small holes in the hardened metal of the corridor as they miss invisible targets, marking gleaming yellow scorch spots when they strike the cloaked defensive drones. What Freeground Intelligence suspected has proven true: the Sunspire has adapted the cloak suits that were developed years before to all her drones. I pick an area above my head that's not being covered and lay down a strafing burst just in case some of the cloaked drones have gotten through. I hit nothing and return my attention to the overall situation. We've lost five more marines; the drones sliced through their helmets at point blank range.

"One tracker grenade aft!" announces a marine.

"One tracker grenade fore!" announces another.

There are two distinct flashes, and the corridor is momentarily filled with fine orange dust. As if drawn by a breeze it dissipates away from us, clinging to anything using stealth technology and lighting them up. The shape of the drones becomes clear for the first time.

They are narrow, half-metre-long machines with over a dozen arms ending in hardened tips and tools. Cutting lasers, heavier manipulation clamps, and an onboard computer make up the contents of the body. They climb the ceilings and walls as easily as they scurry across the deck.

"It's closing!" shouts Lieutenant Crow as he passes through the opening in the Sunspire's hull. A thick layer of organic steel is regenerating at an alarming rate, threatening to leave several of my command crew behind. Without hesitation I take a gamble, setting my rifle to automatic and firing dumb slugs at one side of the hole. Chunks of the metal fly past my flinching command crew, but the hole is just big enough when my heavy slugs run out. "Come on!" I shout, dropping my rifle and reaching through.

I take Isabel's hand in my left, her temporary navigator's in my right, and yank them through the closing hole. The hull seals the three others off. "Blow a hole in this!" I order to any marine who isn't busy firing at a defensive drone. With the heat of the sun striking the Sunspire's hull, it's regenerating much faster than normal. I watch the membrane of thin organic steel thicken as I move Isabel behind me, between myself and several marines.

Mary turns, looks at the regenerating hull, and orders half a squad to concentrate fire on a section of fresh hull. It's too late, it's already too thick. "Not going to happen, Commander, hope they weren't mission critical," she tells me, signalling her marines to cease fire.

I know the shuttles won't last more than a few minutes longer under the heat and pressure of the dwarf star. Those crewmen will be exposed, then their suits will fail. They aren't the only losses. My visor display informs me that we've lost fifteen marines. One of my reserve command crew members bought it when they got caught in the crossfire. Mary, Isabel, and Remmy are fine, however. We also have more marines than we expected at this point, more than enough to go on. I bend down to retrieve my rifle and just as I'm switching it to pulse mode, my suit alerts me that I'm under attack.

I can't hear the defence drone's tiny limbs, but I can feel its tools probing frantically for a way to crack my hardened armour open and tear me apart. "Help!" I shout as I try to fling it off my back.

It wraps its invisible legs around my arm and pins it above my head. The staccato flash of pulse rifles forces my visor to go dark and my arm is released.

"Looks like the tracker dust settled too soon," says one of the marines. "That one was nowhere on scope."

"Thanks," I reply as I clip the rifle's safety line to my chest. I pull a clip from my reserve pack and reload. I'm thankful for the weapon for reasons beyond protection or revenge. Holding it stops my hands from shaking.

CHAPTER 9
DATA PORT

The atmosphere becomes more habitable after we break through the thinnest interior bulkhead we can find. I stop the boarding team in a broad hallway and we get set up for the rest of our mission. We're a full squad down on marines, and the remaining soldiers are ready to tear the Sunspire a new one for what she did to their comrades. With more room to manoeuvre ahead, they bring out the heavier ammunition, just in case.

I use my head's-up display to look at Isabel's scans, which indicate less movement in the adjacent hallways, and just a trickle of power running through this section of the ship. Our marines spray the air around us with the orange detector mist that keeps those cloaked drones visible, but we're only encountering a couple of curious ones now. They get pecked off as they are revealed peeking around corners.

"Remmy, is there any indication that the virus the Amazon uploaded to the Sunspire is still working?" I ask.

"I'm still dark," Remmy replies. "I can't say anything for sure until you get me to a central data port."

"Power plant and propulsion energy levels are still next to nil. I can't get a good read on the smaller systems, but they're probably working on backups," Isabel says. She's doubling as our systems engineer, since we lost ours getting here. Thankfully she's a good officer, and studied the schematics of the Sunspire.

I check Alpha team. They're well on their way to the central aft data port. Lieutenant Urik kept his people moving as they reconfigured. I would only admit it if pressed, but Urik is the better commander. He'll probably reach his data port before we do, so I start thinking about the secondary mission: taking the bridge.

The team is almost finished checking armour, switching weapons, performing scans and collecting data. I return my attention to my immediate surroundings. Their mirror smooth surfaces of the hallway are so perfect they are featureless. Either the seams are so fine that we can't see them without a detailed scan or the Sunspire has grown her shiny blue organic hull over all the finer features aboard. I don't bother tasking anyone to check, and set my own scanner to passively detect doors.

"Group combat shielding coming up, stick together," one of the technicians announces. It's completely new technology to Freeground and no one here knows where it came from, but I love it for this mission. Instead of each suit depending on one energy shield, the fields can merge into a stronger, moving protective barrier. It only takes her a couple of minutes to set it up.

"All right," I reply. "Let's get moving." I can't see the shield with my naked eye, but my visor makes up for the limitations of my human sight, overlaying the energy pattern of the barrier. It looks like a bubble stretched over our group, expanding and retracting as people move further or closer from the majority.

The marines lead the way, rushing down silver-blue hallways. The space is so shiny that the little lights affixed to the sides of our helmets seem to reflect forever. As they move down a two metre wide hall, I can't help but feel as though we're trespassing on sacred ground, and a hateful eye is tracking us.

"We're at the main aft data port," reports Lieutenant Urik over the command channel. He's in charge of incursion unit Alpha, and well ahead of us.

"Congratulations," says Remmy. "Be careful, I have nothing on wireless scans, but that doesn't mean the Sunspire is totally brain-dead."

"I know," replies their comms officer. "Would you shut up and let me do my job?"

A quick look at Remmy's activity screen on my heads-up display tells me that he's moved on, already performing a fresh scan of the area around us. If we were sitting in the common lounge, Remmy would have argued for at least an hour, but he's surprisingly professional in the field.

I keep tabs on Urik's team as my team makes its way across a large open space towards a bank of lift doors. We're not far from the nearest central port, inside one of the large transit centres aboard the Sunspire.

"Wait, something's happening," says Lieutenant Urik. I look to the small window on my heads-up display that shows Urik's point of view. Their technician pauses at the lift interface a moment. "Go, go! Break through that panel so we can get to the interface!" Urik orders.

I miss a step and nearly collide with the marine to my right when I see all the lights in Alpha Unit's area come on. The doors seal them in, and the walls around the Lieutenant and his men start to move like a metal skin.

"Oh crap," says Remmy.

Screams fill the channel as Lieutenant Urik looks to his right and sees heavy metal membranes come together like silver-blue waves and roll towards them. The space between the upper and lower parts are only a couple of centimetres high, and I find myself silently praying that their reinforced vacsuits can handle the crushing attack. They do, but not well enough to prevent injury.

The chorus of screams are so agonised that they seem inhuman. The ripples of organic metal mangle the team and I can hear armour and bones breaking. The lieutenant isn't dead. The medical system reports extreme systemic distress - broken femurs, pelvis, collarbone, four broken ribs, and a punctured lung along with other organ damage - but pain management kicks in right away. "Good luck, Commander," says Lieutenant Urik as the pair of crushing membranes come around for another pass.

Remmy stops and falls to one knee, forcing everyone around to halt. The sounds of the ship crushing the already broken bodies of our comrades are too much. His breakfast comes up in a surge before his command unit can dose him with anti-nausea medication. The hood of his vacsuit suctions up his sick. Compressed water sprays his face clean.

"The lieutenant?" asks Mary.

"Aye," I confirm, offering Remmy a hand up. "Was anyone else watching that?"

"No. My tactical system just updated, crossing Urik's team off," Mary says.

"And I thought comms officer would be a cushy job," Remmy says. "Sometimes I hate being the all-seeing eye."

"EMP," I tell Mary. "I want to shock the walls ahead so we don't run into the same thing at the forward link."

"Yes, Sir," she agrees. "We're coming up to a terminal at the end of the hall, we'll do it there."

"Won't that kill the terminal?" asks a technician.

"Someone didn't do the reading," answers Isabel from behind him. "Main terminals are hardened against EMP, egghead."

"Oh," the technician offers lamely. "Getting the Faraday sheets out."

"Good," I say, noting the technician's serial number so I can demote him as soon as we finish taking the ship.

The cost of taking the Sunspire should start to take its toll on me. Maybe they changed something during my grief therapy, something important, because I feel the loss as though from a great distance, like I'd never met Urik. I had, though briefly. The deaths of Urik and his unit should evoke more feeling. Instead, putting the emotional impact of what happened aside is effortless. It's as if someone went through my emotional inventory and filed down the edges so I wouldn't cut myself on anything sharp. I'm not so subdued that the cost of taking the Sunspire isn't making me angry, however.

We start running again, down another stretch of hallway. "Picking up a sudden surge in wireless activity," announces Remmy.

"Does it match anything we've seen?" I ask.

"Yes, but it's from Third Era archives," he replies. "Thoss machine code."

"What? That hasn't been seen for centuries." I bring the available information on Thoss code up on my display. The Freeground Intelligence database tells me the same thing: Thoss code. "What did you find out here, Sunspire?" I say to myself.

We make our way to the end of the hallway and find a darkened circular space. The temperature is twenty one degrees centigrade, spot on for life support. Then Mary shouts, "Movement!"

"Get under the Faraday sheets," I order.

Red and blue lights illuminate the space ahead. My visor adjusts to reveal larger, walking robots with particle beam emitters mounted across triangular heads that make them look like they are staring at us with angry red eyes. Gripper hands with nano saw fingers rotate at the ends of four long triple-reinforced arms. Six collapsing legs extend beneath as they power up and begin sidestepping around the room. One of the nearest bots lowers its body and head so its sharply pointed chin touches the deck. It is as though its perfectly round, glowing red eyes are looking directly into mine. The thing's mouth - a round blue pulse beam emitter - opens and closes as its protective aperture seals and unseals.

"Fire," I order quietly. "Fire! Fire!" I shout as the one staring at me springs forward.

The marines at the head of the column open fire and spread out. The charging bot lands in their midst, taking several heavy rounds but surviving long enough to yank Mary off the deck and fling her into the open space behind it. As it is reduced to a twitching pile of ergranian metal struts and broken armour, its brothers descend on Mary like a school of piranha.

The marines panic, opening fire on her attackers, ignoring the technicians behind who are trying to get the Faraday sheets over them. The robot's particle beams break through Mary's energy shields in seconds. Grippers with nano saw fingers cut through her armour, flesh and bone.

"Get under the sheet, now!" I grab the EMP charge from one of the marine's backs, set it, and then toss it into the next room. It is Mary's only hope. If the grenade doesn't disable the machines trying to hack her to bits, there won't be anything worth saving. I barely have time to get under the Faraday sheet myself before it seals. A handful of marines, the technicians, and my bridge officers make it with me. The charge goes off.

I whip the sheet aside and check Mary's medical status. She's still alive. The medical component of her command and control unit is inoperable, however. I rush to her side. A half functional bot turns so it can take a shot at me and I fire my rifle on the run, strafing it and the bot beside it. I knock one of the five marines who were caught outside of the faraday blanket to the ground along the way. He'll be at least half useless for the rest of the engagement. His rifle, personal energy shield, and most of his gear are fried.

A few of the other guardian bots begin to move. Little parts close to their armoured bodies at first, but enough for me to see that they are recovering too quickly. My clip is half empty by the time I reach Mary. "We're coming, Commander!" says Remmy from behind. My tactical display verifies it: he picks up a rifle and begins leading my unit forward.

Part of Mary's jaw is missing, she's lost both legs and an arm. Her vacsuit hood has been peeled away and she stares at me - an expression of fear and pain. She struggles to breathe through profuse bleeding, and I do my best to remain detached. "I'll get you fixed up, hold on." I load an emergency stasis dose into my command and control unit and press the nozzle to the side of her head. "See you soon." To my relief, she closes her eyes and the bleeding stops. A quick medical scan verifies that she's stable, in emergency stasis.

I turn my attention to the ongoing fight. It still isn't much of a battle. The bots are still just starting to recover, only a couple of them having reached full mobility. There are several hallways leading to the chamber, however, and I expect more company at any moment. I focus on a pair that come around the transportation hub in the centre of the large, circular space and watch with satisfaction as my heavy explosive rounds shred their metal bodies. My bridge officers fire their sidearms at their highest setting, and it helps, but only just enough to keep the machines at bay.

"Technicians! Move up and interface with that terminal!" I order. "Time to shut this party down!"

The technicians Remmy left behind look warily out from where they're hiding in the hallway across from me, but they don't move.

"Now, Mister!" I reinforce harshly.

"Get your ass up here or throw me your brute force interface kit so I can do it myself," Remmy shouts at them.

The pair of technicians starts to run from the hallway to the terminal behind me. Three bots spring at them, but we cut them down within a metre of the cringing non-combatants. They start cutting into the glassy terminal interface as soon as they arrive. "Transparent ergranian, Sir," Remmy says as he gets his comm kit ready. "It'll take a few."

"Sir, how long do you think the other internal incursion countermeasures will be disabled for?" asks Isabel. She didn't see the carnage at the main aft terminal, but knows some major defensive system took out Urik's team in seconds.

"Two minutes," I lie. I want to believe an EMP will disable the Sunspire's more elegant defence systems, but there's no way to be sure. The lie is to reassure my people, without removing a sense of very real urgency.

My tactical system alerts me to a new threat. There is a wave of small crawling attack drones, exactly the same as the ones we encountered when we boarded, on their way from the starboard side. "Fire team! Head's up! Incoming at nine o'clock."

"Don't worry, Commander," interjects the voice of Lieutenant Davi on my command comm. A point on my tactical map pings and a timer counting down from fifteen minutes appears. "We're on our way."

A marine hands me a clip and shoves two more into my belt. If the scan is accurate, and there really are hundreds of drones coming, I will need them. I add my rifle fire to the fray, laying into the last of the walking bots until it collapses to the deck. I reload as quickly as I can - two point nine seconds from ejection to firing my first round, according to my performance tracker. Glancing at a small performance display on my heads-up display is an old academy habit I haven't bothered breaking. I set my sights on the first of the crawlers and mulch it in three shots.

The fight goes on. Everyone who isn't cutting into the central data port is burning through ammunition, blasting at the wave of small bots. These ones aren't cloaked, but even so, a haze of detection dust lingers in the air just in case something tries to sneak up on us. I'm on my last cartridge when we start losing ground.

Our reinforcements arrive, and if these machines had a pulse I might feel bad for them. A hail of white hot rounds cuts through the moving mass of small, deadly machines as fresh marines fan out into the open space from the starboard hall.

"We're through!" announces the cutting crew.

Remmy hurriedly plugs in and begins uploading. "The Holocaust Virus fix is installing. Here's hoping it works."

"Tell me as soon as you see a command screen," I tell him.

"It's up," Remmy says seconds later, moving aside.

I hand my rifle to a nearby marine who was caught in the EMP. Turning my attention to the main terminal's command interface, I jack my command and control unit in. The Sunspire recognises me as a commander with command codes. "Disarm internal defences," I order as I enter the instructions manually using my comm unit just in case the voice command doesn't take.

"Command authority recognised. Standing down, Commander Patterson," says the computer in a pleasant female voice. I recognise that voice immediately. It's Alice, as she was when Captain Jonas Valent first took command of the Sunspire during her short turn as a shadow ship. Her code was also the basis for the Holocaust Virus, the program responsible for turning the Sunspire into an automated killing machine. The question is, which version of Alice am I speaking to? The helpful artificial intelligence that accompanied Captain Jonas Valent? Or a blood thirsty virus hell-bent on cleansing the galaxy of all humans not allied with the Order of Eden?

I glance at the rest of the large room, where marines are still battling wave after wave of crawler droids. "It doesn't look like they're reverting to repair and maintenance mode, Remmy," I tell him, moving aside.

"It should have worked! They shouldn't want to rip our faces off by now," he complains as he takes a look through his own portable control pad. "They should have reverted to the friendly little-" he stops for a moment, his eyes widening. "What the..."

"What is it?"

"It's an emulator," Remmy says. "The Sunspire tricked the antivirus into thinking it cleared the Holocaust Virus out of the computer by letting it cure a fake operating system."

"How long will it take you to go around it?" I ask, drawing my sidearm.

He shakes his head. "It's not gonna happen. I can only see one part of the real Sunspire's computing system, and it's locked behind serious firewalls."

"How serious?"

"Do you have a century or two?" he replies.

"All right, then we resort to secondary measures," I say.

"What? But that would-" one of the technicians objects.

Before he can finish his sentence I silence his communicator. "Don't you dare tip this machine off," I warn. I select the software package Special Projects developed just in case an incursion unit ever tried to retake an infected ship, and enter my initiation code. It only takes half a second for it to upload to the Sunspire. I yank my comm unit free of the cable connecting me to the panel. "This is happening. I don't care how bad you techs want to study the Sunspire. I don't think this thing will do tricks once it's in your glass jar anyway."

The emulator interface freezes then disappears. Lighting flickers overhead for a few seconds before going out.

"So much for getting a copy of the AI before the ship's computer dies," mutters Remmy.

"Just make sure there's nothing left," I tell him over my shoulder as I begin firing at the nearest silver-skinned crawler. "While the rest of us do the heavy lifting."

"We're setting our platoon's EMP up," warns Lieutenant Davi. "This section should be clear of crawlers and anything else that's looking to rip us up in a few seconds."

"Give us ten seconds to get under Faraday sheets."

I blast a crawler right off a marine's back and shoot it six more times before I hear the lieutenant say, "Now's a good time, get under cover. Fifteen seconds."

My people learned their lesson. They all make it under the Faraday sheets in time and none are caught in the massive electromagnetic pulse that disables most of the crawlers.

The marines do a sweep of the room and set up to guard the five hallways leading into the transit centre. "Congratulations, Commander," says Lieutenant Davi as he crosses the space between us, offering his hand. He's a short man, heavily muscled. It looks like he spends every off hour in the gym. I'm sure he and Mary will get along fine when she's back on her feet. That is, if they let our units work together in the future.

"Thank you. Still a lot of work to do. There's no way of knowing how many more of these," I kick a limp crawler, "are lurking around. That EMP only covered about three quarters of a klick."

"At least you got the Sunspire AI under control," replies Davi.

"That plan failed. We had to force a core wipe. It's going to take weeks, maybe months, to set an operating system running to spec. Until then, she's a hulk," I tell him.

"The captain is going to be pissed," Lieutenant Davi says.

"He and the admiralty can line up and kiss my ass. They wanted the Sunspire, we got her for them. As far as I'm concerned, this was a success, and I'm putting you on record for saving our butts."

"I'm not finished yet, Sir," Davi says with a smile that almost stretcesh the bounds of his vacsuit hood. "We still have to sweep a few klicks of corridors and get some of the critical rooms open."

"Let's hit the armoury first," I say. "I have some marines who were too slow to get under cover during our first EMP."

CHAPTER 10
CLEANUP

The orders come down when we're just setting out for the armoury: "Set up camp around the data port. The Amazon is sending the primary force in to complete the capture."

It doesn't take long to fortify our position. A fine cloud of orange dust is sent into the air. It remains aloft almost magically, or it would seem that was if I didn't know that the cloak detection dust wasn't actually billions of nanobots all programmed to find and adhere to objects using known sensor obscuring technology.

I take a fresh look at the large circular chamber we're setting up in and make a decision. "Lieutenant Davi," I say. "Get your people to start looking for bulkhead doors. I want to seal all but the port side halls off."

"Yes, Sir," Davi replies. "And call me Malcolm"

"Call me Clark once we're off duty."

"I'm going to reconnect with the data port and make sure there's nothing going on in the Sunspire's systems. Anything smart enough to try to trick me with an emulator might have a cold backup somewhere ready to activate if she ever gets wiped."

"Good idea," I tell him.

It takes Lieutenant Davi's team the better part of twenty minutes to find the bulkhead doors for the adjacent hallways. The Sunspire is so streamlined internally that, I can't see them even when his people are cutting into the control wiring. We're coming up on the half hour mark when they finally start closing doors and welding them shut.

With the doors closed it seems like we suddenly have too many marines for the one entrance we're covering. "Always better to have more guests at a party than not enough," I say to myself.

"I hear that," says a marine behind me. "Still hope it's a bore, though."

"So, what's this primary force they're bringing in?" Isabel asks quietly.

"About twenty eight hundred marines and techs," I spare a glance at Mary's stasis bag. I wish she were here to see how we're taking control.

"Why didn't they do that in the first place?" she asks.

"The marines they're sending in are regulars," answers Lieutenant Davi. "We're the traitors and glorified inmates, disposable."

"We're the scum of the fleet," Remy adds wryly. "By the way, our wounded have been marked by a Combat Medic team from Special Projects."

I check the tactical status screen on my heads-up display and only see that our wounded are marked for medical attention or retrieval. "I don't even see Special Projects on my status system."

"Oh, right. I'm doing some creative eavesdropping." Remmy spends another moment checking a few details and nods to himself. "The Special Projects Intelligence Unit have been watching closely ever since we wiped the Sunspire's core. They're already uploading code and have new tech with the med teams."

"Where do I get a Comms Tech like that?" asks Lieutenant Davi. "I'm looking for a replacement."

"Oh, watch what you wish for," Isabel cracks.

"You'll have to ask Doctor Anderson, he put my team together," I reply.

"Anyway," Remmy interrupts. "They say they're on their way here."

"Ahead of the main body of reinforcements?"

"Now," Remmy smiles. "They're Special."

"I take it back," Lieutenant Davi groans. "I don't think I want a Remmy if he comes with that sense of humor."

"Are you sure?" Isabel asks. "You can have this one."

We hold our vigil for two hours as the tactical window on my heads-up display tracks firefights across the ship. The main force of marines encounter whatever we managed to avoid while capturing a central data node. Our anti-cloaking mist picks up a group of over fifty crawlers as they're flushed our way.

They meet a wall of orange detection dust, it looks like they're being smothered by a living smog. The marines fire, and for the first time since we boarded, we have an easy upper hand. The area is clear in minutes, and I don't see the need to waste my ammunition.

Two marines from my team send more detection dust into the air, tossing dispersal grenades into the open that go off with a loud thump and a puff of scattering smoke. Before the entire area has coverage, four fresh squads of marines arrive escorting a medical team in dark blue and white armoured vacsuits. They don't look like the average medical team.

None of them have visible comm units, and they don't wait for us to direct them to our wounded or report on their condition. Everyone near the stasis bags are pressed aside, myself included. They get right to work. From the rear of the group come a trio of medics drawing medical devices that look like caskets. Mary and our other injured are placed inside.

"Commander McPatrick," says a Marine who steps in front of me. I was so intent on watching what the medics were doing I that I don't notice him until he's right in my face. My heads-up display identifies him as Commander Sarlin. "I salute the work you've done and the sacrifices your people have made here," he prefaces with an actual salute, something that is reserved for ceremonies and disciplinary panels in the Freeground Fleet.

I return the gesture, snapping a stiff salute in return. "Thank you, Commander."

"You and your men are to stand down," he says. "I am taking command of this post. Your new orders will be uploaded shortly."

"We do the heavy lifting and then reinforcements take on the cushy job," Remmy mutters.

I turn towards Lieutenant Davi, who is my direct subordinate for this mission and salute him. He's surprised by the gesture and salutes back after a moment's hesitation. I make light of my replacement's gesture and compliment Davi at the same time; "Thank you for saving our asses back there! That was a hot mess and you put it out!" A quote from some movie I heard once, and it cracks most of the unit up. "You and your team are relieved."

"Thank you, Sir!" he barks back, and I suddenly feel like I'm back in boot camp.

I'm grateful for the momentary distraction. This removal from command really is a slap in the face, and if I were concerned about my career I wouldn't be slightly irritated, I'd be down right livid. I'm also waiting to see what this new medical technology does to my best friend. Traditional treatment and recovery would take months for someone with Mary's injuries, but I can only guess that these caskets are here because they're supposed to do the same job in much less time.

My people are pressed aside as new technicians take possession of the data node and no less than a couple hundred marines move in to secure the area. Specialists begin cutting into the walls, looking for more manual control mechanisms I suppose. Others begin work on the tram system and unsealing the doors. I understand the rush to get the Sunspire back on her feet, but this is happening faster than even I expected. Faster than I'd advise.

I get a notification telling me that my new orders are in, and I'm not entirely pleased. HOLD POSITION AND RENDER ASSISTANCE IF IT IS REQUESTED OF YOU.

"Are they starting recovery right now?" Isabel asks, a little uneasy.

"They are," I answer. "And our orders are to watch."

"This thing was trying to kill us less than an hour ago," she says. "Isn't it a bit soon?"

"Other than a few crawlers, it's totally safe," Remmy says. "The computer core memory was totally wiped along with every other connected computing device aboard. I didn't see anything running last I checked."

"And anything we find that can hold an artificial intelligence is being destroyed on discovery," adds Commander Sarlin. For the first time I realize how closely he's watching me and my friends. "Don't worry, we're in complete control."

"Gee," Remmy says with a pondering expression, "whenever I hear that in dramas everything goes to hell in the next act."

Commander Sarlin offers us a stiff smile and moves on to supervise something else.

At long last, the box they stuffed every part of Mary into opens. To the astonishment of everyone around she sits up and steps out. Anyone who knows what her condition was before is amazed at how there isn't a scratch on her. The rest are more than a little surprised to have a nude woman in their midst.

"Really?" She says irritably to one of the medics. "You guys build a miracle box and don't have the sense of mind to add a smock dispenser or something?"

"Wow," Remmy says, starting to clap. "Too bad she plays for the other team."

I can count the number of times I've seen Mary embarrassed on one hand, it doesn't happen easily. She covers herself as most of Beta and Alpha teams applaud. The other two injured marines step out of their pods too, in perfect condition as far as we can tell.

One of the medical team presents her with an armoured vacsuit and she yanks it form him. "If I knew a couple hundred people would be getting a free show I would have done some trimming."

They're given new armoured vacsuits, but not before Mary causes a riot of laughter by taking a deep bow. I'm blocked off from her by marines and medics. When she's dressed and finally allowed to walk over to us she flashes me a great big smile. Pats on the shoulders and welcomes sound from the marines she led aboard.

"I thought I was done for a minute there," Mary whispers. "Thank you, Clark."

I nod. "You're kidding right? I'm not going into exile without you watching my back."

"Likewise," she replies. "What's the status on the Sunspire?"

"They're just doing a sweep and clear. I think we're about to be demoted to ornamental status."

"Not even," Remmy interjects. "When the report on this action is read into the public record back home, it'll be the marine units from the Amazon that get credit."

That subdues the lot of us for several minutes. "A good soldier doesn't sign up for the glory," Mary says. "But not getting credit when we lost so many taking the ship is an insult I'm not going to forget."

"I hear you," agrees Lieutenant Davi. "My comms officer and incursion specialist were killed in the first three minutes of action. They should have their names etched on the Founder Chamber wall."

"I never thought I'd say this," Mary prefaces. "But I think I'm done with this outfit. Give me my dishonourable discharge and drop me someplace where I can get mercenary work." There's real ire in her tone.

On the heels of her comment I feel a calm fall over me, as if someone just dosed me with some kind of calmative. Mary looks at me and the only words I can offer her are; "I don't know."

"I hope that's the conditioning talking," she says. "And I hope you get over it soon."

Within hours the marines of Beta Team - my team - are assigned to other units. They salute, congratulate and pay respects to me and Mary before leaving, but I can't help but feel the cold shoulder from command. I'm qualified to be first officer on the Sunspire, so I should at least be allowed to participate in guarding and securing her.

I wait with Mary, Isabel and Remmy. Lieutenant Davi is in the same spot, waiting with his combat engineer, Bida, for orders. They come two hours later, when the ship transit system comes back on line.

Davi and Bida are sent to one section of the guest quarters in the upper berthing and we're sent to another. If that isn't insulting enough, Commander Sarlin sees a need to send marine escorts along to make sure we get there. The place has already been swept by a marine scan team, but we do it again ourselves anyway as soon as our escorts leave. The place is clear. It's a good thing too; we're locked in.

CHAPTER 11
DOWN TIME

I can't shirk the feeling that I'm back in prison. On the Amazon we weren't allowed to leave the common quarters, and now that we're on the Sunspire it's the same thing, only the section we're assigned to is smaller. There are six guest quarters and one deck watch bunk in our little section of the ship. The techs made sure everything worked before Mary, Remmy, Isabel and me were locked in.

That's where I am now, sitting on a nice, comfortable sofa with Isabel's head in my lap. My hand gently strokes her cheek and neck while we wait for Remmy to return from the guest accommodation room. There's a refrigeration unit there, which was emptied of fresh food long ago, a pair of materializers, emergency medical supplies and other items that guests might like. Other than the fridge, the place was well stocked. The tags say that it was done before the Sunspire turned on her crew.

Isabel and I are weathering the boredom well. We started sharing the same quarters on the third night. My assumption is that some of the social rules don't apply to Intelligence Operatives, or whatever they call the four of us. If I'm wrong, I'll deal with the consequences. What can they do? Drug me? Separate us? Bust me down a rank or two? I'm past it. I watched marines die right in front of me on the last suicidal raid. Mary was almost one of them. We're on down time with nowhere to go, not much to do, and no one from command has paid us a visit yet. Every morning for the last two weeks since we checked into the Sunspire hotel, I've gotten the same orders: "Beta Unit is on restricted leave. Please make use of available facilities."

Two weeks since we first walked into this lounge. If it weren't for fitness meds, I would be losing shape and putting on pounds.

"Well, nice of them to leave us in luxury," Remmy says as he brings a bucket of Mega-Poppers from the food materializer. He drops into one of the thickly padded armchairs and turns his attention to the two metre tall holographic vista in front. The lounge's pair of sofas and five arm chairs are arranged in a semi circle so people can watch the universe go by through the room length transparent section of hull. It's built like the older sections of Freeground, featuring a starry view. We get to see the blue belt, a seemingly endless field of asteroids and planetoids. You'd think that would be interesting, but after two weeks, you get used to it.

Remmy adjusts the transparency level of the hull so the view is muted. It increases the quality the holographic projection. Lately he's been watching a 22nd century Earth drama. I don't really get what he sees in it. The series is called Hole In The Floor, and it's about a group of people who think they are hiding out from a long nuclear winter in a bomb shelter.

Mary wasn't interested either until one of the characters secretly turned to cannibalism. How someone could *secretly* turn to cannibalism in a sealed bomb shelter is beyond me, but I shrug and decide the show is part comedy.

I relate to the misguided characters a little, though. I'm looking forward to running a few simulations once Remy's finished his so-called dinner. The sims on offer from Freeground Intelligence are unlike anything we'd ever seen. The missions are short, and take place in jungles, on uninhabitable worlds with lakes of acid and mercury. There are others, all coded so you don't know what you'll get until you're inside. We know we're being tested, but I'm so bored I don't really care. I wouldn't mind finding out what our score is though.

Aside from old holographic dramas and sims, I've been learning Spanish from Isabel. Everyone on Freeground has some kind of comm unit that comes with a translator, but hearing her speak a few words piqued my interest. It feels like it's going slowly, but Isabel tells me I'm picking it up quickly.

Mary comes out of her quarters and walks over to the sofa. She lifts Isabel's legs, sits under them and begins idly massaging her feet. "What's James doing today?" she asks as Isabel coos. "Enjoy it now, because you're doing mine later."

"'Kay," Isabel replies as I stroke her cheek. She's in heaven.

"James? He was almost caught gnawing on Veronica in cold storage," Remmy says, not looking away from the holographic talking heads.

"I liked Veronica, the show's been missing something since she died," Isabel mutters.

I check the show's info on my comm unit and sigh. We are up to episode one hundred and nine and there's still no indication that one of the characters will wise up and open the hatch, just to see if the nuclear winter is real.

"Boredom getting to you?" Mary whispers.

"El caníbal masticar solo?" I reply, getting a snicker from Isabel then Mary, whose translator interprets my quip as; "Does the cannibal chewing alone?"

"Well, your Spanish is getting better," Mary says. "How about you, Izzy?"

"It would be, if it weren't for the company," she says with closed eyes. "Would like to see more of the ship though."

"I guess this has got to be loads better than where you spent the last year," Mary says.

"Yup," Isabel agrees. "I think I saw six or seven people the whole time I was in prison. Whatever they put in the crappy food kept me from wanting to kill myself or just going crazy, but it all blurs together. Day ten was exactly the same as day two hundred ten. But here? Right now? This is like vacation. There are a couple other places I'd like to be, but I'll take this for a while." She kisses one of my fingers as it comes close to her mouth.

"Can't say I disagree," Remmy adds despite the mouthful of crunchy snacks.

"That's life in Fleet: long stretches of boredom mixed with moments of brisk activity punctuated by instants of sheer terror," I say. "Only, you get regular duty shifts and watches when you're aboard - usually."

"That's about it," Mary nods. "It sounds like you're finally getting back to your old self."

I haven't thought about that in days. It's as though something is forcing me to forget what the empty, dull feeling was like when I was released from grief therapy. Thinking further back is hard, like trying to remember being numb. Numbness is difficult to recall, because it feels like grasping at nothing and expecting a handful of substance. My sister is gone, my parents are gone, but I don't feel abandoned or as if any of it was much of an event at all. In the present, as I look at Mary who is earnestly interested in my well being, I'm suddenly aware of what is going on. "I feel like I'm putting myself back together using available materials."

"Using Spanish and ancient reality television?" Isabel laughs. "We've got to find better building materials."

"That won't be a problem," Doctor Anderson says as he enters. "I hope you've enjoyed this impromptu vacation." With a gesture he shuts the arguing holographic heads down. "As of this moment, the entertainment database is off limits," he announces. "Even your private stash, Remmy."

"Damn. There goes my late night viewing."

"Instead, you're going on a strict diet of First Light crew logs, action reports, and technical specifications. ITD, the Intelligence Training Database will also be available, and I suggest you start with a good look at Uumen. That's where you're going to be on your next mission. You'll be off ship in five days if everything goes as planned."

"That's a Regent Galactic world," Isabel says as she sits up.

"Technically it's become an Order of Eden world, and the Issyrians aren't happy about it. The solar system was originally theirs, and they lost it during corporate encroachment before they fully understood how our corporate system worked. Long story short, all the land is now owned by the Order and our target is hiding there, exactly where no one would expect him."

"Who is our target?" I ask.

"Doctor William Marcelles, one of the lead developers of the framework technology," Doctor Anderson answers.

"I heard about that, it was in a communications watch brief a few years ago," Remmy says. All evidence of the sour expression he had at the news of his beloved drama program being yanked away is gone. "Framework tech was to manpower as the atom bomb was to firepower. We were to immediately forward communications with any mention of it up to Intelligence. Nothing ever comes my way, though."

"That changes today," Doctor Anderson says, bringing up a full height hologram of Jacob Valance. He's wearing a dark long coat with flexible metal bands running across it. Their overlapping pattern hides shield and cloaking emitters that, according to the contraband I reviewed, he developed himself in the field. His heavily armoured vacsuit looks similar to the hardiest Freeground combat armour, sporting the same type of shield emitter bands across its entire surface up to the headpiece. His headpiece is a thickened hood with a blackened transparent faceplate. "Vindyne had Doctor Marcelles develop an advanced version of Jonas Valent while they were both in captivity," Doctor Anderson explained. "We suspect Marcelles programmed something into the copy, but have no way of discovering what that might be. Freeground tried to buy the research and the Valent copy from Vindyne when their corporation began to collapse, but it was too late. Alice, his former artificial intelligence, liberated the Valent copy thinking it was the real Jonas Valent and left him on a ship disguised as a derelict called the Samson."

"Wait, an AI did that alone?" asks Isabel. "She must have had help."

"Alice had somehow downloaded herself into a human host years before. Vindyne programmed the Jonas Valent copy just in case he got loose. When he woke up he thought his name was Jacob Valance, had social, combat, medical, and basic general information to draw on, and no idea who or what he was. Again, that was years ago, and now we know that copy as Jacob Valance, the bounty hunter and mercenary."

"Okay, so how is that info important to our next mission?" Remmy asks. "And will our chances of survival be better than last time?"

Doctor Anderson laughs softly and nods. "Chances of survival will be better. Your field team will be retrieving Doctor Marcelles."

"What will the other teams be up to?"

"They're on other missions," Doctor Anderson replies. "They won't be in range to offer assistance if you find yourselves in trouble."

"What are we facing?" I ask. The idea of going down to an Order of Eden world, where any artificial intelligence could identify us as being non-members is daunting, to say the least.

"The region Doctor Marcelles is hiding in has a low police presence, and light surveillance. He chose his hideouts fairly well, and has made friends out of the issyrian resistance there. Other than that, we don't know anything about what you'll be facing."

"What about the Order? They must be watching the area for people who haven't paid for membership," Mary asks.

"They are, and we've managed to match each of you with identities in their databases. A lot of workers from the nearby Regent Galactic mining outfit travel there during their time off. A contact of mine provided me with the schedule and other details, including the transponder codes of the shuttle one of the miners uses on regular trips."

"That's one hell of a contact," Remmy said. "I want to be just like you when I grow up, Doctor Anderson."

"I'm assuming it's too late to request a new comms officer?" Isabel asks. "I think ours is a little over contaminated by old dramas."

"Hey, that's my cultural education you're criticizing there," Remmy retorted.

"Okay, let's take this a little more seriously, please," Mary says. "So we'll assume their identities and take their ship to the planet."

"Exactly."

As much as I'm getting comfortable despite my boredom, I'm glad it's time to get back down to business. A quick glance at the directory representing years worth of information we've been given tells me there's something bigger going on. The mission details are something we'll have days to go over, but getting extra questions answered after Doctor Anderson leaves is another story. He is already turning to go, with one of those mild smiles on his face. "Why are you giving us all the information you have on Jacob Valance, Ayan Rice, the Samson crew, and even Colonel McPatrick's nephew?"

"I was wondering if you'd get to that," he says, stopping and turning back towards me. "Your obsession with the crew of the First Light, and Jacob Valance makes you perfectly suited to study their activities away from Freeground."

"But why are we studying them?" I press. "Are we going to have direct contact?"

Doctor Anderson thinks before answering, his gaze flicking between the four of us. "I can't answer that right now, it's too early. What I can tell you is that you'll be encountering a few things they left behind. Doctor Marcelles is the first loose end we have to address. Having access to him will be a major boon for everyone, especially the four of you. Intelligence suspects that the framework technology has already been mass produced, meaning that the Order of Eden has an army of regenerating troops at the ready. They can be packed into bulk containers, transported as framework skeletons, then programmed with specific training and directives. There is an excellent chance that each different type of framework will have personalities that suit their tasks. When they're needed the framework constructs can be dropped on site, subjected to incredible stresses along the way, surviving what no human in any suit could. On the ground they would materialize flesh, becoming regenerating human soldiers. A ship normally capable of carrying only a thousand troops could have ten times as many framework skeletons aboard."

"What happens when the job's done and they don't need them?" I ask, even though I suspect I already know the answer. I just need to hear it aloud.

"There is a dematerialization sequence, where the framework skeleton stores the evolved personality of the individual, then hides and de-fleshes if it can't march back aboard its transport."

"I think I'm gonna be sick," Remmy says.

"So Doctor Marcelles may know of a good way to shut them down? Remove them from the battlefield?" I ask.

"We suspect as much," Doctor Anderson says. "You'll have everything you need to find him, but the Sunspire will be out of range, in hiding."

"Right," Isabel says. "What's to stop us from just going off mission and running?"

"We'll find you," Doctor Anderson replies. "One of the other teams would have to take care of you, and trust me, I know exactly which one could do it."

"Contingencies," Remmy says, stretching out in his seat. "Contingencies for their contingencies all backed up by an oh-my-God-it's-all-gone-to-hell backup plan."

"You're not wrong," Doctor Anderson confirms. "I'm sorry, you'll never find out exactly how we're tracking you, and you won't be free until I say you're free. That's the deal that kept two of you from being executed, and the other two from an indefinite prison stay."

"What are we offering Doctor Marcelles?" I ask.

"A chance to get within scanning distance of Jacob Valance, a safe place to work for the rest of his life, and the resources of Special Projects," Doctor Anderson replies. "Getting him back is one of the few objectives with broad support across both major parties. Meeting with our contact on Uumen will be the easy part, convincing Doctor Marcelles to leave might be more difficult."

"But there's almost nothing here about where we're going," Remmy says as he looks through the mission brief.

"That's because we only know the route you'll be taking once you land and roughly where our contact will be. You should spend any extra time reviewing logs from the First Light and Samson crews."

I spend a moment skimming through the mission brief myself and, like Remmy, am surprised at how short it is. Everything we absolutely need to get started is there, but that's all. The Doctor is still here though, so I press on to get more information on another topic. "Can you prioritize this information for us a little?"

"Start with Pandem," Doctor Anderson says. "That's where the Order of Eden started their first gathering colony, committed the worst crimes, and where the most relevant former First Light crew members reunited. The logs get interesting once they're all back on board the Triton."

"Tell me we can watch this holographically," Remmy says.

"Any way you like, just begin with the major events," Doctor Anderson replies as he makes to leave. His stride leaves no time for another question, and I have more than I can count.

It's as if we were all eager for another assignment. Within minutes we're all neck deep in study material. I start with the journey of Ayan Rice the second and Minh-Chu Buu to Pandem right away. Isabel is right beside me, watching my half metre tall holographic projection as the pair have their first conversation at the outset of their journey on Minh-Chu's old ship. "I can't believe they both just left Freeground," she says. "I mean, Minh hadn't finished his stress therapy, Ayan could have been a star as the first perfectly fabricated human being, and they just decided to chase Valent. They couldn't even be sure what he'd be like when they got there."

"Jonas Valent saved their lives, and Minh was his best friend," I tell her. "It makes sense to me."

"I'm sorry, it sounds selfish to me," Isabel says. "Minh-Chu has a big family on Freeground, and he could have gotten back into Freeground Fleet as a decorated pilot. I'd kill for that kind of career bump."

"If there's one thing the First Light crew had in common, it was loyalty," I retort.

"To a fault," she replies. "I mean, they threw away everything and ended up on Pandem? Everyone who was able to get even a glance at the open Stellarnet from a nearby system knows that the place was a world wide slaughter."

"May as well go where the action is," Remmy chuckled. "Turned out okay though."

"Idiot," Isabel sighs. "Skip to the end, bonehead. They're stranded on Tamber, a moon without any police, where you have to scrounge for food, clean water - it's a disaster."

"But they saved hundreds, maybe thousands of people along the way," Remmy replies. I know he's arguing with information that he gleaned at a glance, neither of them have all the facts yet. "That's what these people do, I think. On their first mission they saved an entire colony, Concordia, wasn't it Clark?"

"That's right," I say. "They stepped right in front of Vindyne and saved as many as they could. I met a few. Some of them are pretty happy to be Freegrounders now."

"What did that get them?" Isabel asks. "Vindyne didn't exactly forget and forgive. Within weeks they had Valent in custody, and where is he now?"

I look it up idly and find the logs detailing Jonas Valent's death. My heart sinks. Before I didn't know for sure, but seeing the footage of him dragging the original Lucius Wheeler out of an airlock before a chemical reaction could detonate him like a bomb makes it real. "He's dead," I say quietly.

"See? They just stumbled in, not taking measure of the situation."

"No one knew much of anything current about humans outside of Freeground space back then," Remmy argues. "Most crews would have done the same thing or worse, we were so closed off. We just didn't realize it until they brought back stories of the outside. Their experiences out there were so exciting, so incredible to us that they couldn't be contained. Censoring was pointless, it only encouraged Freegrounders to seek out the truth, and they found it more often than not."

Isabel sits back, red faced, turning her attention to her comm unit. Something in what Remmy said got through to her.

Remmy presses on anyway. "If they didn't stumble around out there, some other corp would have taken us over because we wouldn't have worthwhile shield technology, or know who the players were, or have anyone out there who owed Freeground any favours. The Concordians had friends, and when Jonas' crew saved them, they became Freeground's friends."

"Fine, I get it," Isabel says quietly.

"Better to stumble around in the dark, looking for the door than to suffocate in a sealed room."

"I get it, okay?" she shouts.

"They did the best with the knowledge they had," Remmy won't give up, even though he's won.

"She gets it, Remmy," I say. "We have a lot of catching up to do."

We read summaries and watch logs well into the night, until we can barely keep our eyes open. Remmy tires out first, followed shortly by Mary.

When it's just Isabel and me, and we're starting to fade she looks at me. "Can I ask you something?"

"I've seen some pretty bad arguments start with those exact words," I say with a reassuring smile. "But sure."

"Why do you idolize the First Light crew? Mary told me you've been digging up info on them for years."

I'm starting to realize that Isabel, the woman I fancy over every one that's come before, might not be a big fan of the First Light crew. My answer doesn't come without a measure of consideration. "They took a challenge and made a difference for us, even though they didn't have much of a chance."

"That's just it," Isabel says. "I don't know that they did much of anything."

"Without them we would probably only have a bare understanding of shield technology, our vacsuits would still just be basic environment suits, and there's a whole catalog of tech they brought back and improved."

"It's just technology though. What good is it if they opened us up to Vindyne? The Order of Eden?"

"Without them the Order of Eden or something like it would have swept in and taken us over, no problem." This is starting to look like it might get heated, and I decide it's time to change tact. "But, in a way you're right. The technology can't be the only benefit. I think they also opened Freeground up to other cultures. We even had pretty free access to the Stellarnet for a while. The feeds were a couple months old, but we could see the galaxy for what it was."

Isabel's gaze takes a down turn, she's looking into her lap. "That was them, wasn't it?" she admits.

"I don't think we would have had that short alliance with Lorander either. They taught us a lot during those three years, and we only caught their notice because they saw what Vindyne was doing to people through our distress messages. If the First Light never rescued those refugees from the Overlord, we'd never have sent those. If we were still closed in like we were, we wouldn't have had an advanced warning about the Holocaust Virus either, and it would have hit Freeground before we hand a chance to wipe out all our artificial intelligences."

"Didn't Valent cause that? In the beginning, I mean, by releasing his AI?" she asks.

I remember seeing something about that during the day and call it up after a moment. "Here's evidence that was just sent from Tamber that shows that the Order of Eden included code from Alice to make people think it was Valent's fault, or Valance's doing," I show it to her and, while it doesn't provoke an argumentative reaction, it does nothing to raise her spirits.

"Well, that's good," she offers sullenly.

I shut down the display on my comm and take her hands in mine. "What's wrong?"

A tear rolls down her cheek and she hesitates before answering. "I'm starting to understand." She takes a deep, unsteady breath. "To understand what it's going to be like on our own out there. If we get through the missions Anderson sends us on, we'll get turned out on our own. Then what?" Her teary eyes look into mine, and I see she's terrified. "All I see about these people from the First Light is how they've had to fight, and adapt just to stay alive."

I pull her into my arms and brush her cheek. Isabel lays her face into my palm and cries. "I'm not like them, or as strong as you and Mary."

I don't know what to say, so I just try to keep her talking. "What about Remmy?"

That inspires a wet chuckle. "Remmy's too daft to realize what's about to happen."

I laugh and nod. "When he goes off duty, he really goes off duty."

"Like his brain has a switch," she elaborates. "Wish I had one."

The hard won levity starts to drain, and a realization strikes. I voice it before she slips back down into tears and worry. "You won't be alone," I whisper against her temple, punctuating it with a kiss.

She looks up at me with what almost looks like surprise.

"I'm pretty sure Mary has a crush on you," I inform her.

Isabel laughs and punches me in the chest. "Be serious!"

I look her in the eyes and let it all out. "You brought me back, Izzy. My first big feelings were for you, and now you've got me. You've got me from here to the furthest star, luv."

The kiss that follows my dedication is soft, warm, and slow. "Thank you," she says against my lips when we part. "I think I want to stay just like this," Isabel says, getting comfortable in my arms. "For as long as we can."

I hold her closer until she starts to doze off some time later. I carry her to bed. I didn't think about our impending future enough to be frightened of our freedom. After seeing her fall apart at not knowing what that future would be like, after our missions were complete, I'm forced to stare it in the face.

As I lay her down she half-wakes. Her gentle grip on my arm stops me from standing up. I quietly join her. As she drifts off again I lay wide awake wondering; where is my fear?

CHAPTER 12
INCOGNITO

I learn more in a few days about the First Light crew, what became of them, and how different they were in the time leading up to our mission than I ever thought possible. Through their logs and summaries of events I experience how dangerous the galaxy really was. I follow one of the Samson crew for a while, his name was Ramirez, only to find that he dies needlessly in a battle for the Triton. Within hours of his death a political solution is found. Ramirez and the men he killed all sacrificed themselves for nothing.

Never is it more clear in my mind that you can't always know how much a sacrifice means until it's made. For the first time in my life I question how valiant Freeground's heroes really are. I begin to think many of them are misguided, blinded by fervent patriotism at first. They discover that's not enough, but not without paying the price.

They fight for each other. The bonds that tie those people together are personal. At one time they decided they were as good as family so they sought to renew friendships some time after Jonas surrendered himself. Jacob and Ayan the second seemed to find a new love for each other after they meet up even though, by all accounts, they felt like very different people. To someone from Fleet Command their abandonment of Freeground might seem treasonous. The way I see it, they are going towards each other while seeking a life in the greater universe.

It was their timing that made things difficult. The Holocaust Virus and the Order of Eden were making a mess of humanity. The First Light crew, the Samson crew, and finally the Triton crew's experiences while the virus was spreading is terrifying. Anything with an artificial intelligence can be infected. It would then check the identities of people around it against a copy of the Order of Eden database and attempt to murder anyone who wasn't on it. In most cases, that's just about everyone.

Some families on Pandem did get the chance to pay. While Jacob and his people were there they kept their forensic software running, collecting data. I know I should have felt something as I looked through the reenactments. When I reviewed the death of a nafalli family who were sheltering humans who couldn't afford to pay the Order of Eden membership fee, Mary had to leave. She couldn't watch as three maintenance bots tore them to shreds. When it was over a very young nafalli crept out from a small cupboard. She cried for hours when her parents wouldn't move, eventually falling asleep. When she woke she tried to get a response from her father by patting his cheek and plucking at his eyelids. In the end, she curled up against his corpse and quivered in the cold of night. I should have felt something. My critical thinking should have collapsed and I should have been in tears like Mary, but there was nothing.

I found out what happened to that little girl. She was picked up by survivors and eventually transported to the Triton, where someone named her Zoe. The most recent holographic recording of her placed her with an adoptive mother, and she was visited daily by Ashley Lamport from the Samson, and Panloo Ieem, a refugee. I stared at a hologram of the toddler hanging between their hands for the better part of ten minutes. I didn't feel relief, but some kind of satisfaction at seeing the child happy. If they never sheltered humans, the whole family would have survived. Most non-humans were left alone unless they got involved with unregistered humans.

I'm thinking about Zoe's relatively happy end when we break through the atmosphere and pass over the yellow and green surface of Uumen. Thick forest encroaches on issyrian habitats. Their great clutches, where nutrient rich lakes are contained by domes built from yellow-orange resin are slowly being violated by giant brambles. The brief told me that those habitats were where most issyrians preferred to live. The waters of the clutch extended their lives, facilitated easy chemical communication and was the birth place for their young.

The brief didn't prepare me for the grand reality of it. The clutch isn't just one large dome encompassing the lake, it is several. Some are artfully stacked atop each other, and at the end of the habitat furthest from the encroaching forest you can still see water flowing between the resin bubbles.

Most of the habitats are abandoned. The encroaching forest, designed to convert habitable worlds to a human friendly environment, is taking one side of the lake. Its persistent growth is visible through the domes, creeping along the shore and inward along the murky bottom.

"I can see why there's an issyrian resistance here," Remmy says as he monitors communications for any mention of our little transport.

"I'd get closer, but I don't want to draw attention," Isabel says. "I'd be pissed if someone came along and messed with my habitat too."

"It limits their breeding," Mary says. "By corrupting their waters, the Order is making it a lot harder for the issyrians here to find mates and have children."

"Someone did the reading," Remmy quips.

"We're going to Lyssipa," Mary replies, plucking at her loose fitting, long sleeved green shirt. "I hope everyone else did the reading too, since this place is going to be full of angry issyrians."

Isabel gracefully manoeuvres our ship into a slow descent, following the directions provided by port control. "Why don't they just leave?" she asks.

"Money," Remmy replies. "The issyrians didn't have a firm concept of it when Regent Galactic got here. They were given tons of cash for their land but ripped off for years on everything from building supplies to candy."

"Where'd you read that?" I ask.

"Stellarnet. I've been following independent news from Regent Galactic worlds for years."

"That's why they set you up in our group," Isabel says. "Now it makes sense."

"Yeah, well, they also charged me with more counts of contraband possession than all three of you put together. I'd be in jail for a century if it weren't for Doc Anderson."

The buildings below look like metal and concrete versions of the clutch domes and pods. We get a good look as we descend to our landing pad. Balconies and walkways with hundreds of issyrians making their way around come into view. Even at a distance I recognize that most of them seemed subdued, none have the tall, striding carriage I was used to seeing in the few that visit Freeground.

With a gentle bump our ship sets down on a narrow pad. I check my gear, making sure the pockets of my loose, draw string pants hold a couple days worth of provisions, an emergency medical pack, a few technical trinkets. Under my two-layered long shirt a pulse handgun is holstered in the middle of my back. It's the heaviest legal weapon allowed on the planet.

"Everyone got everything?" Mary asks.

"Yup, don't forget your ID slips," Remmy says.

My thin ID slip is taped securely to my upper forearm. The DNA stamp has been updated so I can match my new name. I remind myself to ask Doctor Anderson who was responsible for getting someone from Freeground so deep inside the Order of Eden that they can modify DNA records.

The moment the single cabin ship's hatch opens we recoil. The air reeks of something rotten, and the humidity makes it stick. I have never experienced anything so vile, and to make matters worse, the air is thick enough for us to taste it, a sickening tang on our tongue.

"Oh my God, what is it?" Isabel asks.

I ignore her and step onto the long walkway that runs along the outer edge of the rounded port building. The outer structure is built for busier days, with small to medium landing platforms spaced out evenly, enough to accommodate a few hundred ships at once.

"I think it's the natural domes, and the issyrians," Mary says as a group of issyrians pass by.

They were unlike any I'd ever seen. The shape shifters always looked regal, almost showy when they were on Freeground. Some of them sported elongated necks, or made their smooth skin glisten as their bodies shifted under their suits in little waves and ripples. You never knew what an issyrian would look like from one moment to the next. I was told they could even take the shape of humans.

These are different. The group that walking past our platform have brown and black spots on sickly skin. The thousands of celia that are normally hidden under layers of shifting skin hang limp along the sides of their faces, arms and backs. One has a dark cavity in his side, as though something dead has been cut away. They all wear painful looking devices that hug them around the middle and circulate fluids through their upper torsos. None of that affects me at all. The shock of sadness comes when I realize that all seven of them, short and tall, are touching each other. Careful prods with flat fingertips on arms, backs, shoulders and faces are shared as they pass slowly. I heard once that it is their custom to do that when they are near death. It is their way of making sure that they are still part of the living universe, and to pass on impressions and emotions chemically. "Everything here is rotting, except for the terraforming forest," I explain.

"Are you all right?" Mary asks, coming to my side.

One of the issyrians look straight at me with big, round, dull blue eyes. I don't know what to do, so I stare back. It doesn't matter which organization did this. The issyrians will remember they were human above all else. When my locked stare with the issyrian comes to an end I look to my new comm. It's a cheap imitation, partially transparent, without emergency medical systems. "We'll be meeting our contact in twenty minutes. Let's get going before we run into something unexpected."

CHAPTER 13
THE HOLLOW CITY

The interior of the port building is worse. The lights are dim, the windows are shaded, and in the centre is a pod of water several storeys high suspended in a transparent vessel. It's made to look like one of the habitats outside, but wisps of green and brown contaminate the fluid within, algae that makes the aquatic section of the port unsuitable for issyrians. Several vicious looking fish swim in and out of the murkier sections of the fluid, I guess they're bottom feeders, natural garbage eaters who are doing their best to clean things up.

"Those are fricken huge," Remmy says, looking at the fish. "That one's over two metres, easy."

We follow a worn yellow line that leads us to the city tram. Once aboard we have the car all to ourselves. "This place looked kinda busy from above, but is almost dead up close. I've never seen a port this slow." Isabel says.

"There's a major port on the other side of the planet," Mary answers. "The human port."

"Ah, right."

"The people we replaced were actually headed there originally, there are resorts for humans on leave, kind of tourist traps."

"I don't mind a good tourist trap," Remmy says. "Shops full of decorative jewelry and authentic regional artifacts that really aren't worth anything. Open bars, gambling everywhere you turn, beaches - fake or real, they're better than sitting in a star cruiser. I think my favourite thing is the entertainment: no one judges what you're into, it's nice and guilt free."

"Sounds like fun," Isabel says. "Only, I wonder what kind of entertainment you're into that is only guilt free in special places?"

"No comment," he replies with a nervous laugh.

The rest of the ride takes place in mechanical and verbal silence. The monorail system doesn't make so much as a hum, and my companions are just as taken by the view as I am. The course the transit car takes sends us hurtling between buildings that look more like interstellar hulls. Their round concrete and metal sides are stained by contamination. Brown, yellow and green buildings are streaked by watermarks that turn their colours to sickly shades. We watch in silence as the view of larger rounded buildings lit by the high yellow sun are replaced by the underside of the city, where smaller pods, or rounded structures piled together rest in shadow.

There we see the masses. The slick ground is mossy and soft, rotting underfoot as hundreds of issyrians make their way from place to place. A few are in sealed suits, trying to protect themselves from contamination. The rest wear clothing much like ours: light woven fabrics in loose fitting shapes. I don't know that issyrians have one specific colour to their skin - I haven't known that many to be honest - but most just beneath us was a sea of muted tones.

The transit car reduces speed and angles down. Issyrians clear the track as we slowly drift into an open air station. There are hundreds of them gathered around a hovering holographic image to our left.

"Be quiet and careful," Mary warns as the doors slide open. The crowd engulfs us passively the moment we emerge from the car. The transit platform is full. It seems to be standing in as a viewing platform for the holographic figure of a boy, who can't be older than thirteen.

Big oval eyes glance our way briefly, only momentarily distracted by our presence. "-right and true," the young speaker says with a bearing that demonstrates a mastery of oration. "Time and time again humanity has proven that it can adapt nature to its needs, now it is time to find a middle ground. That is our calling, that is why the Eden Fleet has joined us along with its master, Eve herself. She believes, as do I, that having the power to adapt something to our needs does not mean that we cannot compromise, that we cannot preserve or restore as much of the natural environment as we can while becoming its master. To be the master of our environment is our destiny, it is our fate, but how we accomplish that mastery is up to us," proclaims the speaker.

"That's the Child Prophet," Remmy whispers. "I've seen a few of his recordings before."

"I've heard of the little shit," Mary says. "How the hell did a little snot-nose found the Order of Eden?"

"He is their messiah. The predictions he makes come true," says one dull eyed issyrian. He's short, and unnaturally thin in the centre. "So they say."

"Figurehead," Remmy mutters. "I'm sure that's all he is."

"Like minded allies are coming to our door," the Child Prophet announces. "It was said that before the darkness a people would treat with the Ruling Order, and it has come to pass. The majority of the United Confederation Governing Council have voted that they will enter into an alliance with the Order of Eden. They have made pledges for all their member worlds, advancing our cause, and joining us in our glorious coming fate."

"Hate fate," says an issyrian somewhere behind me. The phrase is repeated by a few others in the crowd as the hologram fades.

I realize we weren't the only humans in the audience as a trio in worn, dark blue loose fitted protective clothing make their way out of the crowd. "Don't be here, not now." One fellow with a long scar across his forehead says to me in an intense whisper.

I take his lead, following right behind. "No! Don't follow us!" says a woman behind him in a strange, thick accent. "Stupid travellers, you don't belong in Trest."

Something about the size of my fist flies past my head. Rolling across the ground in front of me, it looks like a chunk of dried moss and clay. We hurry away, not running, but making good time alongside the tracks. Running would have been like signaling the crowd to chase us. When I check the rear view on my comm unit I'm relieved to see that, even though a few of them are brandishing chunks of dirt and clay, ready to toss, they are letting us go. One of them hurls a good sized chunk in our direction and it strikes Isabel in the back. The dry clay bursts apart on impact, making it look more dramatic than it is.

"You all right?" I ask.

"Fine. Just wish I could turn around and tell them we have nothing to do with the Order."

I glance about and can only see the deeper shadows under the towering round buildings and dozens of circular houses piled like eggs. Issyrians look out their doors and windows at us and the crowd behind chanting; "Hate fate!" With an over the shoulder glance I see issyrians crowding into the transit car. More than half the crowd manage to fit inside, and from the looks of it they are set to do harm further down the line.

"Come!" says a voice from beneath a low rail bridge. "Hurry, come with me!"

I check my comm unit and nod. "You're Emiss?"

"Yes, friend of humans. You don't all look the same to me. Come before you get into more trouble!"

We do as we are told and follow her through a service grate under the monorail. I almost retch as we turn a corner and we are struck with a sickly sweet smell. It carries a warm humidity that makes me feel like I'm being coated with the stench.

"A few dead down here, sorry," says the tall, thin issyrian. She wears clothing that matches mine closely - a long shirt with draw string pants and simple boots. "It makes it easier to hide, not even patrol drones come here." She rushes us down several tunnels. When the scant sunlight coming through the grates overhead disappears she becomes slightly luminescent, shedding just enough light for us to pass without stepping into the deeper pools or tripping over unidentifiable rotting piles. I'm still sure I'll be sending everything I'm wearing out the airlock the moment I return to the Sunspire.

"Finally," Isabel says as we emerge into an alleyway. "I hate being underground."

"This way," our guide instructs, starting down a narrower alleyway without making sure we're following.

"Wait," I say.

She stopped and turns, looking me up and down with her big, oval blue eyes. "I'm waiting."

"We're new here, very new here," I tell her. "But how could the issyrians let the Order of Eden take one of their solar systems?"

"We didn't know how your commercial system worked. Before we had a chance to learn Regent Galactic owned all the land, and many of our people enjoyed the things they brought, paid too much money. We were too poor to buy back," she replies in a rush.

"What about your government?" Mary asks. "They must have some interest in saving this world."

"We are quarantined. Contaminated, sick," Emiss says as if speaking to a slow child. She rolls up her sleeve to show us a wound that looks like some kind of bacteria was eating at her. "Omira, Doctor Marcelles' friend, tries to help, but no one can help. There are few clear waters."

"So they won't send help because they're afraid of becoming contaminated?" I ask.

"Yes."

"That doesn't make sense," Remmy counters. "I've seen a couple dozen issyrian travellers, they looked perfectly healthy."

"Outcasts, barren folk. They seal their skins and communicate the same way you do, with words, and data. It's a shadow life."

"I'm sorry," Remmy says with unexpected sincerity. "We don't know enough about your people to avoid stupid questions."

Emiss stares at him a moment, her eyes shifting to a more vibrant blue. "It is all right, we have many prejudices. I will try to limit mine to the ones that apply to you in particular."

"Are we near our destination?"

"Yes, just around the corner."

Once we're through the oval door the smell eases, and the air begins to clear. The hallway is wider, cleaner, and there are several issyrians with the back rig that we saw in the port. They look healthier, and I assume the machine on their backs running viscous fluids in and out of their bodies is some kind of filtration unit. Most of the issyrians we see inside are armed, all of them eye us with some suspicion. Parallel to the hall there are three centimetre wide runnels with a thin jet of greenish brown fluid, it never ceases to flow, filling the space with the sound of the forced jet.

"I'm detecting chemical communication," Remmy says. "These issyrians are a lot healthier, I think."

"I didn't know we could detect pheromonal communication," I reply.

"I'm using the medical scanner. I can't tell what they're saying, but they're talking to each other."

We come to a roughly circular central chamber with a domed ceiling. Pipes come in from all directions. Many of them are capped or redirected so their contents flow back into the sewer system. In the centre is a thick column with vessels, intertwining tubes, and monitoring systems built in. There are several alcoves scattered around the room. I watch an issyrian emerge from one with a new circulation device affixed to his back. He looks worse than our guide, with a misshapen head and only one arm. The solid stone of the hallway is replaced by fine grating. Several other issyrians and a few humans - all of them looking healthy and clean - are busy at work maintaining the machinery, or working the controls at free standing input columns. A breeze tickles my skin from below as we move across the space towards a pair of staircases. I look down and see whirling waters. At a glance I can see several small shapes, like fish, darting around beneath.

"This is an incubator and treatment room," our guide tells us, directing our attention down through the floor. "One of the few places on this hemisphere where our children can be born then grow to adolescence."

"Why don't you cover it?" Mary asks. "A lot of things could pass through this grating."

"They must become accustomed to interference, learn to combat contamination. The pools are also monitored so the aggressiveness of diseases can be maintained."

"So you know how to purify the world outside?" Isabel asks hopefully.

That seemed to surprise Emiss, whose gaze lingers before she answered. "No, the Order has contaminated every space on this world. We disease and cure our young so they can evolve to survive. They know pain in youth so they survive as adults."

"Thank you Emiss," says a raspy voice from above. We look to see an older woman coming down a winding metal staircase. "I can handle things from here."

"I wanted to speak to you about the recruiting centre," Emiss replies.

"There will be time later. Why don't you spend some time in a regeneration pod?"

Emiss bows and walks away without another word.

"Thank you," Remmy says as the issyrian passes by him. He's rewarded with a nod.

"I speak for Doctor Marcelles." The tall woman says as she descends. Her piercing grey eyes make quick work of inspecting me and my companions.

"We're here to ask for his help on behalf of Freeground Intelligence," I tell her.

She idly checks a display on a nearby control column. "You have a problem that even Freeground Intelligence, with all their tendrils stretching out into the galaxy can't solve?"

"I wouldn't say they've got a lot of contacts out here," I reply.

"Then how did they find Doctor Marcelles? They have someone out here listening, watching," she returns her attention to us. "You have the look of fresh initiates. You'll learn all about how Freeground Intelligence compartmentalizes, and maybe even how long of a reach the organization has." She turns towards a nearby exit and beckons.

At the end of a short hallway is a makeshift sitting room, where a few humans casually watch news broadcasts from the Stellarnet. "...taken responsibility for the Holocaust Virus, but the British allegations make things interesting for the Order of Eden. As more recruitment centres appear across civilized worlds we see more allegations of the Order of Eden's responsibility for the virus. Most of our viewers live on worlds that have wiped out artificial intelligences in all their systems, making machines safe again. The Order of Eden calls the mass deletion the first digital genocide. If you ask the representatives from the new British Empire, they'll unanimously tell you that it's the best remedy to the Holocaust Virus. The Carthans and Roma Prime Public Affairs office, agree, adding... " the newscaster says.

It's strange seeing a real human actually reading the news. Until the Holocaust Virus, most news casters were artificial intelligences with fairly convincing human images sitting in to represent them. The Stellarnet was the first to come back online. I didn't see much of it because of Freeground censorship, but I saw enough to know that humans were at the wheel again, bringing their creativity and imperfections with them. "Across the core worlds that were worst hit by the Holocaust Virus, new governments are emerging along with the old establishments. Despite the infighting, groups of rebels and combat ready ships are making their presence known. A common message; 'Hate Fate' has been spreading like the virus that brought on these terrible times, and this newscaster expects that these words will become our call to action. They are a direct reaction to the Child Prophet and his message of-" I stop listening. The newscaster seems to be reveling in the misfortune of billions almost as much as the Order itself.

"Have a seat," our hostess invites. "I can have food brought if you like."

"No thank you." I take a seat across from her in the middle of a worn sofa. Remmy and Isabel sit on either side of me. Mary warily lowers herself into an ancient armchair. "No offence, but I'd like to speak to Doctor Marcelles directly."

"He's a little busy," she replies. "My name is Omira Gerring, where he goes, I go, so this isn't just his decision."

"Well, there are some things, like our offer, that I don't think I can discuss with anyone else," I tell her. I decide that would be my last attempt at getting past his gatekeeper for a long while. I don't want to wear out our welcome before we've even had a chance to so much as shake the Doctor's hand.

"I know everything about his past work. Besides, he's listening," she says with a knowing smile.

I take a breath and nod. "All right. I've come with an offer. We can get him in range of Jacob Valance. We're aware that he never got to finish his work with him."

"He finished what was important. The Valance project was a failure in the end, so Doctor Marcelles moved on."

That takes me by surprise. Ever since I found out about Jacob Valance and the framework designs, I was under the impression that it was Marcelles' masterpiece, maybe even an obsession. How could he move on from something so revolutionary, or someone who went on to create his own history? Her statement also takes one of my best bargaining chips away.

"Isn't that a little like child abandonment?" Remmy asks.

"Valance was programmed with what he needed to survive before the Doctor escaped from Vindyne. Judging from the data we saw four months ago, he's still failed to trigger the final phase of his development, so the chances of him ever becoming more than just an average framework with a passable intelligent personality installed are next to nil. We've moved on."

"To what?" I ask. "That is, if you don't mind me asking."

"Applying stable quantum entanglement to medical nano technology," she answers. "It's all theory now, but we're certain it'll be a leap forward when it's applied."

"So your work doesn't have anything to do with the issyrians here?"

"No. They provide a safe place to work and we help them develop a treatment for their people. Their hope is to evolve the new broods into an infection resistant breed that can take the planet back. Rejoining their Houses is impossible now, so that's their only option."

"I'm sure Special Projects will be glad to help. They'd at least provide research data, maybe even send some people down for a while," I tell her. "Or you can rejoin Freeground, and you'll have full access, your own department and a safe place to research for the rest of your lives." It's a risk, embellishing the offer a little and extending it to Omira as well, but she already seems unmovable.

"You have the clout to make that happen?"

"My mission director does, and I know he'd be behind this kind of research," I reply, sure of my response.

"Are you sure you can promise this to me as well? You don't even know who I am."

"I can guarantee Freeground Intelligence would extend their offer to you, especially if you know everything he does."

"In trade for what?"

I don't see any reason to hesitate or package those details. "We need your help in defeating the framework technology. We have evidence that-"

"Stop there," she says, holding a hand up. "I know for a fact that Doctor Marcelles warned Freeground Intelligence, Vindyne, and anyone who would listen about the potential harm that could be done if that technology was misused. The portions of the framework technology that he worked on were meant to augment a living being, not to create an army. Now you're in a new arms race. I can assure you he wants no part of it."

"You can't be safe here. It'll only be a matter of time before the Order discovers this place," I retort. It is only when I watch Omira lean back in her seat that I realize that I've been reduced to being adversarial. The encounter is supposed to be about enticing Marcelles back and it's turning into an argument.

"I'll discuss this with him. Please make yourselves comfortable, just don't wander." Omira is on her feet and heading out of the room before she finishes speaking. She doesn't give me time to add anything, not that I have anything in mind.

The rest of my team know I screwed up an opportunity. Not even Mary looks at me in the awkward minutes that follow as we wait idly. Then, just as Remmy is opening his mouth, about to offer some silence shattering quip, Omira returns. "You have his attention," she says. "Even after all the time I've spent with him, he still manages to surprise."

"That's good for us, right?" Remmy asks.

"Yes," Omira replies. "He'll show you how to kill frameworks one on one, from there your government can develop whatever mass weaponry it wishes to overcompensate with. First you have to do something for us, something very important."

"And dangerous," Mary adds. "Just guessing."

"Your companion is right," Omira confirms, sitting down across from us. "There is a ship called the Fallen Star, it was hidden in the Silvermane Belt, this solar system's outer asteroid belt. Doctor Marcelles wants you to download the contents of the lab computer system and collect some samples that should still be in suspended animation."

"That's what you were after when you came here," Remmy says. "It's what led you to this solar system in the first place, isn't it?"

It was like he picked the question right out of my head, only I wouldn't have asked it. Omira's tense smile tells me it's too soon for details, and I make sure we don't push. "Why can't he go himself?" I ask. That's the important question.

"Something aboard the Fallen Star broke containment. A being that was in storage for another scientist's work. The Fallen Star was a Freeground research vessel, one that was never meant to be this close to any civilized area," Omira replied. "Once he provides your people with the information they'll need to kill frameworks he knows they'll start asking about what was left on that ship next."

"So he wants to be prepared," I reply. "What was he researching there?"

"You haven't earned the right to that information yet, sorry."

"When do we leave?" I ask, watching Mary's reaction in my peripheral. I can tell at a glance that she agrees it's the right move. I'm convinced there's no other way to get what we need out of Marcelles, so it's the only way. I promise myself that I'll gather as much intelligence about the Fallen Star as possible before we make hard seal on her airlock. There's a nagging, bad feeling about the whole thing that just won't go away.

CHAPTER 14
PART 1 – APPROACHING THE FALLEN STAR

Freeground's training focuses on what happens between the stars. In the dark expanse between distant points of light, where anyone could disappear forever in the endless cold vacuum. Boarding missions are the most risky venture in ship to ship combat. I have no shame in admitting that boarding the Fallen Star makes me more nervous than I've been on a boarding mission since I was a trainee. If you're in the infantry, more general purpose marines, or any part of Fleet, you've had at least a hundred hours of simulation time, and many hours of practical time at boarding and disembarking.

As Isabel flies our aged shuttle through the slowly moving outer solar system asteroid belt, none of that training matters. We pass through a clutch of brown and black stone and the more active part of the inner asteroid belt comes into view. A dark shroud of fine, whirling dust surrounds a ring of highly magnetic stone. If it weren't for the scant light from the distant sun, we'd barely see it at all.

The situation is completely different on the scanner readout screens. The fine dust caught in the magnetic ring show up as bright blue and green arcs, clearly illustrating the safe course, and perfectly obscuring anything in the whirling ring's midst. "Are you sure you accounted for drift and collisions?" I ask Omira.

"If you enter where I specified you'll come in right behind the Fallen Star," Omira replies. "The magnetic fields here obscures her perfectly."

"Can we get through without being pulled off course?" I ask Isabel.

She takes a moment to verify her position and trajectory before answering. "I'm going to use a part of the field ahead to pull us in. We should get to a magnetically stable pocket here," she pointed at one of the displays, indicating a place behind a large dark spot. "A magnetic planetoid. I bet the Fallen Star is shadowing behind."

"If we're lucky," Remmy says. "With all that magnetic activity, there's no telling what condition she'll be in."

"She will be largely the way Doctor Marcelles and I left it," reassured Omira.

She wears her confidence like armour. It is almost difficult to speak to Omira, since we entered the belt she seems smug.

The sound of fine particles grating against the hull makes any further discussion difficult. For a moment the shuttle begins to turn sideways. I glance behind me into the main hold and catch Mary's eye. She's beyond nervous. Her gloved hands grip the hand-holds above her seat tightly, and her old fashioned pull-down helmet faceplate is fastened tight.

The dim safety lights and instrument panels are the only illumination as we move deeper into the magnetic ring. I watch as two types of scanners go offline, protecting themselves from being overloaded by the energy surrounding us. I monitor the basic navigational, thermal and field sensors unblinking. We pass into the calm centre of the ring and the rasping of sand against the hull quiets to almost nothing.

Scanning for the Fallen Star's energy readings or for materials that could match her hull are impossible, so I start looking for man-made shapes. Omira is over my shoulder, looking on. At long last she highlights something. "Follow this, it'll lead you to the Fallen Star."

I forward the information to Isabel, shaking my head all the while. "I see a charged rock formation, but nothing that looks like a ship."

"Doctor Marcelles foresaw that," Omira says. "It was part of his plan. Once we're closer and you can get a better image you'll see the Fallen Star."

We follow the magnetic fields like a current. Isabel makes a fine art of carefully applying thrusters and keeping us drifting in the right direction. As we drift towards the large asteroid ahead I look closer at the image of its tail. Long minutes of searching finally lead me to a artificially square angle, at the rear of the ship, I assume. "It's become part of the asteroid," I explain as I zoom in and try to find a docking port.

"The asteroid is a formation of particles from the belt," Omira explains. "They covered the Fallen Star, hiding it perfectly right in the middle of magnetic fields and dust."

"Is it intact?" Mary asks.

I scan for air pockets inside the ship and come up with a floor plan of the three hundred metre long vessel. "A bit of minor hull damage but no breaches. There are two docking ports we can access at the rear." My apprehension and suspicion are starting to become excitement, but I still can't help but let my more prudent instincts lead me. "Isabel, hold here."

"Yes, Sir," she replies, firing forward thrusters to slow the shuttle's approach.

I turn in my seat to face Omira. "Now you're going to tell us what to expect when we board, and what we're going after specifically." My question prompts Mary to release her passenger restraints. It doesn't take a genius to see that this part of our trip could become an interrogation.

"You are after the secret of defeating framework soldiers on the battlefield," Omira replied. "You're trading your services for that information. That's all you need to know."

"We're not boarding unless you tell me how this ship ended up here, it's not like Marcelles could pilot it himself, or as if an entire crew would abandon a ship this size because he left. So, what are we after, and why is this ship abandoned?" I ask. The truth behind my threat is that I'm willing to take Omira to the Sunspire instead of Doctor Marcelles. She may not be our target, but she might be good enough for Intelligence for the time being.

"The answers to your questions will involve you in a much larger situation than you're interested in. Suffice it to say that the administrators aboard didn't want to see their research destroyed, but they wanted the ship to be hidden and protected just in case they could never make it back," Omira says.

That just piques my interest, and I'm about to pursue the issue when Remmy pipes in. "So you're saying that something happened that made all those scientists and officers decide to leave at the same time?" he asks dubiously. "Come on, start making sense, lady."

"I can't tell you everything, there just isn't time," Omira tells us, looking defensive for the first time since we met her.

"Why was the ship abandoned?" I ask. Mary doesn't look impressed by any part of the situation.

"For you to understand that, I have to go back into the Fallen Star's history. It was built by Lorander, during their first alliance with Freeground at the turn of the last century," she started to explain.

"So about ninety years ago," Remmy says. "You're not kidding when you say history. I didn't even know Lorander had an alliance with Freeground back then."

"You aren't meant to," Omira replies. "The Lorander corporation allies itself with whoever will serve its long term interests, or fits their long standing philosophy. Freeground entered into a partnership with Lorander during that alliance, a scientific one, and they began to research a species that evolved quite differently than humans did on Earth. By the time Doctor Marcelles joined the scientists aboard the Fallen Star, she had been in service for over sixty years, and there were fourteen different races aboard. The majority of the crew consisted of issyrians."

"That's the race Lorander and Freeground wanted to research?" Remmy asks.

"One of them, but they were more interested in a distant evolutionary relative of theirs - the edxians. Doctor Marcelles' type of research into high speed living tissue regeneration was more than welcome, it helped them understand the few creatures they'd managed to capture on some of their brood islands. Land masses where edxians deposit their young during early adolescence into adulthood, so they can develop physically, socially and mentally undisturbed."

"I've never heard of edxians," Isabel says.

"They're from way out of the sector," Remmy replies. "Intelligence has almost nothing on them, just that they like to capture ships that wander into their space and the crews go missing. There are a few horror movies that show 'em eating humans, but they're not that great. There was this one part in Meat Adrift where an edxian uses this big sharpened spoon to-"

"We're getting off point," Mary interrupts. "Everyone knows, if you hear clicking and hissing on comms planet-side that your translator can't make out, it's time to call for a pickup. That's what they tell us in the marines."

"Right," Isabel says with a nod.

"Did they get far into their research?" I ask, trying to press things on.

"Yes. While Doctor Marcelles was aboard they made great strides. His work forced him to seek out different colleagues after a few years. He was captured along with several other researchers while on a collection expedition on Myo. By then Lorander had been completely uninvolved for decades, and Freeground did not have the military might or ambition to mount a rescue mission against a superior force. It took years for the Doctor to escape, and that is when he was recovered by the First Light and the Triton."

"Then he was sold to Vindyne," I added. Everyone in the shuttle knew he was held captive again, so he could continue work on the Framework project. "I know he managed to escape after a few years, but no one knows exactly what happened after that."

"He was able to secretly signal the Fallen Star from the Vindyne research facility, and they were instrumental in his escape," Omira explains. "That is where we met, and I've been assisting him since. Things had changed aboard the Fallen Star since he was a part of the crew. The research into the edxians had intensified. Researchers who hadn't been caught for years had become brave, almost brazen in their first hand research. It wasn't long before the edxians caught the Fallen Star leaving one of their brood territories and marked by an entire tribe. They see outside contact with their broods as the worst kind of insult. The Fallen Star war forced to hide. The issyrian crew led the scientists here, where they hid the ship and all their work. They suspended most of their research and put their specimens into hibernation before making landfall on the planet."

"Is there anyone left aboard? A custodial crew?" Mary asks.

"There was," Omira replies.

"Oh, here we go," Remmy says, throwing up his hands. "Let me guess: you haven't heard from them in a while."

"Your snarky friend is right," Omira confirmed. "We haven't heard from them in over a year."

"All right, what are we after, and how much of that ship do we have to get through to pick it up?" I ask, looking through the porthole into the near complete darkness outside.

"From the rear airlocks it's only one deck up and nineteen frames forward. We'll be going to the rear cold vault."

"Cold vault," Remmy says. "Meaning we're going after something in stasis?"

"There are subjects in stasis there, but we won't be retrieving them. We're going after a crystalline data storage unit, very small, very easy to move. It was stored there as a backup by one of Doctor Marcelles' colleagues and now it's critical to his work going forward."

"You're coming with us," I tell Omira.

"I was planning on it."

PART 2 – BOARDING THE FALLEN STAR

Omira fills me in on other details about the Falling Star as we're making sure the shuttle has a hard seal with the docking system. It's a mess. Fine particulates have found their way into everything on the outside of the ship, even the clearest of the docking ports.

She tells me things I'm glad to hear. She has all the access codes, that the researcher who owned the data we're collecting has been dead for two years and they wanted Marcelles to have their work, and that Omira knows exactly where to find it. I don't know if I believe all the good news.

Omira also tells me several things I don't want to hear. The fastest way to the cold vault is through a different stasis lockup. The ship's anti-intruder systems were disabled over twenty years ago because it used to incorrectly identify specimens as attackers. She also tells me that hand scanners won't work reliably. I choose to believe all the bad news and expect that she's holding several things back.

Remmy is busy doing an echo scan of everything past the pockmarked outer airlock door and at a glance I can see that he's actually getting what we need - an updated schematic of the nearest fifteen metres of the ship. He flashes me an uneasy smile. "Sometimes the oldest tech does just fine when the new stuff just can't get it."

"Good work," I tell him.

Omira looks over her shoulder at me as she manages to finish uncovering the manual locking switch for the door. The black and brown dust that was covering it grinds under foot more like sand. "We'll be through in a minute. The key sequence is very simple."

"We're taking this at full speed, right Clark?" asks Mary.

I think for a minute. There are a few ways to approach this kind of situation. One is to take it slow, try to understand your surroundings and make note of every little thing so you can operate using as much information as possible. The other extreme is to rush the problem, only paying attention to what you absolutely have to, with the goal of getting in and out as quickly as you can. I already don't like what I've heard about this ship, and the objective is simple. "Any motion on echo, Remmy?"

"Nothing," he replies. "May as well be a mausoleum."

"We're taking this at full speed then," I tell Mary. "Isabel, you're staying here. Keep the ship sealed until we're back."

She looks over her shoulder at me. "I'm going to have to, the airlock coupler is telling me that the section you're breaching is set up as a issyrian fluidic environment."

"What?" Remmy asks.

"You're going for a swim," Isabel tells Remmy with a grin. "What did you think those flow jets on the back of your suits were for?"

Remmy looks at the arm length, low profile rectangular boxes on the back of Omira's suit then at me. "You sure I'm not needed more here, boss? I mean, how complicated could their computers be, really?"

"Secure your helmet so we can start our suit check and get going," I tell him.

Remmy got the ship's lighting and basic environment systems working within minutes of us boarding. I'm still surprised anything works. The lights running in lines down the middle of the floor and ceiling barely pierce the murky soup we propel ourselves through. The hum of the mag-jets on my back remind me that this isn't just water, it's a thicker, nutrient rich compound the issyrians use in most sections of their own ships. I don't know anyone who has ever been aboard and issyrian vessel, or has gone for a swim in a place like this.

The stuff doesn't touch me, thanks to the environment suits Omira set us up with. Judging from the brown and green streaks running through the stuff, it looks like something went bad while the ship was in hiding. "What would an infection from this stuff do to us if we caught one?" I ask.

"You could end up with an easily treated skin disease, or develop an aggressive phage. Just don't get it in your eyes, that's where the worst infections start," replies Omira.

"Environment systems are purifying the flooded areas," Remmy replies. "Looks like this stuff will be clean in about twenty minutes. Pretty good system."

"Issyrian environmental systems are almost as good as Freeground's," Omira says as she takes a corner.

With the jets on it's more like flying than swimming, the suit keeps most of the pressure of the liquid running over it off of us. I can still hear the viscous stuff moving across my helmet though. We move too quickly for comfort. Boarding operations happen slowly because you're supposed to clear rooms as you come across them, follow a schematic, make sure you don't leave systems or closed doors behind to bite you in the ass. We move like we're raiders following Omira like she's about to lead us to a treasure hold.

It's hard not to imagine that there are eyes lurking in dark, open doors just out of sight. The scanners can see more inside of the ship thanks to the hull's shielding, but they don't see half of what they normally would. It wouldn't take much to hide from us, watch us go by from behind a piece of equipment that was left on. We pass through a pair of shielded doors the crew left wide open and I get a glimpse at the main reactor control room. In that moment I can see the status displays indicate the ship is sitting at full power thanks to passive collectors on the hull. They must be pulling juice from the magnetic fields outside. I let it distract me for just a second, almost long enough for me to miss Omira slowing right down. There's something different about the colour of the liquid. The reactor room and the corridor we pass into beyond has black and brown swirls.

"Oh no," Remmy says as we catch up to Omira.

I see them then, three issyrian corpses, or what's left of them. Something chewed away most of their bodies, leaving thin, almost wispy tangles of cartilage and spiky spines. "Did you know them?" I ask as I watch Omira gently touch one of their soft, cartilage skulls.

"I knew all of them," she answers coldly. "They flooded this part of the ship as quickly as they could, according to records."

"Probably to keep whatever did that away from them," Mary said. "Any idea what it could have been?"

Omira worked at the station for a moment, navigating the holographic file menu as if it wasn't distorted by the liquid suspending her over it. A flickering image of a six limbed, shelled insect appeared with several paragraphs of what I assume are research logs. The image stabilizes and I can finally make the terminal's projection out clearly. "Specimen oh-three ninety eight," I read aloud. "Is that image life sized?"

"No, they stand about half a metre tall when they're down on all six legs, about a metre and a half when they're on their hind legs. The human scientists called them land piranha."

"What's a piranha?" Remmy asked.

"Fish that can strip a human of flesh in seconds if you're unlucky enough to be swimming near a school of them," Omira answered. "They're kept as pets, and sometimes used to keep specific artificial habitats clear of other organisms."

"Why would you keep something like that alive and on board?" Remmy asked, pointing at the predator's image. "Couldn't you study them dead?"

"There was a team studying their behaviour before the ship had to shut down," Omira answered as she looked over her shoulder at Remmy. "They have to be alive for that."

"Goddamned scientists. I guess these are some kind of edxian babies or something too, right?"

"No, they're a jungle insect found on brood worlds. The children left there like cracking their shells and eating them alive."

"Remind me to download a map of brood worlds," Mary says. "So I can keep as many light years between me and them as possible."

We move on. I make sure I'm right beside Omira as we pass through the dimly lit corridors. The liquid is clearer thanks to the environmental systems purifiers, and it isn't long before I see our destination. It's an old vault door like I've seen in period films from a couple centuries ago - when the right kind of metal could be trusted to keep intruders out if it was thick enough. "How many people were left aboard?"

"Seven issyrians," she replies. "Six of whom are accounted for."

"Dead," I say.

"Yes," Omira replies.

"I'm sorry,"

"For what?" Omira asks as we slow to a halt in front of the round, three metre wide vault door.

"They were members of the crew, thought you might know them."

"Yes," Omira says. "But everyone who remained behind only did so because they weren't smart enough to leave."

Remmy and Mary come to a halt behind us, and I notice they've pulled me into a private proximity radio channel, excluding Omira. "Everything is off here," Remmy says in a rush. "The chemistry of this stuff, the cumulative data on Omira's vitals, this ship, nothing is exactly what it should be."

I glance at Omira, who must know there is a private conversation happening behind her, but is paying attention to the vault's security interface, ignoring us. I turn to Remmy. "Start at the beginning," I tell him. "What's wrong with the water?"

"This isn't water, it's more like a gel, but that part is normal," he replies. "Near the bodies we saw back there I picked up evidence that the issyrians weren't the only things that died in the area. Something else, something with a total different chemical makeup from the issyrians bled there."

"Okay, so the issyrians got a chance to fight back," Mary replied.

"No, way too much blood evidence was left over in the fluid. Forensic software couldn't reenact what happened specifically, things were stirred up too much, but it was clear on one thing: something or someone dragged those land piranha corpses out of there."

I think for a minute. There's no telling what Omira is hiding, and I'm starting to get the feeling that sending her aboard the Fallen Star alone would not only have been safer for my people, but the only reasonable decision on the table. I rest my hand on my pistol and look to Mary, who takes the cue, holstering her pistol in favour of unslinging the rifle on her back. "Okay, let's move on to your next point, Remmy."

He hesitates a moment, maybe finding the opposite of reassurance in the fact that I'm taking him seriously. "Omira's vitals work on a pre-programmed response," he starts, whispering despite the fact that there is no way Omira can hear what we're saying over a private channel. "At first there was no way to tell, but I've left my passive scanning software running since we left the Sunspire, and after collecting enough data she's the anomaly. When she should get excited her pulmonary and cardiac responses elevate by exact degrees, same thing when she's at rest, when you've had arguments with her, it's like it's all pre-programmed."

"Highly disciplined people or people with systemic regulation can have the same symptoms," I reply.

"I've seen that before," Mary agrees. "But Omira is different. I looked over Remmy's numbers and was about to tell him he's paranoid, but then I crossed it with our deception tracker: she shows no physical signs of lying, or even that she's holding something back from us. Not once, not since we met her."

I didn't have to make a conclusion aloud, we all knew Omira had made an art of holding information back. I opened a general channel. "How long until we're inside?" I asked Omira.

"The airlock beyond this chamber door is filling up so we can transit to an air atmosphere without flooding the secure research area. It will be another two minutes, you and your team can continue discussing all the reasons why this ship makes you nervous."

I don't bother denying her accusation, instead I ask her about what I'm pretty sure Remmy's next concern is. "I was wondering about that, why is this ship so well armoured?"

"This is an exploration vessel, and it was built before combat shielding was common. The hull had to have many layers of different types of armour so it could survive near contact with solar phenomena and other types of intense stellar energy. Basically, it had to be able to hold up against anything a manoeuvring field couldn't repel."

"Internally. The floor plan of the ship so far suggests there are at least two more airlocks like this one," I tell her, pointing at the vault door. "My guess is that this ship is segmented. Not only that, but there's a full hangar on the port side. This ship is made for extended missions off ship, and to handle quick craft retrieval."

"It is an exploration vessel," Omira replies.

"I've seen schematics for research vessels, they have compartmentalized labs, but there is actual heavy armour here. The hangars also tell me that it wouldn't take much to turn this into a small carrier. What were you people doing?"

"I wasn't one of the researchers," she tells me, turning her attention back to the vault. "Get your nerves under control and stop your people from chattering please."

It takes all my training to keep my temper in check. What helps in that moment is the desire to get my hands on a huge find inside that vault so I can trade it for my team's freedom. "How far inside that vault is what we're looking for?"

"One level up, about thirty metres in," she tells me flatly.

"We're going to move fast Omira, no sight seeing," I say.

"Agreed." The outer lock door opens and we swish inside. It closes, leaving us in a small, ghostly lit chamber as the liquid drains out and the air pressure equalizes with the inside of the vault.

"This is what intelligence is like, Clark," Remmy says. "The higher ups only give us the information they think we need to get the job done."

"And we don't get to talk about how many people we lost or how fucked up what the people we work for were doing when it's all over," Mary adds on a private channel. "We better walk out of here with something big. I want out."

I nod, but stay focused on the mission. Long range plans aren't on my mind right now.

PART 3 – THE VAULT

This was a laboratory. In the near-blindingly bright light we discover that it's become a slaughter house. Black and dark blue blood is spattered across the white and grey walls. The deck plating is scarred and pitted with signs that something with enough strength to dent metal won a fight here.

"Looks like we missed the action," Mary says, looking around, her rifle tracking with her eye line.

"I just threw up a little," Remmy replies. "You'd think ration bars tasting the same coming up as they do going down would be a good thing, but it really isn't."

"It's this way," Omira says.

"Are we going to try and figure out what happened at all?" I ask her. "This doesn't match up with the expectations you set for this mission."

Omira stops and looks at me coolly. "You can't put this mission on pause like one of your simulations."

"I've been on more boarding missions than you could imagine," I tell her. "And my experience, my instincts are telling me to turn this around and get my people back to the planet. Even better, I'm thinking we should take a loss here and get back to the Sunspire."

"That wouldn't benefit anyone," Omira says.

"Better to go back empty handed and alive than not at all," I reply. "There's way too much blood here for three or four issyrians."

"It's not issyrian blood either," Remmy says. "Scans as those beetle-piranha things and something else."

Mary takes point as we make our way up a claustrophobically narrow spiraling ramp, and I start feeling like I'm forgetting something. No matter what I do, how hard I concentrate as I retrace my steps, I can't remember what it could be. The walls are still smeared with blood, the non-slip red and blue checkered floor is streaked with drag marks. "How long ago did this happen, Remmy? Get a reading."

"I've already got one, started analyzing a few minutes ago because our forensic software lags like a one legged man on these old hand scanners. Looking at the preliminary results, I can tell you that these things were dragged up, not down."

"That's what I wanted to know," I answer, eying the way behind. I wish someone would turn out the lights, somehow the stark white medical lights are showing me too much. The stains tell a violent story.

"Door opening," Mary announces above me.

"We're entering the vault proper, on the level above," Omira tells us.

"Contact, three p-beetles," Mary whispers into her proximity radio.

"Good nickname," Remmy says. "They notice you?"

"No," Mary replies.

Remmy sees over the lip of the ramp into the next chamber before I do and reels as though someone sucker punched him from the left. Before he can think too much about whatever's up there I get him thinking about his job. "What's on that scanner's live screen? Describe it to me."

He fumbles for a moment but gets down to business before long. Before I get to see whatever has him rattled. "Massive energy drain. It's keeping the lights down, coming from two frameworks."

I get my head above the deck and see the p-beetles first. They are three quarters of a metre long, with split, segmented torsos covered in black and dark blue-green carapaces. The two halves come together at the base of an upper segment bristling with serrated appendages. The head glistens in the faint light, a collection of eyes, pincers and mandibles.

Somehow the p-beetles broke two large stasis containers. In the flickering half light I can make out one nearly skeletal corpse hanging within. There is another on the floor, three beetles are feeding ravenously, biting deep, ripping flesh from bone with jerks of their heads. Their twelve legs strain and scramble against the deck as they fight for leverage so the chunks of rend flesh can be bigger. I make eye contact and immediately wish it were only a corpse.

A very human twitching mouth and wide eyes stare at me as a framework copy of Jonas Valent suffers through the feeding, alive, regenerating as the p-beetles feast. A strangled cry croaks from his throat as one of the creatures yanks a section of bowel free. The stub beneath his shoulder twitches to move an arm that hasn't regenerated. His efforts are reduced to a momentary squirming in a pool of old gore. With one leg half eaten, and his arms missing, there's not much he can do.

"That's the power drain, frameworks that are regenerating while these things feed on them," Mary concludes.

"Yeah," Remmy says. "There's another deeper in."

I can't watch this. My thumb turns the safety on my rifle off, and I take aim at the Jonas framework's head. Shooting him in the head will end his suffering until the framework regenerates and his personality is reloaded.

"Don't!" Omira says in a harsh whisper. "If they're busy feeding on these we can get by with minimal interference."

"I can't stand by and-"

"These models were never programmed, I doubt they even know what's going on," she says.

I lower my rifle as one of the p-beetles whips its head towards the framework's face and begins eating with renewed verve. Those framework eyes told a story of suffering, but I have to turn away. Strategically Omira couldn't be more right. I have to think that if Jonas Valent was here he'd do the same thing. The rest of this chamber is huge, it looks much bigger than it did on the schematics. There are at least dozens of other stasis tubes, mostly intact from what I can tell in the failing light.

"Remmy, is our way clear because of what's going on?" I ask.

"Yeah, there's about fifteen p-beetles in another corner around a framework in the opposite corner. It's hard to get a good count because it looks like they're fighting over, um," he hesitated. "Food on the other side. Three more p-beetles are just wandering around, but I think we can get around them if we stick to the larboard side."

We don't disturb the feeders in front of us, don't save that framework suffering a hellish eternal cycle of regeneration and consumption. It doesn't feel right. None of it does.

I look at Omira, she's unaffected. I can't help but think that she's either a butcher who has seen worse or doesn't have the emotional tool set to even comprehend what we just saw. Mary makes eye contact as we round a row of four metre tall containment tubes. Her expression is a wary one, she's nervous, a bad sign.

Closer to the mid-larboard side of the chamber I start seeing computer terminals. They're ancient, but still running diagnostics on copies of Jonas Valent, Lucius Wheeler and three other specimens I've never seen. Some of them are being slowly programmed with memories, others are in full stasis, while a few more are getting raw code burned into their brains. As I'm turning away I see a readout of a containment unit that simply reads; ALICE, and something urges me to stop.

Remmy notices and looks as well. "Wait, this isn't like anything I learned about neural programming," he whispers. "They're working this through in layers, trying to apply an intact artificial intelligence on different physical versions of her brain without adapting the software."

"Why is that weird?" Mary asks.

"They're trying to adapt the brain to the viral version of Alice instead of adapting the software to the grey matter," Remmy replies. "It shouldn't work."

"But it did, that's how Alice got free," I tell him. No one knows for sure, no one ever got close enough to confirm that. It's still a scientific fantasy that some people like to believe, however. I guess some humans just want to think that we are brilliant enough as a race to write software that's good enough to run on God's hardware.

"Yeah, I'd love a first hand scan of her," he looked a little deeper and nodded to himself. "Wait, there is translation software here, but it's old Vindyne stuff." Remmy looks around for a moment then to Omira. "That's what this is, Vindyne neural rehabilitation research carried on past its prime, isn't it?"

"This isn't why we're here, we have to move on," she replies.

"You're just continuing it using frameworks, but why?" Remmy asks.

"You'll find your answers up ahead."

Remmy looks back at the terminal and flinches at the sight of something, I can't tell what it is because it's in a swimming holographic sea of code, but it's got him alarmed. "Wait, new root found?" He says, alarmed. "This time stamp matches our boarding op, what the hell?"

Omira rushes towards him, trying to get to the terminal before he can read more. Mary steps in her way and handily trips her off her feet. Our guide doesn't have a chance to try to get back up before Mary's boot is firmly planted on her chest. "We have to move on!" Omira hisses.

Remmy returns his attention to the data stream and rewinds the feed. "This program started running when we boarded because it detected a new framework processing node," Remmy says. "Just one, and it has a Freeground serial number."

I stare straight at the flowing code, and should be able to understand what I'm seeing, but it's a river of gibberish.

"Can you tell which one of us it's in?" Mary asks.

My instincts suddenly start telling me it's time to move on. I can barely hear the conversation continue as my eyes start sweeping for p-beetles and I retrieve my hand scanner. Before I know it, I'm saying: "Mary, let her up," and I'm moving to help Omira to her feet.

"Didn't you hear me, Clark?" Remmy's asking, but he's just holding us back with technical details.

"Get your eyes on your scanner, we've got to finish this," I tell him.

He stares at me, Mary's staring at me too, but after a moment they return their attention to the task at hand. Mary's talking, but she must be on a private channel to Remmy because I see her lips move, her expression harsh, but there's nothing coming out.

We make our way between rows of frameworks of Wheeler, Valent, and a couple others I don't recognize. Their faces, suspended in amber liquid, seem contorted to me, and I sometimes get the feeling that they're aware of us. I feel like a thief creeping past the foot of a sound sleeper's bed, praying they don't awaken.

We drop through a hatch in the floor, I don't even remember it being mentioned, and end up in an isolated hallway. It's narrow, the lights are too bright, like a clinic, and the floor is covered with rotting carapaces. Something's gotten to the p-beetles, the diners became dinner to something nastier.

"Aw, man, this can't get worse," Remmy complains.

"Hey, at least we can't smell this through our suits," Mary quips in return. She only cracks jokes when she's nervous.

Omira presses on and I take up a position at her right side. Our goal is near. The crunching and cracking of dead matter under foot doesn't deter us. The lights dim to twilight intensity in the next room. The gore ends at the threshold, and the lounge we enter is clean. Mary brushes me aside and draws her rifle, Remmy draws his sidearm and takes a kneeling position beside her.

I can't see what's got them so alarmed. It's an empty room.

"Snap out of it!" Mary is shouting, but at who I couldn't imagine.

Omira looks at me with the first real smile I've seen from her. "You can wake up now."

At the command my head hurts so bad that my knees give out. I realize then that Remmy and Mary were trying to tell me that the computer was interfacing with framework tech implanted in me. I can feel it, and recognize it as a thought that is not my own, but threatens to press everything else out. "What the hell is going on?" I ask no one in particular.

"You're being reprogrammed, some kind of neural mod," Remmy says, getting down on his knees in front of me and looking into my eyes.

"Astute conclusion," says an unfamiliar voice.

I look up and try to raise my rifle at what I see but clumsily grasp at the stock instead. It's almost an issyrian, only its covered in semi-transparent hard plates. It looks like they've grown from somewhere under the skin, dark amber scabs that formed armour. It makes the issyrian look carnivorous. "The framework programming system on the configuration deck above us is only trying to find a way to reprogram your neural implant. It seems someone has been limiting your scope of perception, and suppressing a few of your memories," says the creature.

It begins prying the rough chitinous plates off its face, revealing a visage that looks partially human. "Memory suppression, what-" I'm interrupted by such a surge of pain that I crumple to the floor. As I twitch I can't help but picture the framework of Jonas Valent being devoured above. Emotions come flooding into my awareness. The anguish of knowing my sister was executed, the betrayal at being exiled, the guilt of seeing Mary drawn into this with me, and of love - long lasting love for my sister. It's all painful and I'm barely aware of Remmy and Mary putting themselves between me and everything else as I thrash under the pressure of realization.

My head starts to clear and Omira starts talking. "Freeground evidently needed unquestioning soldiers, and they made one out of you," she tells me. "Anything you've experienced since you entered their custody could be a lie. Those emotions you're probably feeling were all on a suppression list, a very long one."

"You were dead inside, friend," says the issyrian thing as it slowly steps closer. More of its face is visible, but I still can't make out who it is. "But this lab contains software that's far more sophisticated than whatever Freeground used, so we're setting you free."

I'm thinking of my sister, of the last time I saw her for real, at the spaceport. "Couldn't you have done it gradually?" I ask, veiling my grief pangs with an attempt at levity.

"Your objectivity and drive to complete your mission were also reinforced by Freeground's neural programming. You have been conditioned carefully to perform your duties. Now all that is unraveling," Omira tells me.

"Is it true, Clark?" Mary asks. "Is that what's happening?"

I make my best attempt at pulling myself together and start getting to my feet. "Feels like," I tell her. "I'm sorry for where I've gotten us."

She fixes me with a confused expression for a moment and whispers, "It's okay, better here than a prison cell."

My vision is clearing, the pain is starting to subside. I look to the issyrian then and recognize the face of Doctor Marcelles. His slowly growing smile is the last thing I see before the lights go out.

PART 4 – SEEING CLEARLY

I wake up and I can't move. Combat reflexes kick in regardless, and I take in as much as the scene as my rolling eyes can. I'm in a lab that still looks like the vault but much cleaner.

Mary comes into view. "You're back with us," she says with an uncharacteristically reassuring smile that tells me that everything is not okay. The only time she tries to reassure people is when everything's gone sideways.

"Why can't I move?" I ask, feeling trapped.

"The wires Intelligence put in your head kicked back when their programming was almost overwritten," replies Mary. Isabel steps in beside her, taking my hand and squeezing it.

"Your friend is right," explains the creature I saw last time I was on my feet. "Crude, but her description isn't inaccurate. I tried to overwrite their programming with software that you could interface consciously with, something you could control instead of the other way around and Freeground Intelligence's program locked us out and disabled you. Setting you free won't be as easy as I expected, I'm afraid."

"You're trying to remove their control devices," I confirm.

"Yes, if I'm going to re-enter the web of Freeground Intelligence, I'm going to need friends," he says as he runs a scanner across my face.

"We're still on your ship, Doctor Marcelles?" I hazard a guess.

"Yes, the Fallen Star."

"The piranha beetles?"

"They are my food supply. Part of an experiment, and quite delicious once you master capturing and preparing them. Sort of like crab."

The food chain of the beetles feeding on human frameworks, and the Doctor feeding on the beetles crosses my mind and I consciously press it aside.

"They took our grey matter grafts out, Clark," interjects Remmy from somewhere out of sight. "I think we're in good hands for once."

"I've never met such an optimistic Intelligence Officer," I mutter. The crack brings a smile to Mary and Isabel's faces, but Isabel adds a tear while she's at it.

"So, what's the fix, Doc?" I ask Doctor Marcelles.

"I'm going to start a framework conversion," he replies without missing a beat. His dark, smooth face comes into view then, and I wish it hadn't. Not even his eyes are human anymore, they're bigger, and a solid violet colour. The top of his head is too broad, and his body is covered in amber plates that affix somewhere beneath the skin. "I woke you for consent."

I can't help but be surprised, and I suppose it showed.

"You look astonished," Doctor Marcelles laughs. "Even scientists of my caliber take the wishes of their subjects into account. Besides, I don't need to have another angry framework to deal with."

"Chances?" I ask.

"Excellent. It'll happen in your sleep and that framework derivative graft work that Freeground put in your head will be gone or replaced with something you can control," he replies. "And remind me to ask you why you think they only used a framework graft on you, and not your comrades when it's all done."

"I'll try to remember," I tell him. A framework conversion. I know what it is, that our Freeground eggheads don't completely understand it, but would love to get their hands on someone with the tech. The thought of being one myself - being immortal and nearly invulnerable - is so exciting. At the same time, I know its a great big step away from being human. "Alternatives? What other choice do I have?"

"I let your friends go so they can take you back to Freeground Intelligence and I stay here," Doctor Marcelles says flatly. "I won't be delivered to anyone by soldiers who aren't in control of their own thoughts or can't answer my direct questions themselves."

When he puts it that way I can't help but agree. My head does feel clear, and I feel a grief pang and the stirrings of very deep anger at what Freeground did to my sister. My mind is free of Intelligences' control, and I decide I don't want to go back to being a puppet. "How do I know you're not going to do something even worse? I don't want to trade one master for another."

"Doctor Marcelles would never take control of another intelligent being," Omira bursts from somewhere to my left, well out of sight. "He researches the diversification of life and how to prolong it, not how to control or master a person."

"That's enough," Doctor Marcelles says over his shoulder.

"I've looked through the research logs here, Clark," Remmy says, appearing beside Doctor Marcelles. "As far as I can tell, it's true."

"We also scanned each other for devices after our grafts were removed," Mary says. "We're clean. I trust him."

"That's good enough for me," I say. "Make me my own man again."

"Excellent," Doctor Marcelles says. "I'll give you a moment alone with you friends while I make preparations."

"See you soon, Clark," Mary says. "We'll be outside."

I smile at her and try to nod, but get nothing out of my neck muscles. "See you on the other side."

That leaves Isabel and I alone. "You've gotta make it through this, I want to know the real you, Clark. No strings."

"I'm looking forward to it," as I say that I'm not actually sure I am.

"They said something a while ago, Remmy tried to keep it quiet, but I overhead," tears well up anew, and I hurt at the sight of her in so much pain. "They said that you falling for me was just part of a program."

"No," I reassure her. I don't know if my response is a reflex or the real deal.

"Don't lie to spare me, Clark, I've gotta know."

"It's all real," I tell her. I hope I look more sure than I feel about it. She's beautiful, even when she's in tears, but I dig for how I felt before and come up with nothing.

"Thank you," she says, kissing my lips lightly. "Because it's so real for me, I love you Clark."

"Time to go," Omira says as she steps into view. "The sooner we begin, the better."

Isabel reluctantly releases my hand and moves away.

"See you soon, Clark," Omira says as she gently closes my eyes with her fingers.

CHAPTER 15
THE REPORT

The view of the Gamma Surro asteroid field was best described as unremarkable. Remmy still found the slow turning, drifting hunks of brown rock hypnotic anyway. There was nothing else to do as he waited for Doctor Anderson to finish reviewing the first hand report. Nothing to do but wear a hole in the floor as he paced in Anderson's office and grow more nervous by the minute. For Remmy Sands, being quiet was a challenge, not knowing exactly what his superior officer was seeing, and waiting on his opinion was torture.

"He died while Doctor Marcelles was trying to reprogram the neural net Intelligence installed," Doctor Anderson said as he looked up from his reader.

"Yes, Sir," Remmy replied quietly. He took a seat across from him, feeling guilty at his enjoyment of the plush seat. His friends were still on Uumen, in squalor. "Doctor Marcelles tried everything, but the Freeground Intelligence safeguards did too much damage."

"Well, the evidence confirms your report from one end to the other," Doctor Anderson said. "Except there's a current status statement missing." He seemed at the same time disappointed and saddened by what he'd just experienced second hand.

"That's why I'm here instead of Mary Reed, Sir," Remmy replied. "She wanted to transport his remains herself, but someone had to stay behind and monitor the mission on the ground. I also thought it would be good for her and Isabel to build goodwill."

"So you're in negotiations with Doctor Marcelles?" Anderson asked. "He left the ship and went to Uumen?"

"After we told him how bad things got for his former crew mates and the rest of the issyrians down there he felt he needed to help them find a way to re-purify the planet."

"Is that even possible? The scans you took make the new forests on that world look more like an aggressive fungus," Doctor Anderson said.

"He seems to think he can fight fire with fire," Remmy shrugged. "Doesn't change the fact that he's not interested in paying the Sunspire a visit, or returning to Freeground unless you give him your support with the issyrians. He's re-defined the term 'gone native' I think."

"I'd say so. I wish we could get involved in this, but even the proposition is problematic," Doctor Anderson said, standing and crossing to the window. "Captain McPatrick and Freeground Intelligence Oversight agree that a policy of non-involvement is best for the Sunspire and everyone back home."

"You don't think so," Remmy said with a smirk.

"I can't engage in that conversation, Ensign. What we're saying right now is going on record, and I can't let it be mentioned that there is any consideration for the option. We're both bound by their decision in this," Anderson retorted. "Tell me Mary hasn't done anything to ally herself with the fighters down there."

"Mary hasn't done anything to ally herself with the fighters," Remmy replied, straightening up and repeating the words mechanically.

"So, how are Mary and Isabel continuing their negotiations with Marcelles and pursuing a goodwill mission if they aren't joining their cause?"

He knew this question was coming, and how important it was that he offer the right answer. There were ears listening in live, there always were. "Mary is assisting with the maintenance of their weaponry and fortifications. Isabel is helping them patch together a couple old transport ships. They're making themselves useful when Marcelles is busy researching the forest Regent Galactic is using to convert the planet."

"Is that all? He's that focused?" Doctor Anderson asked.

"Nothing I saw indicated that there was anything else cooking, Sir," Remmy replied. "At least, nothing he's directly responsible for."

"He's not trying to directly cure the issyrians?"

"Not that I saw, but I didn't stay for long after we got back to Uumen, I was hot to get back up here," Remmy replied.

Doctor Anderson sighed and shook his head. "What about defeating framework technology? Did you get us anything on that?"

Remmy removed an old fashioned two centimetre long data chip from his pocket and flipped it on Doctor Anderson's desk. The silver chip landed almost in the middle and bounced low, stopping near the edge. "There it is," Remmy said with a grin. "He didn't seem to care much about that info. It was almost as if he was sure someone would figure it out any day."

Doctor Anderson walked to his desk and tried to scan the chip. "No receiver node on it," he commented. "A little paranoid about getting scanned at a distance?"

"Wouldn't you be?" Remmy replied. "Imagine if some orbital monitoring satellite picked up data on defeating frameworks as we were on our way away from the planet. I'd be having a completely different kind of briefing with some Regent Galactic hard ass."

"Actually," Doctor Anderson started as he plugged the chip into his command and control band. "They'd probably hook you up to a neural scanner and take you on a guided tour of your recent memories by asking you pointed questions."

"Wow, they don't fool around these days," Remmy said. "Have you seen one?"

"One of their scanners?" Doctor Anderson said as he reviewed the contents of the chip on a screen of projected light. "I've only seen the versions Intelligence finished testing last year. Freeground is set to start using them officially next month."

"Then I guess I picked a good time to leave," Remmy said. "Even though they'd probably just get a stream of disappointing nights out and increasingly disturbing porn if they scanned me."

Doctor Anderson couldn't help but chuckle and shake his head. "In that case, I'm glad they didn't do a neural profile on you." He ejected the chip and put it in a desk drawer. "You're right, everything we need to make framework killer weapons is here. That's mission accomplished for you and your team as far as I'm concerned."

"So you don't need us to bring Doctor Marcelles here?" Remmy asked.

The hatch slid open. Captain McPatrick and a short intelligence officer with pin-prick eyes entered. "Ensign Remmy Sands, I'm not surprised you fell short," the Fleet Intelligence operative said. "Call me Shannon. I am here to bring you back down to basics. You don't have the luxury of failing, especially now."

Remmy didn't bother standing or offering her any sign of respect. If she hadn't come in speaking like she was a dissatisfied slave owner he would have stood at attention, but she was immediately the most irritating thing he'd ever seen.

Shannon went on, looking straight through him with those beady eyes. "I'm calling bullshit on all the details of Clark Patterson's death and everything that follows. I also don't believe your team spent next to no time discussing politics or complaining about your place in the Sunspire's mission while you were still aboard. I smell an editor in this report, Ensign, and if we had time I'd charge you with tampering."

"The whole report is taken from his neural recorder. The one you guys implanted and didn't tell him about," Remmy barely concealed his irritation. "How could I modify a recording taken by tech I don't understand? Hell, not even Marcelles could figure out how to reprogram it without killing him. Want more details? Then get to the morgue and scan his corpse," Remmy spat.

"The events of his death aren't as important as what I suspect was omitted from the record," Shannon insisted. "What about political discussions? You can't tell me that you spent weeks between missions without talking about Parliament in detail, or complaining about your situation."

"Patterson wasn't a very political guy," Remmy said. "And you speak about him with respect. He died because of something your people did to him. He was in the service all the way."

Shannon snickered. "He died because of tampering which Doctor Anderson should take responsibility for. He knew Doctor Marcelles wouldn't leave Patterson wired, so he sent your team to get him fixed. We knew it, so we let it happen just to see if Marcelles could do it. He may have failed, but there's evidence that Marcelles has technology we want."

"Yeah, and I just delivered it," Remmy said. "You want to kill frameworks almost as fast as you can kill anyone? There's the step-by-step on how it's done."

"The Intelligence Oversight staff and I are positive that whatever you've given us is only the beginning, especially if Marcelles has become an issyrian-human-framework hybrid. We've never seen anything like that before, never even simulated it," Shannon replied. "That kind of advance can't be ignored."

"So you want him more than ever," Remmy said half to himself. He expected something like that to happen, but hoped it wouldn't. The last thing he wanted was some new team following him back to Uumen.

"We're sending Lieutenant Samuel Davi with you this time. He and three of his team will go along, monitor your progress and take over if they see it is necessary. If you fail, your contract will be terminated and you will be on your own. You may leave, Ensign Sands."

"Oh, please, oh please drop my leash and let me go into the wild," Remmy said with an impish grin. "On a world where humans get free meals, board and good pay. That would be just terrible."

"We'll have your citizenship revoked," Shannon said slowly. "I doubt you can come up with one hundred thousand credits for a new one before one of their machines gets to you."

Remmy's mood turned sour. "You people have no sense of humour."

"Get us Marcelles," Shannon said. "Then I'll show you my pleasant side."

* * *

Doctor Anderson watched Remmy retreat from the room. It was like watching himself, only a few people alive knew him when he was that young, when he had a wandering, active mind and a sense of humour that he used to hide behind. Don Quixote would have been proud of the youth Carl Anderson was, and disappointed with the man of productive schemes and hard focus that Doctor Anderson became. Remmy brought memories of his first stint in Intelligence back, and wondered if Remmy survive to meet his own Jessica Rice.

There were noticeable differences between Doctor Anderson and Remmy, however. Remmy faced greater challenges at a younger age and rebelled in grand fashion. He also saw the politics in the Intelligence community for what they were: a constant power struggle. People like Remmy Sands got caught in the middle, often crushed underfoot. That brought his thoughts back to Commander Patterson and his fate. "Doctor Marcelles can't resist an interesting patient. That's why I sent Commander Patterson's team to him."

"Wasteful," Captain McPatrick said. "If he finished a couple more missions I would have started giving him time on the bridge. Out of all the rejects and malcontents we've taken in for this tour he was one of the few I could see myself endorsing for re-entry into Fleet proper."

"Which would have led to you flipping the switch, turning off the suppressor Fleet installed and setting his grief loose on him," Doctor Anderson said. "He would have never gone back after facing the death of his sister."

"It would have been done gradually," Shannon said. "Especially since the grief therapy was slipping. The neural latticework was the only way to stabilize his personality, to get him in shape for our needs."

Doctor Anderson looked to Captain McPatrick. His expression was stony, he didn't like forced conditioning, cybernetic or not. He believed a soldier should be able to stand on their own, think on their own and manage themselves. Old school, the kind of thinking Doctor Anderson didn't always like, but found easy to understand and respect. Shannon was from the new school of Intelligence. "So, if I start improvising are you going to slip nanobots into my food? Have a latticework built in my brain so you can pull my strings?"

"Your failure would be costly, but your mission on this ship isn't so important that I couldn't turn it around myself. I'd just present my report to Parliament as another failed New Liberal initiative."

"And let all the work I'm trying to do to connect Freeground with the galaxy go to waste," Doctor Anderson said with a sigh. He leaned back in his chair, sparing a glance at Captain McPatrick.

"Don't look at him," Shannon said. "He's under Fleet Intelligence oversight just like you. The return from retirement is conditional for you both."

"So you've reminded us more than once," Doctor Anderson said. "So, other than hijacking my operations on Uumen and restricting me from going down there myself, what special instructions do you have for me today?"

"Nothing else. I just wanted to make sure Ensign Remmy Sands was given all the right details." Shannon turned on her heel as if she were a statue on a turntable and left.

Captain McPatrick was about to follow when Doctor Anderson cleared his throat. "Doctor?" He asked, stopping.

Doctor Anderson waited for the hatch to slide closed behind Shannon before saying; "starting to understand how your nephew felt when he was commanding the Sunspire yet?" Doctor Anderson said. "Oversight wrapped around one leg dragging you down?"

"Doesn't mean I'm going to break away from the fleet and abandon Freeground," he replied in a low growl.

"Give it another month. No one can carry an Oversight officer on their back forever."

CHAPTER 16
LONGSHADOW VII

"I hate dome cities," Coral said, looking up at the expansive transparent metal and support beam dome above. The dark surface of Longshadow VII filled the airless sky beyond the dome. Small clusters of light marked cities on the surface, a stark contrast to the pitch black sections where there were pits large enough to see clearly from their distant orbit.

"Why? Is it the thought of getting sucked into space if one of those panels break loose, or is your claustrophobia acting up again? No, wait, you're getting the spins whenever you look up because all you see is the surface of Longshadow Seven and your brain keeps telling you that you should be falling, or that you're upside down," Kipley offered.

"They call that vertigo," Judge added.

"Don't help," Coral said. "Either of you."

"If we could have taken our C&C units with us this trip, you'd be medicated by now," Kipley said. "Can't believe a chick like you is letting a case of the spins get her all out of joint. I thought you were rough-and-tumble tough."

"Never sleep again, Kipley," Coral growled.

"Why? What's she gonna do?"

"You might wake up on the wrong side of an airlock," Judge replied with a too-wide grin.

Longshadow VII's third moon was the settling place for the builders of Longshadow prison. This was where they retired to when the dark planet below was ready to open its doors. The moon base, called Preacher's Landing, served as an observation and supervision site for the prison planet.

The blood on the walls had been washed away by her new owners. The holocaust virus struck long before Davi and his team arrived. An entire Order of Eden battle group orbited the moon, never far from the city-base.

What was more important about those ships was the people they brought. Tens of thousands, enough for the Order of Eden military to take control of the ghost city Preacher's Landing had become. Everyone in Davi's five person team was uneasy except for Judge, his second in command. A gust of air struck them in the face as an airlock door opened to admit them onto a larger, tube enclosed street.

"Welcome to Preacher's Landing," said an android with human features. His skin was flexible, probably well synthesized to feel human, only it had a sickly grey sheen. "You are the four hundredth and twentieth group of travellers to stop here since the Order of Eden liberated the station, congratulations. Do you have any questions?"

Davi breathed an inward sigh of relief, glad that their fake Order of Eden identification cleared the android's scans. "Where is the Bloated Barfly?" He asked.

"That establishment is adjacent to the main Port, not far from the terminal you just came from. If you take sub-car road thirty three and announce your destination you will be taken directly there."

"Thank you," Davi said. He started for the side door beside the android that read: SUBTERRANEAN ROAD 33

"Since you are one of the first groups to visit here since new ownership, you can receive fifty percent off all accommodations," the android rambled with an inviting smile.

"Thank you," Judge said as he passed by.

"Ask me how! Did you know that the Longshadow system has many tourist attractions? Try a shuttle safari, where you can see the dragon dogs of Longshadow Seven and how mines operated in ancient times, all in one day!"

Judge looked directly at the android and said; "Thank you," with a note of finality that brought the machine's promotional rambling to an end.

The lower streets were carved from dense, rust coloured stone. Lightweight hover vehicles swept past trundling wheeled transports. The heavy load bearing tires made a deep hum as they rolled down the hard road. Yellow lights shed only enough illumination for someone to safely see by. The rest of the light came from old signage advertising for shops along the row, most of which were still empty. Their owners were dead, or had escaped and those broken store fronts looked like cavernous wounds, hollow and dark.

"Looks like we missed the fire sale," Jack Kipley said. He was a whip thin man, who was constantly checking every corner.

"A little respect," retorted Miir Coral. "Most of the shop owners were murdered when the virus made AI's go berserk. This is a tomb as much as it is a street." She wasn't what one would expect a covert marine to look like, with golden hair and a figure born out of fashionable genetic manipulation. She was conceived during the fad to have petite, shapely daughters. Fortunately, her small size served her well in her job. More often than not she was the one who was able to venture where no one else could fit.

"Sorry," Kipley said. "Did you know someone here or something?"

To Davi's relief, Coral didn't reply. Extending that conversation with someone as impossibly dense as Private Kipley was pointless. He was one head trauma away from being declared brain dead, but an incredible fighter. "There's the Bloated Barfly," Davi said as he saw a holographic image of a robust bottom shifting on an almost too-small barstool hovering in front of one of the few lit shop windows.

"Looks like a prime night spot," Stanley Foster said. He was the other half of the genetically altered duo in Davi's group. He was conceived around the same time as Coral, and it was fashionable then to have tall, square jawed male children. He was fully a head taller than Davi, who was of average height, and very happy his parents didn't care about offspring fashion.

"We're not going inside to meet someone special. This is a kidnapping, remember?" Davi replied.

"What?" Kipley replied. "Seriously? We sneak in through a huge hole in the Order's security, walk right past I don't know how many port patrol guys on the way here without any trouble, and now we don't even get to sit down for a drink? I mean, if we're not going to see some real action this trip, we may as well get glossed, they must have a serious selection in there, with the Order stocking the place."

"We got in so easily because of the guy we're retrieving," Judge whispered. "Where do you think our Order of Eden idents have been coming from?"

"Oh, so this is the guy," Kipley said.

A crowd of technicians in filthy yellow and brown jumpsuits emerged from the bar ahead.

"Did you even bother reviewing the mission brief?" Coral asked in a harsh whisper.

"Enough to know where we were going and how long I have to watch your backs for," Kipley said. "Don't need to know much more."

"I'll never get used to the idea of you being a member of *Intelligence* when the word could never describe anything you do or say," Coral said.

"Quiet," Judge told them as the technicians came within earshot.

Davi made eye contact with one disheveled woman with half slumbering eyes. She looked like she had been drinking something other than alcohol, something that was probably concocted in a laboratory. He didn't see a hint of suspicion in her eyes, only the evidence of a temporary paradise of altered perception. If everyone in the pub was half as intoxicated as she was, the mission would go off without a hitch. "Judge, you go ahead and check the place."

"Aye, be back in a minute," Judge replied.

Before they ran into anyone else, they were through the side door of a burned out shop on the row. It took a moment for his eyes to adjust to the dark. When they finally did, he took a look around. There had been some looting, but not nearly as much destruction as he expected. "Law took control here fast," he muttered as he pinched the edge of a silky blouse hanging off a display.

"It's like the owner closed up shop and pickers just took his cash and the more valuable jewelry," Coral said. "I knew things were bad out here, but I never wanted to see this myself. You look at how much work went into this shop and know someone, maybe a whole family cared about it, they worked here day in, day out. Now they've been killed, or pressed into service in the mines, and it's just…" she sighed, taking the dark interior in. "Empty."

"At least it's not New Vickers," Kipley said. "If this were a shop there, you'd find the shopkeeper and a few customers smeared across the walls. Now that was an eye opener. Almost like seeing Pandem like the First Light guys did."

"At least there was still fighting when they got to Pandem," Foster said. "New Vickers was just a never ending slaughterhouse. Androids rounding up leftover humans so they could get loaded into slave transports."

"Or so they could give them a hundred K and join the Eden side," Kipley added. "Never seen anything more messed up than someone giving a 'bot a bunch of coins, getting a hot meal and turning slave driver all in one hour. Totally fucked up."

Davi remembered watching that, and somehow it didn't surprise him. It should have, he should have had more faith in people, but when one of the prisoners paid his way into the Order of Eden from the marching line and turned on his fellow captives within the hour, it just made him want to leave. They watched that processing station, where androids and robots infected with the holocaust virus stripped starving humans, de-loused them, met their minimum survival needs with salvaged food and medical supplies then marched them into cargo containers.

Davi and his men didn't do anything about it. They were there to gather intelligence, not be seen or caught fighting a hopeless battle. Otherwise he would have wrecked the whole installation himself.

They accomplished their mission before leaving. The *TRF Peter* had dropped several transit shuttles, probably looking for supplies, or offloading dissidents but the ship itself was long gone. What happened to the people aboard their shuttles was a mystery. They were missing, most likely dead or taken into custody. Two of the three shuttles had already been cut up into scrap, the third was clamped to the landing platform, it's doors hanging open and systems running as if it were expecting the owners to return any moment.

Davi was snapped back to the present as Judge returned. "Our target is sitting next to the door with a cyborg. There are about a dozen more people inside, only three we have to worry about - they're hard shell."

Hard shells - it's what they'd started calling the Order of Eden soldiers who wore heavier armour plating. Their metallic dark green armour made them look like they beat up a giant cockroach and stole it's carapace. "What about the bar?"

"Automated dispensers, no android servers either," Judge replied.

"Okay, this is almost too easy," Coral said.

"Want to hear the punch line?" Judge asked. "There's a door at the back leading upstairs - though an empty dance floor into the main port."

"You're shitting me," Kipley said. "Straight retreat to home free? It's like this guy wants to get taken."

"Maybe," Davi said to himself. "How did you know his buddy was a cyborg?"

"Metal plates instead of a skull cap, and a sensor array instead of eyes and a nose," Judge replied. "Probably has other augments too."

"That's disgusting," Coral said, cringing. "How can someone do that to themselves?"

"Maybe his lid got shot off and all they had were antique parts?" Foster offered.

"Didn't look like Plague Age tech," Judge replied as he checked the charge on his stunner. "More like the Home Machinist's Self Improvement Kit. I think we should hit him first. Not with stunners either, that would probably just make him angry."

"You're right, the cyborg wasn't on the mission plan," Davi said. "Coral, Kipley, use rippers. Hit that cyborg until it's a pile of scrap and meat."

"Knew I'd get a chance to use this on this hop," Kipley said as he pulled his ripper, an old fashioned blade shooter out from under layers of clothing. It was a snub-nosed version of an ancient design that fired one point five millimetre wide blades that were thirty to fifty microns thick. On the lowest setting the weapon's projectiles zipped through the air at just under the speed of sound. On the highest setting, the blades could move at many times that speed and pierce medium-heavy personnel armour. The clip he slipped into the grip was filled with rounds that would slip through skin, or even thin metal before shattering into tiny fragments that tore through the body. It didn't use a power cell or explosives so it passed as non-lethal on most worlds' port scanners.

"Foster and I will grab the target, Judge will clear the room," Davi looked to Kipley specifically. "When you finish with that cyborg, help Judge, but make sure you switch to your stunner. The intel on this world tells us specifically that most of the law enforcement doesn't see infighting as much of a priority until they have a death on their hands."

"What about the cyborg?" Kipley asked. "We're going to shred him like coleslaw."

"There's no helping that, and he'll probably survive anyway."

"Definitely," Judge added. "Looks like his brain is cased in some kinda heavy armour. Too bad he couldn't afford to do the rest."

"Right," Davi said. "Everyone set?"

He waited for nods all around then let Judge lead the way back to the club. It was a run down watering hole with faded plastic seats and walls that featured more grime than paint. Their target sat near the door with his cyborg friend facing them. He wore a dark green long coat over well made, clean city dweller's clothes - a loose shirt and dark pants. He was out of place, wealthier than anyone else there by far.

The cyborg had his back to them. Judge started things the moment they were all through the door. He expertly tossed a pair of stun grenades towards the back of the room where several unsuspecting patrons were having a few drinks. One landed in a pitcher of Naganto Red ale, the other glanced off of a drinker's shoulder.

Davi leveled his stun pistol at the kidnapping victim, a well dressed, well kept man wearing a crossover belt and a pair of holstered heavy pistols. Silence descended upon the bar room, and it felt as if it took Davi an hour to check his aim and squeeze the trigger. It couldn't have been more than two heartbeats. The instant the bolt of energy flew from weapon's emitter and stunned his prey, the world around him started up again, only in fast forward.

The stun grenades went off, disabling most of the patrons at the other end of the club. Coral and Kipley opened fire on the cyborg, sending flesh and bone fragments from the half-man's torso, neck and arms spattering across the table. Judge took stun shots at patrons who scrambled for weapons or scurried for cover, he didn't make the distinction between anyone running for cover or drawing a weapon. There was no time.

Davi knocked the nearest table over so it rolled between himself and the cyborg. With all regard to speed and little to safety, he snatched his target's long coat and dragged the stunned man behind cover.

He caught a glimpse of the half-ruined cyborg getting to his feet as though whole sections of his torso wasn't hanging in tatters. He caught Davi in the side with an inhumanly quick kick, sending him half way across the width of the bar room. A bar stool stopped his progress across the floor abruptly, and Davi knew immediately that the light armour he wore wasn't quite good enough. At worst he had three broken ribs, at best he'd feel the bruises for days unless he got treatment. Either way, breathing was painful. He pulled a patch from his pocket as quickly as he could and slapped it onto his cheek. A cocktail of pain killers and a rush of emergency nanobots surged from the it.

He looked up in time to see the cyborg stand up, his head hanging at an awkward angle on his bloody neck. His remaining arm - made of old metal, gears and wires - snatched Coral by the forehead.

She fired into its face, only to scrub the flesh away from the half machine's visage, revealing an armoured skull beneath. Kipley buried the muzzle of his weapon into a rip in the cyborg's back and bashed the thing's encased spine with his free hand. The shock was enough to drive it to the ground twitching.

Davi heard a sickly crunch. The cyborg's hand had closed around Coral's head. Whether the act was involuntary or intentional didn't matter. The metal fingers mingled with blood, bone and grey matter. Kipley's boot came down on the cyborg's spinal support column, finally crushing the case protecting critical veins, muscles and nerves.

"Coral!" cried Foster, about to abandon his attempt to pick up their kidnapping target.

"She's gone!" Davi said. He pulled a three centimetre long tube from his pocket and dropped it onto Coral's body. In a few minutes all identifying features would be corrupted, making it impossible for anyone to get useful DNA trace. He joined Foster and pulled one of the unconscious kidnapping target's arms across his shoulder. "She'd want us to get out of here alive," Davi told Foster. "Let's go."

Foster was in complete shock, his mouth hung open, quivering as tears blurred his vision.

"Foster! There's a backup!" Kipley said as he took cover behind the upturned table and pulled Foster down. He started firing at the three patrons who were holding out, firing back with lethal pulse sidearms.

"A scan? She was scanned before we left? She never told-" Foster asked, hope dawning in his face.

"You know her, she didn't want to jinx the mission!" Kipley said.

Davi dragged their target behind the table as quickly as he could, sparing a warning glance at Kipley, who rolled his eyes and returned his attention back to the firefight.

The table Judge took cover behind began turning white under the heat of pulse rounds. "Converting clip!" he shouted, dropping the stun weapons' main mechanism from the stock of the gun and setting the internal trigger's timer. Judge tossed the improvised grenade but didn't make the shot thanks to the restricted space he was in.

Kipley jumped out from cover and landed almost on top of the stun grenade. He slapped the blinking device so it skidded and spun across the tile floor. It exploded before hitting the back wall, catching him in the outer radius, but exploding with their assailants in the centre.

Judge stepped out from his deteriorating cover, checking the corners as he approached Kipley. He checked his twitching squad mate and stood up, grinning. "He's good," he announced. "Ought to shut him up for a while, give him the spaz's for an hour or so."

Davi and Foster moved ahead, carrying their target between them. Judge tossed Kipley, who was only barely unconscious, over his shoulder. They moved as quickly as they could, heading down the hallway at the back of the club. It wound up in a tight corkscrew until they passed through a pair of doors. The dance floor wasn't abandoned, but filled with party supplies. Several decorators were busy at work, setting up for some grand event.

Davi and his squad mates stopped dead in their tracks. Wary eyes and surprised stares greeted them. "Where's the party?" Kipley said unsteadily.

"Told you the dance hall was closed honey," Judge said, slapping Kipley on the rump loudly. "Sorry, he just had to see that the place wasn't open even though he's too drunk to stand, let alone dance." He started for the door on the opposite side of the hall. "Mind if we cut through? Need to take our drunk friends home."

No one made a move to stop the group, and had to make a real effort to stop himself from laughing at Judge.

They spilled out into a run-down section of the port. There were other bars, cheap restaurants, and an open meal gallery. Who would be impressed with the view of Longshadow VII's more dug out side, where the light of smelting fires and open pit mining were visible, Davi would never know. It was the main feature of the gallery through the transparent ceiling. Beneath there was a sea of cheap tables and chairs surrounded by booths and storefronts serving badly materialized or long-preserved food. A few even offered food from forma, a tasteless protein and grain substitute that could be retextured and shaped into different dishes. It was cheaper than materializer food, but the telltale signs that your meal was made from forma were difficult to get past.

The few diners didn't pay them much attention, especially since Kipley was starting to put on a convincing act as a drunk. "Put me down, I want a drink!" he shouted. They dumped most of their weapons in trash bins on their way through. Davi, Foster and Judge kept their rippers.

Davi braced himself as they entered Lander Section C14, where their ship waited. There were two port guards leisurely standing in the disembarking centre at the end of the hall. The doors leading to seven landing platforms surrounded them. In the centre was a scanning pillar, the reason why they dumped their used weapons. If it detected recently fired energy weapons they would have been stopped cold.

"Had a bit too much of a good time?" one of the port guards said through a smile.

"Yeah, figure it's time to hit the bunks," Davi replied.

"Hold on, let me check the scan," the other guard said, projecting the results from his chitinous gauntlet. "Gotta do these random audits sometime or they'll dock my pay."

Davi knew they'd detect no trace of inebriates in Kipley, and find signs of a stunner on the man hanging between him and Foster. The whole mission was seconds from going completely wrong. He reached into his pocket and retrieved a medical sprayer. He stumbled intentionally, drawing the attention of the guard who wasn't fiddling with the scan results. "Sorry, can I get a hand here?"

The guard was already reaching down to help, and Davi took the opening, spraying the guard fully in the face with the contents of the long range injector, it started blinking.

"Son of a bitch! What the-" the guard stumbled back, wiping his face.

"I just hit you with half an ounce of nanobots that are programmed to start chewing through your brain stem. They'll stay dormant if you clear us to leave," Davi explained, holding up the blinking injector. "This light tells me when you're out of range, and I can't activate the 'bots. We get out safe, your body flushes them from your system. If we don't, I give them the go-ahead and your brain gets cut off from your body. I hear it's pretty painless."

The other guard drew his weapon, his look of alarm and confusion disappearing under his armoured visor as it lowered. "Don't move!" he shouted.

"Are you deaf or stupid?" Kipley slurred. "Fuck this up and your hombre gets dead."

"I said don't move!" shouted the unscathed guard defiantly.

"My bet's on stupid," Judge commented.

"O-okay, hold on," said the guard with a head full of nanobots. "We've gotta let 'em go Sam," he told his partner.

"Fuck no! This is our first chance to bag terrorists and I'm not going to pass it up because of some nanobot bullshit. For all you know that bastard could have sprayed you with water and iron filings."

"Iron filings are a lot bigger than nanobots, dick head," Kipley said.

"Get on the ground, now!" shouted Sam the guard.

Davi slowly started to lower to the ground, but made eye contact with the guard he'd infected as he rolled the blinking injector between his fingers. The guard looked at him nervously then snatched his weapon from it's holster and fired at his panicked comrade. He got three shots off before Sam turned his attention from Davi to his partner.

The firefight was over before it started. The infected guard already had the upper hand and blasted Sam wildly, who fell in a smouldering heap.

The infected victor turned on Davi then, the steaming muzzle of his weapon pointed directly at him. "Now you're stuck with me, no way you're leaving me here to get killed or shipped to a mine on Longshadow."

"You got it, just let us through," Davi said.

"Not part of the plan," Foster said.

Davi got back under the arm of their kidnap victim and watched as the defecting guard opened the hatch that stood between them and their ship. "Judge, take his weapon."

Judge put out his hand and accepted the guard's weapon. "What's your name, son?"

"Terrance, Terrance Gerani."

"Welcome to the crew, Terry," Judge said. "Lead the way, quick."

Terry did exactly as he was told and opened the inner airlock door for them.

It didn't take them long to settle into the shuttle. While Davi wasn't looking Judge had put Terry in manual handcuffs and stripped him of his helmet. "When do these nanobots get deactivated?" he asked nervously.

"Right, the nanobots," Davi said. He clicked the button on the injector.

Terry the former guard went wide-eyed for a moment before passing out.

"What the hell?" Kipley slurred from where he sat across from Terry. "Killed him anyway?"

"No, he'll be out for about two days though," Davi replied. "This is an old emergency stasis dose, from before your time."

"You have a twisted sense of humour," Judge chuckled.

The deck of the disguised needle-type shuttle shook as the mooring clamps decoupled and the ship accelerated towards the stars. Davi joined Kipley in the cockpit and started checking the navigational calculations. "How long until we're in a wormhole?"

"The emitters are charging now," Foster replied. "About twenty five seconds. Doesn't look like anyone's targeting us from the orbital station."

"Three retrievals in a row," Davi said.

"You gonna finish that thought?" Foster asked as he set the target for the wormhole emitters.

"Nope," Davi replied. "Just realized it would be the biggest jinx of my career."

"I just hope this kidnapping is worth it," Foster said. "I can't believe they didn't tell you who he was."

"Some high level mover and shaker in the Order who likes slumming it," Davi replied. "Lucky for us."

CHAPTER 17
FRESH PAIN

Their course took them through the Spilt Sun Nebula, a precautionary measure. Kipley was in an upper bunk sleeping off the last tics of the partial stun. Judge was putting together the abridged version of their after action report and Davi was watching Foster open the fifth and last wormhole.

As soon as the wormhole opened, Samuel Davi sent a signal to the Sunspire requesting classified information.

"What's that about?" Foster asked, pointing at the older dates on the file list.

"I have a hunch about who our guy here is," Davi said. "If I'm right, he'll appear in some records but have no file of his own."

Foster locked the controls as the autopilot took over and made a record request of his own. Davi didn't notice until the records were downloaded - they were Coral's. "Don't you think events are a little too fresh?" Davi asked.

Foster looked at him suspiciously and opened the file. "I want to see this scan Kipley was talking about." The small holographic display flashed red and a recording of Coral in uniform appeared. "Sorry folks, there can be only one of me. If you're seeing this, you've looked for an emergency revival scan, or something like it. It wouldn't matter if you found one, since one of my last wishes is that no one try to re-create me. There's really not much point, since the source is already dead, and I wouldn't benefit from an imitation running around. Like I said, there can be only one. I hope you liked having me around. See you in the big after."

Foster looked for records of a scan again, despite the message and punched the terminal when he didn't find one. "Motherfucker lied!"

Davi tried to get a grip on Foster before the man rushed from the cockpit to the main cabin but missed. "Judge! Stop him!"

To Davi's surprise, Judge didn't lift a finger. Foster pulled Kipley out of the upper bunk, sending him straight to the deck. "You lying piece of shit!" he howled as he followed him down and pummelled Kipley as he woke up.

"Get him offa me!" Kipley shouted, trying to fend him off.

Foster managed to get one last, devastating shot in before Davi managed to pull him off. Kipley sat up, a fount of blood pouring from his smashed nose. "What the fuck?" he asked, incredulous.

"You told me Coral had scans, that she had a body waiting!" Foster said.

"I assumed! Hell, a connected chick like that had to have something set up," Kipley replied.

Judge pressed an emergency medical injection into the side of Kipley's neck and looked at his nose. "Get your hands out of the way," he said. After a moment's inspection he nodded. "Want me to straighten that up or let the 'bots do it?"

"Whatever," Kipley said, spitting blood onto the floor.

Judge straightened Kipley's shifting cartilage back into place with quick, expert fingers. All the while his patient pounded on the floor and grimaced. "God dammit! All this for a piece of ass!" he shouted when Judge's work was finished.

Davi barely caught Foster before he lunged at Kipley again.

"What? Someone had to get you moving when she got her head crushed, you morose bitch!" Kipley said. "If it weren't for me you would have just stood there moping and gotten yourself killed."

"That's enough," Davi said, putting himself between the two. "You're confined to the cockpit for the rest of the trip," he told Foster. "And I don't want to hear another sound from you, Kipley."

"Save a guy's life and-" Kipley started.

"I *will* sedate you," Davi told him.

A chuckle from an upper bunk silenced the room. "Glad Olonz isn't seeing this. He'd be pretty embarrassed you lot were the ones who took him out," said the man they kidnapped. He surprised everyone when he swung his legs down over the edge of the bunk and leisurely sat up, his restraints falling away. "What? Never seen a two-point-one before?"

"You should have been out for another six, maybe eight hours," Davi said. He looked the man over and judging from his crooked grin, couldn't help come to the obvious conclusion. "You wanted to be kidnapped."

"Well, at least one of you has his wheels turning at full speed," replied their willing captive. "You owe me a first officer."

"Olonz, the cyborg?" Davi asked.

"Yup. Guy managed to live almost a hundred years, finally signed on to a nice ship with a manageable crew, and two newbies from Freeground assume he's not willing to go quietly because he's got a shiny head. Anderson knows how to pick 'em."

"Sorry," Davi said. "Bad intelligence. I'm surprised we got out at all."

"I'm not. There are so many holes in Order of Eden security that you might have had a chance without the fake idents I transmitted to Intelligence before you left the Sunspire." Their captive pulled a thin, palm sized case from his jacket pocket and polished it on his shirt. "The Order depends on people who paid their dues to be on their side. They think because there are millions of people buying into their religion and their organization that the smaller gaps in security will close themselves. Gotta love the honour system. You could have gotten through that mission while waving Freeground colours and singing the Revolution Song."

"Then why the kidnapping scheme?" Kipley asked.

"He spoke," the captive said. "Get the sedatives."

Judge laughed and pulled a patch from one of the medical bags. Davi waved it off as it was offered to him.

"Figure out who I am yet?" asked their passenger.

"Haven't done the scan yet," Davi replied. "I'm guessing I won't have to."

"Right. That brings me back to the question: ever see a two-point-one?"

"Two-point-one what?" Davi asked, suspecting he already knew the answer.

"Framework," the captive said as he held the polished case up to look at his reflection. The features on his face shifted, though not in the same way Davi had seen with issyrians. Bone, muscle, and cartilage changed without causing any obvious pain.

When the transformation was complete Davi recognized the face immediately.

"Holy shit, Lucius Wheeler," Kipley said.

"I've had worse greetings," Wheeler said with a smirk.

It took a lot to make Davi nervous, and realizing that they had one of the ten people in the galaxy every dark ops officer was warned about in their possession was enough to put him on full alert. "Shut it down," he told Kipley directly. "We're transporting a package. We never saw what it was, it never communicated anything to us, and we have nothing to say about it."

"Oooh, shut 'er down!" Kipley laughed. He was always amused when he was given a gag order. It would bother Davi if he didn't know from experience that Kipley would keep his mouth shut. The man would hold that secret until his dying day, or until Command released the gag order.

"Fucking great, we have a priority one," Foster said from the cockpit. "Thank God we're coming up on the Sunspire soon."

"Then we've got eight hours on a cot, then straight back on mission," Kipley said. "I bet ya."

"Hell no, if they're sending us right back out, I'll get myself pulled," Foster said.

"Easy," Judge placated. "I know it looks bad now, but we carry on. That's what we do."

For a moment, Davi considered who he would want on his team, Kipley or Foster. Wheeler was watching the whole scene with a smile on his face, like it was a great big show for his benefit. Foster was one of the best techs and sharpshooters Davi'd ever seen, but Kipley was skilled in close firefights, something they ran into more often then long range combat. He glanced at Foster, who was busy checking their course as Judge tried to convince him that he'd be able to hold together. Foster was broken; it wasn't something a night on a cot would fix. "I'll recommend you for removal from duty. Psych will back me up, you'll get your ticket out."

Foster turned in his seat and stared at him for a moment, obviously surprised. "You'd do that?"

"You need out, I get it," Davi said. "They'll treat you and reassign you."

"I've got some mad anxiety," Kipley interjected. "And a death wish. Think you can get me out?"

Davi fixed him with a look and Kipley retreated. "Shut 'er down," he muttered to himself.

"We'll see how much time off they give us between missions this time," Judge said. "You'll have time to think it through, Stanley," he told Foster.

"Bet you a hundred credits we get sent right back out," Kipley said quietly, twitching involuntarily as though he was punctuating the point.

"Shut it," Judge growled.

"Now this is a team," Wheeler laughed. "If I need anyone aboard your ship, you bet I'll be requesting you."

CHAPTER 18
REALITY UNFILTERED

"See? I told you they'd send us right back out after we handed our package over to that Intelligence bitch," Kipley said with a big grin. "You guys owe me one hundred credits. Each."

"We never took the bet," Judge replied.

Remmy couldn't help but smirk as he watched the team assigned to him go on with their banter. It seemed as though no one really liked Jack Kipley, but he kept prodding Samuel Davi and the one they called Judge. He'd met Davi before on the Sunspire, and couldn't help but wonder what he and his team had gone through since then. Their team had been whittled down, with a few dead and one pulled from duty, sent into mental treatment.

He watched the three of them as Davi flinched at their shuttle's sudden dip towards the surface of Uumen. The new members of the team were as awe struck as Remmy was when he first saw the strange features of the issyrian side of the planet. The run down port loomed larger in the forward window as the pilot took her time decelerating. "So, three missions so far?" Remmy asked Davi.

Davi glanced to the pair of soldiers beside him before answering. "Four," he answered, looking a little nervous.

"What type?"

"All retrieval," Davi replied. "Except for the first one, taking the Sunspire."

"Ever replace your intelligence officer?"

"No, Shannon put me on double duty."

"Ah, she seems like the efficient sort," Remmy said.

"There was a lot missing-" Davi started saying, but the last half of his statement was drowned out by the sounds of the outer panels popping under the strain of changing altitude.

"What?" Remmy asked.

Davi looked alarmed but pressed on anyway. "There was a lot missing from your report," he said. "Or at least that's what it looked like."

"All the relevant details were there," Remmy said. "Except for how bad it really is on Uumen. If they knew they would have pointed the Sunspire in a new direction and hit the thrusters."

"Oh," Davi said. "How bad is it?"

Remmy smiled and changed the topic. "So who were you retrieving?"

"No one I can talk about, sorry," Davi said.

"Fair enough. Anyone who has anything to do with what's going on down here?" Remmy pressed.

"No one I can talk about," Davi repeated. "So what can we expect to find down there?"

"Just keep your eyes open and respect everything you see, especially if you don't recognize it. Oh, and forget everything you think you know about issyrians," Remmy added.

The fifteen man transport was devoid of conversation for several minutes as it skimmed the tops of the trees and crossed lakes filled with rotting clutches - the former homes of thousands of issyrians. One of Davis' guards leaned towards Remmy, an accusation in the offing. "You've been here almost a month, is it true you've gone naive?"

Remmy smiled at the soldier and shook his head. "You mean, gone native?" He looked to Davis. "Scraping the bottom of the barrel for recruitment?"

Davis shrugged, half smiling himself. "His name's Kipley, and we're all very proud of him for being able to form complete sentences." His insult earned him a warning glance. Davi obviously didn't take it seriously. "He's right, though, there's a rumour."

Remmy looked past Davi to some of the native vegetation that hadn't been destroyed yet. The forest the issyrians planted on the planet centuries before was a mess of intertwining vines that were metres thick in some places. Translucent leaves fanned out from the uppermost sections like shards of green-blue glass. There weren't half as many blooms as there should have been. The forest was dying, and he never had the opportunity to see what was under that canopy of knots. "Going native here would have been an amazing experience thirty years ago," he said, remembering the recordings he'd seen of issyrians riding sky hoppers between cities, or swimming through the waterways with schools of children. "Going native now, well, that's something else. They've taken us in here though. Don't even mention Clark's name, they're still grieving."

"Did they actually have enough time to get to know him?" the tall, square-jawed soldier asked. Remmy remembered his nickname from the brief - Judge.

"Issyrians respect the sacrifice he made getting Doctor Marcelles back to them," Remmy replied. "Losing the opportunity to show their gratitude is just as bad as losing a close friend. Their honour can't be satisfied, so they've built a couple of shrines. A few hundred visit daily."

"What are they so grateful for?" asked Davi.

"We brought Doctor Marcelles back for them, and as soon as he arrived he joined their underwater habitat." Remmy recalled the memory of Marcelles quietly submerging himself. He was stoic, set with a purpose that no one guessed at the time. "He taught them a lot in a way that none of us could. Issyrians communicate best on a chemical level through water. Marcelles explained it to me as overhearing someone's emotions."

"What exactly did they learn from Doctor Marcelles?" asked Kipley.

"You'll see," Remmy said. "For now, just try to take in the sights." He pointed through the forward viewport to their destination, small in the distance. "They used to have the run of the planet. Now everything is diseased and they have to retreat to the cities. This is one of the only safe ports for issyrians."

"The packet didn't say anything about diseases," said Kipley.

"You obviously missed the section about this world growing more and more toxic to all things issyrian. Birth rates are down eighty four percent and the life expectancy is under thirty. We're headed to one of the few spaceports that are safe for their kind. The rest have been overrun by human settlers. Business is booming for them. If you can harvest or cultivate a natural resource - hell, if you can hold a shovel - there's a job for you here."

"There wasn't anything about issyrians not being welcome in other ports," replied Davi. "There were images of a pretty mixed populace in the file."

"Things are pretty peaceable until the smallest thing goes wrong," Remmy admitted. "Then you get something like this." He activated the projector on his comm unit - something that was more of an entertainment bracelet than the Freeground issue comm unit - and started a holographic playback between them. Three issyrians knelt on a well travelled metal deck, surrounded by humans. "This was recorded two weeks ago in one of the upper levels of Port Saunders."

"Yeah, we saw the intelligence on the human ports," Kipley said. "What did those three do?"

"They were returning from a labour camp," Remmy replied, focusing in on the three issyrians. They were sickly in colour, one had an aspiration device installed against the side of his head. A tall human in a tattered Order of Eden West Keeper's uniform circled them slowly before kicking their joined hands apart savagely. The dark green and blue plated suit made him look hard and imposing compared to his captives. The issyrians cringed.

"I don't think I want to see this," said the soldier who hadn't spoken since he'd entered the shuttle.

Remmy let the recording continue. "You have to understand what's going on. The disease is just the beginning of what the humans here have done."

"The Order of Eden you mean," replied Kipley. "Not all humans are responsible for this."

"Watch," Remmy said, regarding the holographic playback. The West Keeper stopped behind them and pulled a hilt from his belt. He activated it, silently summoning a metre long blade with a silver sheen. The audio cracked as the recording of the crowd's cheers overcame whatever receiver was used to capture the moment. An issyrian glanced behind and, startled at the sight of the blade, grabbed his fellow's arm and tried to find his feet.

The silver sword cut through his arm and half way through his leg in one swipe. Green, blue, and yellow blood sprung from grievous wounds as the West Keeper savagely tore into all three of the screaming issyrians. "That one is carrying fertilized eggs," Remmy pointed as an issyrian who had been eviscerated from behind collapsed, a flood of gel spilling from her. Several soft, fist sized globules slid across the cold floor. "They were almost large enough to be introduced into a clean clutch, if she could find one."

"Turn it off," Lieutenant Davi as the West Keeper worked feverishly to cut the life from the resilient issyrians. One of them appealed to the crowd, the middle one struggled as the soldier eagerly cut into him, and the young mother desperately tried to reach out to her young with her good arm.

Remmy let it play until one of the eggs burst and an issyrian who hadn't found its shape yet formed a mouth and learned how to scream. "Tell me they don't have every reason to hate us."

"You've gone native," Kipley said, suddenly and inexplicably furious. "It's true, you care more about these shifters than you do about getting intel that can save your own people. I'm here to save Freeground, to keep us alive and out of all the political bullshit that's happening out here."

"Freeground has discarded us," Remmy said, keeping his voice down and his temper in check. "Even if you found the answer to all their problems they'd still find a way to shut us out and give credit to some Puritan Party breeder who will retire from the military to run for office in the next term. I've seen the future, Kipley - anyone with a mind of their own has - and you aren't in it."

"They said we can earn our way back," Kipley replied. "And no other squad has done better than us. I'm not going to fuck that up by getting involved with a bunch of aliens."

"Do you realize how much we could learn from the issyrians?" Remmy shot back. "You think framework technology is impressive? They have technology and an understanding of harmony that we haven't dreamed of yet. The only reason this world is being overrun by humans is because the issyrians didn't know anything about human greed, or our bullshit sense of entitlement," Remmy replied. "Oh, and we're the aliens here."

"You keep talking as if we have something to do with this, but we're from Freeground, and we know how to live together just fine," replied Kipley.

"Then what the hell are you doing in the ass end of space with no way of getting back home until the political will changes?" Remmy replied. "I read your file, Jack Kipley, you're a fuck up with assault charges who hasn't fit in for about sixteen years. Do you think anyone wants you moving in to their neighbourhood?"

It looked like Kipley was about to get to his feet until Judge put a hand on his arm. "Fuck you," he said with so much hate that Remmy actually regretted pushing his point. "Just fuck you, man," Kipley finished as he looked away.

The sound of the shuttle setting down on a landing platform resounded. "What did they do?" Judge asked as they prepared to disembark. "They had to do something to piss off the deck officer."

"Those three were workers, they were just trying to make a few credits to get extra food and supplies for their household," Remmy answered as he pulled rain ponchos from a net overhead. "The day before a group of resistance fighters bombed a garrison on the other side of the planet, in New Gibblin. Put the Order of Eden's nose out of joint so they ordered voluntary executions."

"Voluntary executions?" Kipley scoffed. "That doesn't even sound-"

"It's where West Keepers volunteer to execute random issyrians," Remmy interrupted. "Most Keepers are happy to do it. It takes a special kind of asshole to rise to that rank. I hope I get a chance to kill one before I leave."

"Oh yeah, easy," Kipley said. "Kill a senior officer and get the whole damned Eden Fleet down on us."

"Not so far," Remmy replied. "Mary's already killed three in her spare time."

"You really did leave a lot out of your report," Davi said.

CHAPTER 19
GONE NATIVE

"I think I liked grabbing Wheeler more," Kipley said as he walked alongside Davi through the outer tunnels of Trest.

"Shut your hole," Davi replied. "I know you don't respect the job, but you've got to keep a lid on our last few missions. They're classified for a reason." He'd said it before, and was beginning to think that Kipley would never learn. It was a good thing he was hell in a firefight, one of those marines who liked the violence too much.

Samuel Davi tried to focus on Remmy and the pilot who led them through the labyrinthian complex. There were more issyrians than he expected. The Freegrounders were ignored by most as they passed. The few that paid attention ensured that they made eye contact. A couple of them seemed curious, the rest regarded them with sneers that put any human's expression of ire to shame. Half were carrying small arms that looked like they were found or captured, making the threat of being shot to pieces if they made the wrong move very real.

The smell was overpowering. Samuel had to turn on his cybernetic air scrubber so he could breathe normally. It was the only thing he had left of his life before - a little backup breathing device that was implanted for a mission to the wrecked world of All-Con Prime. He thought he had seen the worst air of his life there: sulphur dust, toxic compounds they hadn't named yet, and the rot of an entire army. The issyrian stronghold, really a collection of utility tunnels and dug out rooms, was so much worse.

"You're Isabel, aren't you?" Jack Kipley asked the pilot, who remained in her flight suit - helmet and all. It looked like a crude version of their vacsuits.

Other than the fact that she was female and roughly the same shape as Isabel Fonte, there was no certainty that Kipley was right. He could be discovering a whole new way to insult an issyrian, for all he knew.

"I watched the whole neural transcription of you, more than once," Kipley said enthusiastically. "I'm a huge fan."

The helmeted pilot turned to him and stopped. "You don't belong here. None of you do."

"Hey, I'm just a tourist, sister," Kipley replied defensively.

"No such thing. You have fewer rights than the dead, watch your step," she told him.

"Okay, sorry," he muttered.

Her words made up for what she lacked in physical presence. It was difficult for Samuel to suppress the notion that the half light seemed darker, and the walls felt closer.

Davi decided it was time to begin digging for a little more information. "I'm still wondering; how did you alter the report without fragmenting the neural record? I've never heard of anyone succeeding before."

"Who says the record was tampered with? Doesn't this look familiar?" Remmy asked.

It was true; the caves they were passing through did match what Patterson experienced. Everyone's perception was different, so there was some room for his experience to differ, but what Davi was seeing passed. It still didn't explain the changes that took place since Patterson's death. In the space of three weeks, the three people left in his team managed to integrate into the issyrian underground, and Davi couldn't say why, but he'd find it intriguing if he weren't stuck right in the middle of the situation. "I'm surprised you weren't locked in a room for a month for debriefing."

"What they want Marcelles for is too important," Remmy explained. "Or maybe they're just sore about losing him in the first place, I don't know. The more time I spend here, the less I care about what Intelligence wants and why. I think losing Clark has a lot to do with it. Whether it was the way they rewired his head or just the way he was, he kept on mission. I couldn't help but admire that."

"So, even though you've been here for weeks, you're still on mission?" Davi asked as quietly as he could.

"No, I'm telling you I found a mission here, and what I couldn't say on the Sunspire is that I'm going to see it through," Remmy replied.

"What's the mission?"

"You'll see," Remmy said.

"I was sorry to hear about Patterson, he was a good man," Davi said, setting his other questions aside for a moment.

"We miss him," Remmy replied.

"So if the record was right, why do these issyrians seem…" Davi considered his next word carefully, afraid to insult anyone who might overhear, "different?"

Remmy dropped back so he could walk beside Davi. "Most issyrians don't like to fight. They don't even get angry really, especially since disputes are handled quickly when they're in the pond."

"But this is different," Davi said, urging him to continue.

"Yeah, they look pissed," Kipley added.

"No filter between your brain and mouth, is there?" Remmy asked Kipley. "Not much of a brain, either."

"I run and gun just fine," Kipley growled in return. "That's what matters."

"Shut it down, Kipley," Davi said. He turned back to Remmy. "You were saying?"

"About?" Remmy asked, then remembered what they were talking about before his exchange with Kipley. "Right, angry issyrians. They get vengeance, and loss, especially here, but it takes a long time to develop into something they feel like acting on. They usually run from problems. Issyrians are pros at founding colonies, they can do it just about anywhere. They can't escape this though, the Order is keeping them here so they can be exterminated."

"So they're cornered and getting, well, pissed," Davi concluded for him.

"That's true, but it's not how they found their anger. Someone had to show them how to be angry, what it's like to want real revenge. When Doctor Marcelles joined the purified clutches down here he shared his emotions. No issiryan has felt human anger, or our brand of - what did he call it?" Remmy asked no one in particular.

"Indignation," answered the pilot who led the way.

"Right, indignation is the word Marcelles used," Remmy continued. "From that point on, things changed. If we weren't here, these guardians would have torn you to pieces by now. Ever see an issyrian grow claws?"

As he rejoined the pilot in leading the way, Davi caught a glimpse of an issyrian grinning in the shadows, holding his hands up so the steely, nine centimetre long claws glinted briefly. They were listening, they were watching, and any misstep would lead to a sudden end, no matter how well prepared they were.

"No way we're making this work with plan B," whispered Jed Rembrant. Everyone called him Judge, a nickname that came straight out of boot camp. "The report was off, or things have changed, big time."

"They can hear you," Samuel Davi said in the lowest whisper he could manage. Broad blue, green, yellow, and red eyes turned towards them as they came to the central chamber. It was as shown in the report, the only difference was the light level. There was only just enough illumination coming from the corners so they didn't trip over each other. The sounds of rushing water underfoot drew the eye to the dark roiling pool beneath the open grates. "We have to assume we're being overheard."

"Doesn't matter," Judge said. "The Intelligence bitch walked us into a shit storm that's just over the horizon. We put our cards down or have 'em pulled for us. We've got nothing that can surprise these people."

"By surprises, you mean the two cloaked soldiers with you?" Remmy said as he turned around. "Freeground hasn't invented the cloaksuit that can fool a few thousand issyrians."

Samuel Davi didn't know whether to take Remmy's smile as good humour or a sign that things were about to turn bad.

"And there it is," Judge whispered with finality. "Our hand on the table."

"No malice intended," Davi said. "Also not my idea, but I'll be accountable for it. It's my job to take the fall."

Two Freeground marines appeared bearing rifles to match their cloaksuits.

"You're going to clear your suits' personalization settings and security codes, then strip," Remmy told them. "I always wanted a high grade cloaksuit."

Isabel removed her helmet and shook her head. "Estúpidos soldados," she muttered, walking off towards one of the many adjacent halls.

"The one named Samuel Davi will come with me," said an issyrian Davi immediately recognized as Emiss, the guide who brought Patterson and everyone else in the first group to Trest, the city of the Issyrian Underground.

"Coming with you, boss," Judge said, handing his weapons off to Kipley.

"Wait, me too," Kipley replied, trying to pass Judge's sidearm off to one of the officers who were removing their cloaksuits.

"No, you're not," Davi said firmly. "You're going to go wherever they tell you, keep the commentary to yourself, and do exactly what they tell you to do."

"Aw, hell no!" Kipley said, anger mixed with panic. "This mission is blown already and you knew it would go sideways from the start. So you forget to warn me then leave me alone?"

Judge fixed him with a look that could stop a tsunami and grabbed the neck of his cheap, fluorescent blue shirt. "Stop, listen, learn. You got me?"

Kipley swallowed hard and nodded. "Yeah."

Judge let him go and rejoined Davi.

Emiss was different from the report. Her skin was so dark blue it reminded Davi of the flesh of a black olive. She walked ahead with little concern for the pair following her. The air cleared as they passed through an elbow in the hall that created a barrier with forced air that nearly blew them off their feet. They passed many rooms with humans. They were as well armed as the issyrians, and visibly destitute.

"Nothing in the report about this," Judge said.

"Nope. Shannon was right."

Emiss twitched at the name, hundreds of fine celia momentarily appearing then standing up on the back of her neck and head.

"You know of her?" Davi asked, relieved at possibly finding an easy entry into dialog with their guide. "You've heard of Shannon from Freeground Intelligence?"

"Yes, I was told about her," Emiss admitted. They came to a broad set of double doors that were pockmarked by chemical corrosion. "Here, the purification room."

The doors slid open and Emiss invited them to proceed ahead of her. "Who are you taking us to see?" asked Davi.

"Someone who is more popular than he ought to be," Doctor Marcelles said as he made his way down a long metal stair that rattled with every footfall. It was almost exactly like the large chamber they saw earlier, only cleaner, brighter. Issyrians of every size could be seen through the grate underfoot, swimming in cleaner waters. "Samuel Davi and Jed Rembrant," Doctor Marcelles said once he reached the bottom. The hard plates that covered him in the neural recording were gone. He still had dark, blade like protrusions that ran parallel to his leftover human skeletal structure, but they were sleek features. His face looked more issyrian than human, but it was still unmistakably Marcelles. Unlike most of the issyrians they'd seen since arriving on the planet, the Doctor seemed at peace, even cordial.

Davi struggled through his surprise and shook the doctor's hand. "It's good to meet you. Ready to come home?" Davi asked with a smile.

"To Freeground? That hasn't been home for a long time," he replied, shaking Judge's hand. "But I will go with you conditionally."

"That's more than I expected," Davi replied. "What conditions?"

"Not so fast, Freegrounder," Marcelles said with a knowing smirk. "My questions come first. What is your mission here? You can't have come just for me."

Davi hesitated a moment, becoming very aware of the other issyrians who were slowly gathering.

"You're choosing your details carefully," Marcelles said, taking a step back. "Which only means you hold back. That's not encouraging."

"Our orders are to bring you back with us, and failing that, we're to capture any data or samples here. Leave nothing the enemy can use behind," Davi said.

"Go with you or die," Marcelles translated with a nod. "Have my life's work pillaged. The people I love assailed in their own home. How long did they give you?"

"Three days," Davi said.

"Barely enough time to pack," Marcelles said.

"You can't go with them," Emiss said, her eyes narrowing at the visitors. "The truth they're telling makes me wish they were lying."

"Is it?" Marcelles asked Judge specifically. "Is everything you're saying the whole truth?"

"We're not here to join in on a fool's war," Judge said. "Intelligence doesn't believe in your cause, only what you can teach us."

"A fool's war," Marcelles repeated. "What if I could tell you that there is a way to make this world useless to the Order of Eden? Turn the forested paradise they're trying to create here into a hostile hell?"

"I'd say-" Davi started.

The doctor interrupted him, his long fingers falling on Judge's shoulder. "I'd like to hear my answers from this one."

Judge seemed neither impressed nor surprised by the preference and replied; "Scorched earth. That's the Order's answer there. What they can't have they'll ruin for everyone else. Probably mine it to the core and leave the burning rock behind."

"See? Direct! Straight to the core of the matter," Marcelles said to Emiss. "This man must be a recent addition to the ranks of Freeground Intelligence."

"That doesn't mean we shouldn't try," replied Emiss. "We have the capsules, we even have people in place."

"You're right, of course," Marcelles said. "Even though Judge here may be right, something must be done. The people here have created a biological weapon that will introduce several diseases into the ecosystem. The forests the Order have been planting here would be destroyed. There is a lack of biodiversity in the plants that they use, and we will take advantage of that vulnerability. After they are destroyed, the issyrians will be left to purify the clutches."

"We could not have done it without you, Doctor," Emiss reminded him.

"They would have figured out a replication and delivery system eventually, my contribution is miniscule."

"How can we help?" Judge asked.

Davi shot him a warning glance.

"Hypothetically," Judge corrected. "I have to consult my C.O."

"Once your own people here trust you - Remmy, Mary, and Isabel - then I will find a place for you in our plan," Doctor Marcelles answered.

"What's your timetable?" Davi asked.

"There is no reason to wait. I'll consult the surviving elders, but I suspect they'll agree that we can accomplish this within your three day limit."

"Why Port Gibblin?"

"If a capsule went off there, the contents would be carried across the entire hemisphere by their atmospheric terraforming towers," Doctor Marcelles said. "It is the perfect target, and with your well made fake identification, you might have enough time to pull it off."

"Why not send your own humans?" Davi said. "I'm sure they'd clear security."

"Remmy, Mary, Isabel, and I are the only humans here."

CHAPTER 20
INTERESTING GUESTS NEED NOT APPEAR

Doctor Carl Anderson's office had increasingly become the last place he wanted to be. Shannon insisted their status updates take place there. She didn't have an office, insisting she learned more about people by visiting them instead. He had never disagreed with one person so frequently in all his life. The Intelligence Officer operated in the interest of progress regardless of the cost in manpower or moral standing.

"So, how large does a team have to be to get Doctor Marcelles off that planet?" she asked.

Doctor Anderson already had the emotional leverage in the conversation. He was the more experienced one in the room, and after losing so many officers, criminals or not, he had grown bold with her. One word in the wrong or right direction and the frustration she'd been controlling would come out in some indignant declaration. It was time to provoke her, set her off and see what came out. He put his feet up on his empty desk. "We could always send a platoon of cloaked marines in, maybe lend them a hand with the upcoming mission. You know that old saying; 'if you can't beat 'em…'"

"This mission is holding everything back," Shannon said. "If we get involved with this planetary war we'll be choosing the wrong side against the Order of Eden. We can't afford to make any move that can be seen as a declaration of support for the issyrians. The people I represent specifically instructed me to ensure that we don't get involved in exterior politics."

"A selfish clause on any mandate, not to mention short sighted," Carl Anderson said. "We know our advanced cloaksuit teams can assist the people we have down there without being detected by Order of Eden sensor grids. We even have the ships to get them there."

"We don't know anything for certain. The testing you've done has been very limited," Shannon replied.

"Because you won't let any of our teams get close enough to Order of Eden installations to perform real tests," Doctor Anderson replied. Talking in circles infuriated the Oversight Officer.

"Don't try to lure me into an argument, it'll get you nowhere," Shannon said. "The Order has issyrians on their side as well. Healthy issyrians who benefit from intensive medical assistance," Shannon retorted. "An assault would fail, evidence of our involvement would surface."

"So even though the nano recorders we smuggled in on Davi and his people have shown us that the strike and fade tactics they're using down there are working, and they're planning something big that will go down with or without us, you're not going to give me a few men to help seal the deal? If they fail, the consequences could be worse than our direct involvement."

"There are over sixteen million humans down there. Many of them are soldiers, more of them are recruits, and the majority of them are hardened colonists. One platoon wouldn't make any difference. It would make a big difference to this ship, however. We'd be down to two platoons of trusted soldiers, further unbalancing the ratio of trustworthy military to traitors and malcontents aboard. Your train of thought does not lead to a guarantee that we will come out of this endeavour with any real improvement in our abilities to fight off a framework incursion, or to bolster Freeground Nation's defensive position in the galaxy."

"You and the Purity Party are paranoid," Doctor Anderson said, not for the first time. "This framework army that's got you so terrified doesn't exist. No Intelligence Officer, no matter where they are stationed, has ever seen evidence of framework soldiers. The framework army Freeground Intelligence has been predicting for years hasn't materialized. They are not willing to spend the resources when they have a ready supply of Order of Eden recruits. It's that army you should be worrying about."

"It's a real threat," Shannon insisted. "We can't trust your suppositions."

"We can't trust paranoia either," Anderson replied. "We'll have to agree to disagree, from the looks of it. Now, what brought you here?"

"I wanted to tell you in person that Clark Patterson's team has officially been written off. If they return to this ship, they'll be treated as deserters," Shannon said. She stood and started for the door.

"You don't have that power. You're oversight, remember?"

"When there's evidence of wilful sedition, I can order you to dissolve and disavow a team," Shannon said. "That's what I'm doing. You're also being assigned to review a deal that was made a couple of days ago. I'd do it myself, but as you pointed out, I only have conditional command authority."

"Wheeler," Doctor Anderson said. "Why me?"

"I know you have history, but you are the only one who has the rank to approve the deal," Shannon said. "Have you reviewed the materials?"

"He's trading his claim to the Triton for permanent amnesty with Freeground Nation and standing rank with Intelligence," Doctor Anderson said. Giving Lucius Wheeler more power and a safe haven was against everything Anderson felt for the man. He was the only person he'd known in all his years that he would never be able to forgive. "You could submit this for approval next time we're clear for a burst transmission."

"You'll do this now because he has put a clock on his offer," Shannon said. "As Wheeler put it, he can only remain aboard the Sunspire for so long."

"I'll put it through after I check the written component for surprises," Doctor Anderson said.

"You're not going to meet with him? He seems very interested in speaking with you," Shannon replied.

"He's lucky he's not under guard. Captain McPatrick isn't fond of him either." Doctor Anderson cleared his throat and shook off a rising wave of irritation. "Like I said, it'll be done, but I'm noting that there was significant pressure from Oversight. Hopefully this will come up for review when a new party is elected."

"That won't be for a very long time, Doctor," Shannon said.

"We'll see."

CHAPTER 21
ERRANDS

"Why does he look so nervous, Samuel?" Mary asked Davi.

Davi looked over his shoulder to Kipley, who was looking every which way with fearful, wide eyes. The rough-hewn round tunnel around them glittered under the light of naturally bioluminescent plant life growing out of the walls. The stones in the walls looked like the insides of sea shells, flattened by heat then rounded by rushing fluids. The looser soil had turned to glass. "He's afraid of mirrors," Davi replied with amusement.

"Fuck you," Kipley spat back in a whisper. "Could be anyone hiding on the other side of these walls, watching us right now. We'd never know."

"Picking anything up, Remmy?" Mary asked.

"Just the people we're meeting and us," Remmy replied. "Jitters over there is crazy. These walls don't hide anything, I can get a clear scan of all the nearby tunnels for over ten klicks."

"So, what did this?" asked Tamera, one of the Intelligence cloak troops that was discovered when they arrived.

"This was once the main transit arteries between several clutches," Emiss said. She led the dozen armed issyrians who were responsible for this trip. The humans were just going along for help. Davi was sure that Kipley, Judge, Tamera, and Stanley were being tested. Whatever they encountered on this trip had to be handled gracefully, or they'd be counted out when it mattered. He paid close attention to Emiss; she seemed to be one of the active leaders, and familiar with Mary. "Water flows between clutches, like your cities. It is our main form of transportation, communication, and a demonstration of trust. If all the clutches are healthy, then the cities in a network thrive. If one clutch becomes diseased, the others can purify it, heal it."

"But if they all face disease?" Judge asked.

"Then the clutches must be drained, or isolated," Emiss said. "And our waterways become still, then dry - like this." Emiss picked up a handful of loose soil and glass chips and let it slip between her fingers. "Dead."

"Better find a better system," Kipley muttered.

Judge slapped him across the back of the head.

"Hey!" he said.

"Stop talking," Judge said with a glower.

Kipley was about to reply but thought better of it, and swallowed his words.

"I'm sorry this happened to your people," Davi told Emiss.

"You don't understand," Emiss said. "Outsiders can never understand," she replied before picking up her own pace and walking ahead.

Davi thought a moment and looked around. The tunnel didn't smell like the sewers of Trest, but he couldn't help but recognize that there was a lot of dead plant life between the glittering features of the wall. The transit-way had been dry a long time, dead a long time. "What am I not seeing here?" he said so Mary, Remmy and his own people could hear.

"The clutches aren't just cities," Remmy said. "They're collections of organisms. The issyrians communicate with their environment, including the living things that build their homes."

"So there's a builder class we're not seeing?" Davi asked.

"No, animal intelligence sea mammals, from what we've seen," Mary said. "Think of something like an octopus that builds a nest, like a spider builds a web, lays their eggs, raise their young then moves on. The issyrians learned how to influence them into building nests that make good homes, and a lot more. That's just the beginning. Purdai are the main species that they use, but there are hundreds of others."

"Just like a spider isn't the only type of insect that can spin a web," Tamera added.

"Right. Plant life provides everything else," Remmy said. "The thing is, the issyrians communicate through chemistry, and that gets caught in everything. When they die their bodies become part of the clutch too. So, lost relatives who live a long, natural life in or around their clutches aren't forgotten. We have our religions and what we think an afterlife is like, they have clutches that keep them healthy for centuries and consume them once they die. Knowing that future generations will be able to feel their presence along with all their other ancestors is their immortality."

Davi didn't have to say anything, he just nodded. Death was never absolute for an issyrian unless they were isolated from their clutch for a long time, or if it was destroyed.

They walked in silence for a while before Mary turned to him. "So, how did you get reassigned to the Sunspire?"

Davi knew the question was coming, it wasn't something he liked to talk about, but knew he'd have to share. "I was married to a good man," he replied. "He'd love this, actually. Jovral had great taste."

"Jovral? That's a Lorandian name, isn't it?" Remmy asked. "I didn't think Freeground was associated with Lorander that long ago."

"They weren't," Davi said. "He changed his name during our brief alliance with them a few years ago. He thought it was a lot better than Bart."

"He's right," Remmy chuckled.

"Anyway, Jovral wasn't a military man. A little too delicate for the service, as he used to say," Davi said. It was difficult to talk about him, but he pressed on. "I tried to keep most details of my job away from him."

"Were you transferred out of the regular forces because of your relationship?" Mary asked.

Davi shook his head. "We were married before the Puritan Party was voted in, there was nothing they could do. That was, until one of my subordinates produced evidence that Jovral was cheating on me while I was deployed."

"Happens to a lot of us," Judge said.

"Yeah, and a divorce would have satisfied the higher ups if my subordinate didn't also have evidence that Jovral had long discussions about my post with his lovers. Seems he knew a lot more than I thought."

"I'm sorry," Mary said.

"Well, Jovral was sentenced to twelve years, a slap on the wrist. I was sentenced to twenty five. They put him in civilian prison," Davi took a long breath and let it out as he tried not to think too much about what he was about to say. "He lasted five days before his bunk mate smothered him in his sleep. They say they didn't know the man was a Puritan fanatic, but I'll never believe."

"Sons of bitches," Kiply said.

"I was coming up on four months in prison when they pressed me into service on the Sunspire. Intelligence says they want me back in the regular service, I just have to prove myself, but there's no place for me on Freeground."

"Yeah, you must hate them after what they did," Kipley added.

Davi could barely hold down the urge to pistol whip him. "I'm a patriot, you half-wit fuck up. I always will be. If I knew that getting back into the service would change Freeground for the better, I'd move worlds to get back in, but they'll never stop watching me. If I so much as litter near the Parliamentary Chambers, they'll throw my ass in jail or send me to the furthest end of Freeground space to some asteroid post. Instead, I'm going to have to make my way alone, like you."

"Samuel," Judge said, calming Davi down. "Don't be so sure you'll be alone out here. We all need someone to watch our six."

"Don't know what your problem with me is," Kipley said peevishly. "But the ape-man is right."

"Now you're overestimating your place with us when we get free," Judge told Kipley. "You still have to earn a spot on that shuttle."

"What did he do to get pressed into service?" Remmy asked, nodding at Kipley.

Judge pulled Kipley into a headlock and proclaimed, "he thought it would be funny to drop an empty grenade into his C.O.'s lap at a bar near post."

"And you?" Mary asked Judge.

"I got disavowed on mission," Judge replied, releasing Kipley. "But headed home anyway. Had to see my three girls, even if it took years of good behaviour in the stockade."

"What kind of mission?" Remmy asked.

"Snatch-and-grab on Persephone Four. Got there in time to see our guy get killed, was caught in the open, and Intelligence thought I was the one who exposed our target as a Freeground spy. I didn't get close enough to mess things up that bad, but once Intelligence makes their mind up about something, there's no changing it."

"I thought you served with Davi?"

"I did, but went into special ops when he got locked up. Then, bam, first mission goes south," Judge replied. "Just the luck."

"Who was Freeground spying on?" Remmy asked.

"Never heard of the Persephone system before?" Judge asked. "It's the nearest solar system owned by Regent Galactic. It's probably been completely converted to Order of Eden by now. You think Freeground Intelligence is keeping their distance from the Order? Guess again."

"So you've seen Regent Galactic civilized space?" Remmy asked.

"Only one city," Judge answered.

Everyone stared at him as they waited for him to elaborate, especially Remmy. After sometime he finally asked. "And? What was it like?"

"It's a lifestyle experience tailored to suit your every need," Judge said in an uncharacteristically chipper tone. "That's what the artificial intelligences like to tell the more talented residents, but everyone has more than they need unless you're talentless and luckless. It's pretty easy to earn a lot of credit with the corps there, but living there is expensive, so you need to keep working to keep your credit level up. The poorer you are, the fewer freedoms you have."

"Sounds like a great place to live if you're talented," Remmy said.

"Yeah, but talent isn't everything. You have to be pretty social," Judge said. "From what I saw, some pretty intelligent people went real deep into debt. Companies used to buy people for their debts, or jail them. Now they join the Order of Eden, who clears their debt in exchange for a long service contract."

"Seems they've got so many ways to trap people," Mary said.

Davi hadn't heard the stories of Judge's time in Regent Galactic space, but wasn't surprised. The big soldier wasn't typically forthcoming about his experiences unless asked a direct question. Silence settled over the group until they reached a bend in the tunnel and met their contacts.

"Clear waters, Mentor Losame," Mary said, raising open arms to an issyrian that Davi found difficult to look at. The better part of one side of the man's head was held together by a fine latticework of rods and strands. If it weren't for the transparent helmet he wore, and the suspension fluid within, his head would fall over onto his crudely shaped, bulbous shoulder. Most of the people with him were undergoing similar, but less grisly repair processes. They were the roughest looking dozen issyrians Davi had seen. They carried large crates like pack animals. Extra tendrils extended from their torsos to the ground to add strength and support. It never occurred to Davi that being a shapeshifter could provide extra strength, but these diseased ones proved it.

"I am glad to see you, Mary," replied Mentor Losame.

Emiss touched Losame's chest with her bare hand and nodded. "It's time for you and your people to come with us. The humans are moving in to the cities west of here."

"I would be hesitant," Losame said. "Except there is already a raid planned on the old spawning pools."

"Mentor," interrupted a healthier looking issyrian. "They have humans with them. They cannot be trusted."

"I felt your objection before it was spoken, Itirit," Losame replied. "Your ignorance would blind us to opportunities, like trustworthy allies."

"Can you give us directions to the spawning pools?" Mary asked. "I'd like to do something about that."

Emiss' group of issyrians started to take some of the supplies and share the load as she regarded Mary. "That is above the call," she said. "It also may be too easy for you to lose life."

"If you want Mentor Losame's people to have an easy time getting to Trest Under City, they'll need a distraction. Besides, we need equipment."

"Then I'll leave the decision to you, as you've been correct in your actions until now," Emiss said.

"I'll give you directions," Mentor Losame said. "Thank you very much."

"We need weapons anyway," Mary said. "And these humans need to stretch their legs."

"We're starting a firefight?" Kipley asked no one in particular. "That's the best news since I got here."

CHAPTER 22
MAKING A DIFFERENCE

Davi recalled the images of issyrian homes from Patterson's neural report, and upon seeing them with his own eyes, at street level, he realized that the man hadn't taken a good look. A lot of the report indicated that Patterson was so focused on his mission that he missed a lot of details.

The stench Davi and his people encountered in Trest was in the winding streets, but to a much lesser extent. The homes were bulbous things, round globes piled atop and against each other and dried. Impoverished, seemingly bored issyrians peered at them through dark oval doorways.

"This is Rolue, a city built in the bottom of a dried lake," said Emiss as she returned from telling several households that there was a raid coming. "Their homes are made from incubation sacs, they harden when dry."

"So these are all kids?" asked Kipley.

"No, idiot," Emiss said as she split off again, heading for the next cluster of homes. Expectant issyrians waited for her with worried expressions.

"Their children are dead," Mary said flatly. "Their broods need to incubate in an underwater clutch."

"What the hell is a clutch anyway? I thought it was some kind of bag," Kipley replied.

"It's a group of eggs. Issyrians fertilize in groups, so the children belong to the whole community, it's one of the reasons why they're a peaceful people by nature."

"Nasty," Kipley said with a shudder.

"Best if you stop talking now," Judge growled.

Emiss returned to them, looking more anxious. "The Order soldiers have been seen just ahead," she said, pointing up a pathway.

"That's our cue, time to buy these people time," Mary said.

"Are you sure these can be trusted?" one of Emiss' issyrian companions asked, eying Kipley up and down.

"They'll fight for you, don't worry," Remmy said.

"Or I'll kill them myself," Mary added.

They began the quick jog up the path, between green and brown stained issyrian homes that were quickly emptying. "Sir, I have to advise you," Tamera said in as low a whisper as she could manage while being heard. "If you open fire on Order of Eden soldiers you'll be in direct violation of your orders. There will be no way you or any of your people will be able to return to the ranks of any arm of Freeground military."

"That's if you and your Gretch report us," Davi replied. "None of us have neural recorders, they wouldn't let any of us near them if we did."

"He's right, this can be swept right under the rug," Remmy said. "Just in case any of you really want to go back."

"You don't?" Kipley asked Remmy.

"Hell no, there's a mess here. If you have any heart at all, you'll want to help out. Maybe if I survive this, I'll be able to go see that great big galaxy out there too. Why would I want to go back to an overgrown space-can?"

"The fucking smell alone is enough to get me wishing I was back in that can," Kipley said. "Don't get me wrong, I'll fight for you because I follow Davi's lead - he keeps me alive - but I can't wait to get back home. Freeground might be an old can, but she's safer than this place, probably any place."

"That ends if you open fire here," Tamera reinforced.

"We'll see if you get to make that report, bitch," Kipley said so casually that it caught most of them by surprise. "Sleep with one eye open."

Davi wasn't surprised. Kipley could be easy to talk to one moment, and borderline psychopathic the next. "Stow it, Kipley. This mission is staying out of their reports because it's the only way for us to gain the issyrians' trust in a short amount of time. We'll just make sure the Order doesn't find out that we were from Freeground, that's all. Just a bunch of travellers who sympathize with the people here."

"You can't dictate what I tell Intelligence, nor is it my place to decide how they act on the information I give them," Tamera replied.

"Keep that up and I might start agreeing with Kipley," Judge told her.

"We don't have time to discuss it," Davi said. Mary was listening to everything from where she led the group at the front. He had to bring this to a close in the issyrian's favour. "This is happening right now. You only have a few seconds to decide if throwing in with these people is worth the mission's objective. If you think there's another way, or you can't help, you're on your own."

Tamera thought for a moment, looking from Davi, to the ground at her feet, to Mary and back at Davi. "It's the only way to gain the issyrians' trust in time."

"Tamera," her Gretch objected from behind her. "This is premeditated and exactly the situation we were supposed to prevent."

"Not at the expense of the mission."

"That's not specified," he replied.

"You're new to field Intelligence, so I'll spell it out for you," Tamera replied. "When you're on your own, stripped of mission critical resources, like our cloak suits, emergency beacons, and high-trans comm gear, then you have to think on your feet and do the best you can."

"Yes, Ma'am," he replied.

"You're here and you can help a few hundred people escape whatever these soldiers have planned," Mary said. "This is how people really make a difference out here. I know it'll be hard because it's the opposite of Freeground Intelligence's 'watch, wait, and withdraw' strategy, but I'm sure you'll get the idea."

CHAPTER 23
FIRST OFFENCE

The panicked shouts and screams ahead were all the group of humans needed to get them moving faster up the hill. A gust of wind sent fine sand down the path and into Davi's eyes. He never missed his combat vacsuit more. He'd be helmeted and well protected if they were on a sanctioned mission, but he was getting the feeling that he'd never see that combat armour or orders sanctioned by the Freeground Military again.

They reached the top and took cover in a couple of entrances there. Looking down the hill they could see retreating issyrians to the west and, just around the bend, two squads of Order soldiers in dark blue and green carapace-like armour were marching purposefully. Davi scanned the houses on the corner down the hill and spotted a crowd of issyrians gathering, slowly starting to move away from the oncoming soldiers. "They won't see them in time!" he said, pointing out the cover at the bottom of the hill to Judge and Kipley.

"I'll take point," Kipley said as he launched into a run.

Mary almost lurched after him, following his lead, but Davi grabbed her shirt and shook his head. "Wait until I finish counting to ten," he told her. He watched Kipley expertly duck from one good cover point to the next with impressive speed. "Now, go!" All the humans followed Mary and Davi as they followed Kipley's path.

"He's good. I'm surprised," Mary said.

"Best point man I've ever served with," Davi replied as they ducked behind a crumbling wall, halfway down the side of the hill opposite the one they'd climbed. As soon as Davi broke cover he saw Kipley signalling for them to rush down the opposite side of the street. He was already setting up on a firing perch above one of the rounded roofs. The soldiers wouldn't see him; he was dug in and well under cover.

"Too bad he's a complete ass outside of a firefight," Remmy said, out of breath.

"Guy doesn't fit in anywhere else," Judge replied. "He'd have a chest full of medals if he didn't fight the chain of command."

They finished their run to the corner and easily found cover between the cluster of small homes. Davi was able to climb atop one, across from the one on which Kipley perched. The soldiers would pass through the intersection right in front of them. They came within sight, and were within firing range of their rippers when he saw their leader, a man in heavier armour signal the double column to stop.

Two issyrians burst from one of the homes just ahead of the soldiers, and without hesitation one soldier stepped forward with a large bore rifle and fired. The slow moving round that popped from the weapon sailed through the air and burst right behind the soldier's target, throwing a cone of webbing material forward. The issyrians were stunned by an energy burst and trapped in position as millions of strands caught them upright.

"This is a capture mission? What are their plans for them?" Davi asked.

"Medical research, Doctor Marcelles says. Maybe to develop new medical tech," Remmy said.

The heavily armoured soldier in the lead pointed at Kipley's position then the cluster of homes that Davi and the rest of the humans were hiding in.

"Fuck, they caught us on a scan," Mary said. "Take 'em down!"

Davi opened fire on the lead soldier, his weapon whirring as hundreds of tiny blade-shaped particles surged from his ripper handgun every second. The projectiles shattered against his target's armour, sending micro-shrapnel in all directions around him in a thin black cloud. Other soldiers fell to the sudden attack. Two soldiers knelt behind cover and fired their rifles once, the concussive pops overriding the sound of screaming rippers for a moment.

Davi fired several bursts at their positions, forcing them back under cover and watched the big shells sail overhead out of the corner of his eye. One burst against the side of the house Kipley crouched on. The other hit him dead on. He was knocked off balance, about to fall when the web caught him and held Kipley in place on the back side of the home while stunning him with electrical shocks several times.

It was a small victory, and in the end it didn't count for much, since the group of Order soldiers on the street were practically shredded. "I see two under cover," Davi announced, pointing for a moment then resuming his burst fire at the short wall they hid behind.

"One escaped to the street side nearest us," Judge said. "Remmy, confirm."

"Confirmed on my scanner, he's already put a block between himself and his commander," Remmy replied.

Davi couldn't believe his eyes as the commander rolled to his feet, leaving parts of his shredded armour behind. Davi tried to open fire on him in time, but missed as the leader joined the two soldiers who had taken cover early and remained to fight. "How is he in one piece?"

"Framework," Remmy said. "Highly programmed, they call them Order Knights."

"Intelligence says the Order doesn't use them in leadership positions," Tamera said.

"Well your intelligence is wrong again," Remmy replied. "Forget everything you think you know, Freeground is behind again, and that includes the Intelligence division."

"Especially Intelligence," Mary said, her eyes searching the three-way intersection below.

"What happens now?" Davi asked as he weighed the situation. His instincts and the lack of issyrians below told him that it was time to leave. "What does an Order Knight do when they've lost the battle?"

"We've never seen real evidence of one until now," Remmy said. "We tore that guy apart, no way he gets up unless he's got regeneration tech built-in. Framework quality or better." He looked at his hand scanner a moment longer before bashing it against the rooftop. "Uh-oh, game over."

"What's up?" Mary said as she fired a burst at the enemy's position. Her shots pockmarked the short wall.

"We have incoming, and whoever it is doesn't want me to see a damn thing. I've got sensor fuzz two-point-four kilometres out, they're using an EM jamming field."

"Air support, we're leaving," Mary announced.

"How do we cut Kipley down?"

"Very carefully, with rippers," Remmy said. "Try not to de-limb him, I'm a really bad medic."

Judge and Mary remained where they were so they could keep sporadically firing on the Order Knight and his two soldiers, forcing them to remain under cover. The rest rushed across the street to Kipley. Tamera and Davi shot the hardened webbing around Kipley while the rest kept watch. After a long three minutes of careful blasting, Kipley fell to the ground in an unconscious heap. "We're good! Let's get out of here!" Remmy shouted.

Judge and Mary made good time dropping from their rooftop perch and rushing across the street. "Carry him," Davi told Judge.

"Third time I carry his ass back from an engagement. I should start charging," Judge said.

A roar in the distance announced what Remmy stated aloud, "We're out of time. Sounds like at least four troop carriers." He held his hand scanner up between the grey sky and his eyes, using it to magnify the view. He jerked at what he saw and was visibly seized by panic. "Run!"

Before anyone could follow, Remmy was ten steps ahead, sprinting back the way they'd come with an urgency that dismissed Davi's need to question. As he turned and launched into a run after Remmy, he felt the concussive shock of an explosion in his chest, and the ground battered his feet as it shook. A glance behind him revealed only a dust cloud rising in the distance. The explosion was a kilometre away, maybe more by his estimation.

During Davi's long military career, he'd logged countless kilometres running mostly in short bursts. He'd run from the enemy at length a few times before, once on All-Con Prime during one of the enemy's last-gasp retaliations before Freeground affirmed their victory there. The rolling tanks and vicious infantry had them on the run there until Freeground reinforcements arrived two hours later. His lungs burned, muscles ached, and his head rang by the end.

Davi almost wished he was back there; he'd rather face that danger than what he felt coming behind him as they ran down narrow streets and rushed across openings between houses. The ground pounded the undersides of their feet, pulses of air and sound making Davi's head ache before long. The clusters of homes around them cracked like eggs. Many began to collapse.

"Any resistance! Please come in! Retreating fighters need pickup at this location!" Remmy repeated in a raspy scream into his hand scanner. It was easily adapted to transmit, and had a greater range than the simple communicators they brought with them from the Sunspire.

"They're jamming everything," Remmy said to everyone and no one in particular.

Davi was thankful that he was one of the rare type that could panic for hours, and use that as fuel to run for just as long. Even though Remmy seemed nearly beyond reason, tears clearing paths through grime down is cheeks, he was still using his hand scanner to map their way back towards the old tunnels they'd come from.

He didn't hesitate for a second when the entrance loomed before them, half caved in, and ran inside. "Wait!" Mary shouted after him.

Davi took the opportunity to look behind, and counted Tamera, her partner Gretch, and Judge bringing up the rear with Kipley over his shoulder. The man's stern expression and far away stare told Davi that he could keep going for another hundred klicks, or until his body failed him. A trail of dried blood led up the side of his face past his hairline.

Davi and his group followed Mary through the entrance and to their relief they were confronted by an overburdened cargo truck. A few hundred issyrians were loading onto its flat bed, and Remmy was already being hauled up by his belt by a particularly large one. A few other civilian hover cars were already accelerating on ahead.

"Hell of a day," Judge said as he dropped to one knee and let four issyrians take Kipley from his shoulder. "Find us a place to retire after this, Sam," he told Davi, looking more weary than anyone he'd ever seen.

Davi offered the man a shaky hand so he could get to his feet and nodded. "Consider it done," he managed between gulps of air.

CHAPTER 24
PROVEN

"You see what happens when you engage without knowing the first thing about the field?" shouted Tamera. Davi had seen it before, senior officers who got caught in the line of fire for the first time, or first time in a long time, and then completely unravelled when they were safe at last. He sat down and leaned back in one of the plush seats strewn about in front of a trash heap resulting from the constant servicing the issyrians shuttles and ground vehicles required. They were in a makeshift hangar in what Davi imagined would be one of the larger caverns in Trest.

Judge sat down beside him with a groan. They had only been there a couple of hours, and Davi's legs were still aching. He couldn't imagine how Judge felt. "I'm listening," Davi said with a sigh.

"You're reported!" Tamera said. "Don't go back to the Sunspire, because they'll just ship you back to Freeground for execution after they read my report."

"They don't do that to us folks," Kipley said from where he lay across a row of four seats that had been dislodged from one of the civilian shuttles. "Man, I think I'm gonna throw up."

"Still a little sick from that stun?" asked Isabel as she emerged from the rear of the nearest shuttle with Remmy. Issyrians worked on the smaller ships under her direction. She had the training to make repairs on most of the simpler civilian vehicles there.

"Ulp," was Kipley's response as he suppressed a retch.

"He says he's feeling pretty sick," Judge said, reaching over and patting him on the belly.

Isabel and Remmy laughed at the casual antics, while Tamera found more fuel to fume on. Gretch, her partner, quietly seethed behind her with his arms crossed. "This is serious! I'll make you exiles!"

The issyrians nearby were getting distracted, looking at them from where they worked around, under, atop, and within the three nearby shuttles. "Shut it down, Tamera," Davi said calmly. The last thing he needed was to escalate things by raising to her level.

"I will not shut this down," she growled back.

"Shut 'er down!" Kipley cried mockingly.

"We'll go back to the Sunspire when it's all over and done with," Davi said. "And then they'll probably give us something cheap so we can leave, get to the nearest alien world and make our way."

Kipley inadvertently punctuated the statement by leaning over and vomiting in three agonized coughs.

Judge patted him on the shoulder. "There, there," he chided.

Kipley replied by giving him the finger.

Remmy scanned him momentarily and nodded. "Yeah, he's just got really bad stun sickness. Bet the room is just spinning right now."

"Fuck you, too," Kipley replied, wiping his mouth with a discarded rag.

"That's Kipley-speak for 'hell yeah,'" Judge said.

"How do you expect to live as exiles?" Gretch asked as Tamera threw up her hands in surrender. "You don't know anything about this sector, and I doubt you'll get any financing from Freeground."

"I've dropped in on a couple of worlds not too far off," Judge said. "You really didn't spend much time reading my file, did you?"

"Adding up to a few weeks of experience at best," Gretch retorted. "Not the kind of experience that can lead to a good beginning."

"Are you chastising out of concern, or are you just enjoying the sound of your own voice at this point?" Davi asked.

"Seems a lot of Intelligence Officers like how they sound when they're bitching," Judge added.

"I'm just telling you how things are out there," Gretch said. "You're not going to survive."

Kipley hacked a last splatter of fluid onto the cavern floor and looked up at the Intelligence Officers. "I ran first, I shot first, so blame me, you dumb fuck," he rasped. "Your report's nothing but bullshit if you don't put the blame on me first. These idiots were just covering my dumb ass."

Gretch's eyes went wide, and Tamera shook her head. "He's right," she said. "We could put him up as the aggressor in this," Tamera said. "We don't gain anything by presenting it any other way."

"You're agreeing with them now?" Gretch said, surprised.

"No, they dragged us into this and it was wrong to get involved, but we can still present this in a way that will get them away from Freeground for good with a few credits, so they can survive on their own."

"So, what? Are we following them from here on out?" Gretch asked, incredulous.

"If it will get Doctor Marcelles' cooperation, then yes. That's the only way to salvage this mission for any of us," she replied. "And it's the only way to avoid getting us both busted down to able crewman for what's already happened."

"That's right," Kipley said with a grin. "You guys are our babysitters, if it all goes tits up and none of us survive, you're on the hook for it."

"I hate you people," Gretch said, dropping into a seat.

Mary interrupted Kipley with her entrance, something for which Davi was more than a little grateful. Even in his current condition, his comrade would push for the fight to go on. He loved a good argument almost as much as he liked a good fistfight. "Well, that did it," Mary said as she stepped into the semicircle with Emiss behind her. "You're on the op with us in Port Gibblin tomorrow."

"You have earned our trust," Emiss added. "And we need you."

"Shut 'er down!" Kipley shouted. His nausea forced him into a lunge, and he coughed up a spatter of bile. "Fuck, I thought I was done."

"Is he going to be all right?" Mary asked.

"Stun sick," Remmy replied. "He'll be sick for a couple more hours then sleep for ten."

"Be back up just in time to get our teeth kicked in by the fucking Order," Kipley said as he laid back. "Gotta love a little trust."

CHAPTER 25
PORT GIBBLIN

The forest around them looked much older than it should have. Davi had seen simulated spaces that featured forests with ancient redwoods, as old as the oldest colonies, and couldn't believe the powerful appearance of those old trees. The bark's texture spoke to the centuries they survived, with as many scars and unique markings as anything that old should have.

The forest planted by Regent Galactic on Uumen was a strange thing in comparison. The trees were metres across in some places, but the bark looked strangely smooth. If they weren't moving at over two hundred kilometres an hour on an anti-grav skid craft, he'd reach out and touch one.

Davi let his hand rest on the butt of his ripper handgun. It was only the first object that helped make his experience on Uumen the strangest thing in his life. He'd seen several alien worlds, but from behind a Freeground Military vacsuit visor.

The civilian clothes he wore were a mix between woven fibres that were harvested from the same forest they sped through, and flexible safety plastics. The jacket he wore was dark violet, and was originally made to protect from splashing molten metal in some foundry he'd never see. Most energy and heat based weapons would have difficulty piercing it. It was the best type of armour he could wear on their mission; anything heavier would raise suspicion.

More so than their clothing or weaponry, the humans on Uumen used a mode of travel that seemed next to crazy. Instead of using shuttles or hub-controlled public transit, they preferred to use antigravity vehicles that travelled only one half to two metres above the ground. They called them skids. The humans and the issyrians who were friendly with them used them because all flying vehicles were tracked and registered to a pilot. The issyrians and friends used them to escape notice. It wasn't impossible to use flying vehicles within planetary space, but the less they had to log fake or suspicious flight paths, the better. On a cosmic scale the skid wasn't moving quickly at all, but travelling so close to the ground was exhilarating. Davi watched as Kipley flinched in his seat at the passing of every near by tree trunk.

"Don't worry," reassured Isabel. "The issyrians say that these are used on colonies across the galaxy. Besides, this is a luxury model with an advanced navigation system." She pointed at the holographic overlay between her and the roughly hewn road ahead. Roots crisscrossed beneath in a tangle of wood and ravaged brown fruit.

The luxury craft had seen better days. It carried seven passengers plus the pilot and, judging from dents and score marks, it was likely that this wasn't the first mission the little skid had been on. "I was sure we were all going to die when Isabel took the controls for the first time," Remmy said over his shoulder. "But now I'm only half sure."

The wind rushing over the energy field shielding the top half of the car nearly obscured the last part of his statement. Davi wished it had. "What did he say?" Kipley asked, wide eyed.

"We're all going to be fine," Davi said.

"Oh," he replied.

Davi looked to Judge. "I'm starting to enjoy this," he said.

"I think I left my stomach in Trest," Judge replied.

Davi noticed the large man's white knuckle grip on the edge of the seat and laughed.

"When I get to Chan Lin I'm going to buy myself one of these," said Mary. "Or maybe a bike version. That's gotta be even better."

"You're suicidal, woman!" Kipley exclaimed. "At least with this we've got a buffer, and a few inertial dampers. The bikes I saw back there were just seats strapped to engines!"

"Yeah, I'll definitely get a bike," Mary concluded.

"Why do you want to go to Chan Lin?" Davi asked. He'd never heard of the place before.

"Most of the humans were saved by the other races there, especially the nafali. They already signed treaties, started up a new alliance. There are jobs, peaceful cities, and a new military forming. I hear even Lorander Corp is taking an interest," she replied.

"I might just join you," Davi said.

"You might not have a choice," Remmy said. "If this goes bad, a lot of the issyrians might try to make a break for it, and they'll set their course for one of the Chan Lin system's outer colonies. Most won't make it, but it's the nearest friendly space that'll take issyrians from a banished house."

"Banished?" Davi asked.

"The Great Issyrian Houses in these sectors see this world and the people here as contaminated thanks to this forest and the diseases Regent Galactic brought with them. Everyone here is an outcast," Remmy replied. He didn't look away when he finished speaking but seemed to search Davi's expression for a particular reaction before saying "remind you of anyone?" then facing forward in his seat.

Davi was starting to understand why it was so easy for Remmy, Isabel, and Mary to find their place among the issyrians. As he watched the brown trunks whip by on either side of the skid, he realized that he had been starting to see things from the issyrian perspective more and more. The plight of Freeground Intelligence and his mission seemed less important all the time. As for Remmy's reference, he could only imagine that he was reminding him of how Intelligence invaded and manipulated the mind of their former commander, Clark Patterson.

Going native was a real possibility, especially if what he suspected about his own situation was true. There was no way Freeground Intelligence let him and his team operate without neural implants. He only hoped he didn't get the controller type they built into Patterson.

In the blink of an eye he was past the tree line and beneath Port Gibblin proper. It was impossible to tell whether it was night or day beneath the superstructure of the main port buildings. "Holy shit, here we go," Kipley said with an anxious smile.

"We have to stay inconspicuous until we get the signal," Mary said.

Kipley's hand came out from under his loose shirt, where Davi assume he'd stashed his ripper.

Isabel took tight turns on the spiral ramp that led up into the belly of the main brown and grey metal structure made Davi dizzy.

"Oh God," he heard Tamera say as she closed her eyes and swallowed hard.

The skid came out onto a flat platform section, brightly lit by recessed lights and reflective walls. Dozens of ships marked with black and yellow X's across their hulls sat idle. "This looks like an impound," Judge said to no one in particular. "I've never seen so many small ships held in one place."

"They transport the bigger ones off world, who knows where they go from there," Remmy said as they slowed down.

They came to a stop around a corner where the busier segment of the port started. The largest class of ship they had seen so far - corvettes under one hundred metres in length - were lined up in rows. The hangar seemed to go on forever. Crews from across the sector and beyond tended to their daily business of maintenance, loading, and repair. From a quick glance Davi could see that most of them were either loading cargo or making major repairs. No one was unloading.

"Resource harvesting from the planet," Isabel said as she slid the door to the skid forward and stepped out. "Blue crates are raw foods, green are compressed biomass, and we don't know what the other three colours are."

"The other skid just arrived in their sector," Remmy announced quietly. "We're on time." He led them to a lift that sent the group of eight up to the fifty fifth floor, where Davi was confronted by a sea of colour as soon as they stepped out onto the public transport dais. The swiftly progressing lines to and from the bank of transit pods reminded Davi of the animated model of the human vascular system he referenced constantly during his basic medical training. People moved in and out of the transit hub as if it were a beating heart. In the main gallery below there were thousands of people dressed in styles of clothing that he would have never imagined. The sight of so much variety in one place, and the crush of people was more than he'd ever seen anywhere, especially on Freeground.

The stores were islands of products, barely walled in so everyone could get a good look at them. They sold everything from hot food to toys. Larger stores lined the oval market space. Their signs were simple, static two dimensional affairs. They didn't have to be any more than that from the look of things; people were constantly entering while others were emerging with colourful bags, some of which projected holographic advertising that spoke and pointed towards their point of origin. "Hey! Looks like you could use some new shoes, fella! Treadwise is right over there, go check it out," said one of the holographic ad-men as he was projected by bag in a passer-by's hand.

"This is fucking ridiculous," Kipley said. "A hologram just told me to get a burger down there because I look hungry. How the hell did it know?"

"Marketing is an art," Remmy said. "Just like interrogation."

"We didn't go to the same art classes," Judge replied. "We're really going to pull this off here?"

"It's the best place," Remmy replied.

"See that pillar?" Isabel said, pointing ahead and above.

Davi looked through the gallery's transparent roof and saw a pillar blocking part of the blue sky above. It extended well out of sight. "That's one of the atmospheric modification pipes," he guessed.

"Exactly. One of the primaries.The main feeder lines are right under that Americana joint," she replied. "Looks like you can get that burger."

Remmy and Isabel led the way down the stairs and to the red, white, and blue burger stand. It was a circular bar with stools set around it. The kitchen was in the centre, where Davi saw them frying potato strips and grilling meat products of all kinds.

"It smells like they're burning meat in hot lubricant," Tamera muttered.

"This is fucking authentic, don't you know anything about history?" asked Kipley. "Once upon a time people knew how to eat."

"But everything that isn't green or chipped here was alive once," Isabel countered.

"Nope, not really."

"Don't you know where meat comes from?" she retorted.

"He's right, check it out." Remmy pointed to the holographic Flipper Boy sign above as images of headless chickens and cows danced around the letters. "Headless livestock."

"How does that even work?" she asked.

"Who cares?" Kipley said as he stepped up to the counter and selected a combination with two hamburgers and a basket of chicken nuggets. "Animals are for eating."

"They grow the meat and organs in vats, connected to artificial support systems. They don't actually grow headless animals," Judge answered as he posted his own order: a variety basket of breaded chicken, ham, and beef.

"Is that all they serve here?" Isabel asked.

"I'll order you some coleslaw. If it's anything like the stuff in the period pictures, it's just salad," Remmy said as he sat down between Isabel and Davi.

Davi took the time to take in the crowd again. While some of his people seemed easily distracted by the exotic food, he was still astounded by the mass of people with individual tastes in clothing, dialects of speech, and music he overheard as they passed. "This is how humans should live," he said to himself. "Why isn't it like this on Freeground?"

"We all get the same education until the GAT," Remmy said as he was handed a basket filled with steaming fries, topped with a disc of meat trapped in a dripping bun. He handed a bowl of dressing-soaked shredded vegetables to Isabel and a small container of fries to Davi. "Here, they're potato fries."

Davi accepted, and decided to wait for them to cool before he tried one. He remembered the General Aptitude Test faintly; he took it when he was ten. That was probably the least of the similarities that all Freegrounders shared in their experiences growing up. Unlike most of the people on the Sunspire who were exiled from Freeground, he never felt his choices in entertainment, career, or most other experiences were limited. If there was one thing he could change about Freeground, it was the new breeder mentality, which hadn't been mainstream long.

Sitting on a stool at Flipper Boy, watching a sea of individuals walking around, he couldn't help but wish his husband were sitting beside him. He'd love the vibrance and endless variety.

They had a chance to eat their food and sip their sugary sodas. Davi couldn't get past the first taste test, it was so intensely flavoured that he thought he was trying to drink syrup. "What's the signal we're waiting for?" he asked Remmy.

"You'll know it when you see it," he replied. Without a word he looked over his shoulder and nodded slowly. "Watch that storefront."

How Davi hadn't noticed it before, he couldn't imagine, but once he followed Remmy's gaze and found an Order of Eden Support Centre, he realized that the Issyrians were about to take the opportunity to make some kind of statement. There were four lines of people waiting to enter the busy social centre, and there wasn't a guard in sight. He spotted soldiers mixed in with the crowd throughout the gallery, but none specifically watched the Order of Eden Centre, which he thought was strange. "Is that a registration centre or something?"

"Nope, everyone you see here is either registered or not human. Those centres are for people who want to find jobs with the Order, or advance towards Living Paradise. The hundred thousand credits us humans pay for protection from the Eden Virus and registration is only the beginning," Remmy replied.

"So if I wanted to become an officer in their military, or gain civilian rank, that's where I'd start," Davi replied.

"Yup, that would be your gate to the Promised Land. Immortality in paradise and elevation to a whole new plane of existence are yours, but only if you jump through their hoops. Most people who sign up become civil servants, or low pay workers, a few become military."

"You have some pretty good intelligence," Tamera said.

Remmy brought up the public computer directory screen on the counter and pressed the Order of Eden logo in the corner. The green and blue planet logo spun and enlarged, stopping as it overwhelmed the display. It was an electronic pamphlet with testimonies and a directory offering more information than any of them could get through while they waited. "They turn out more propaganda every day," Remmy said. "It's good entertainment."

Davi turned his attention towards examining the area between himself and the Order Support Centre. There were permanent trash receptacles, a ramp-way leading below, and a few holotransmitter posts no thicker than his arm.

"Checking for cover and forming a plan?" Judge asked him quietly.

A shiver ran up Davi's spine before he could answer, and he flinched visibly. "If this mission kills us, our death will come from the sky, or through that door." He tried his first fry and couldn't help but appreciate the texture, the richer flavour of the salt and other, unidentifiable seasoning. He thought the treat would help hide his rising anxiety, but he was wrong.

"Easy there, Lieutenant," Judge said. "We've made it through retrievals that would have made most infantrymen break rank."

"With a few losses along the way," Davi replied. "Not just in death, either. Foster cracked so hard he got dropped from the unit. He's probably still back on the Sunspire, getting grief therapy."

"You know what they say," Judge replied. "One in nine people can live as a soldier for longer than two years. The rest just fall apart and fall out. Foster lasted a long time for a softie."

"Shouldn't have been in the service in the first place," Kipley said, wiping mustard and catsup from his lips with his sleeve.

"They should draft you back into service as a part of the exam," Judge said. "If they can stand you for a day, they pass."

Davi interrupted the impending spat. "What's the distraction we're looking for?"

"Keep watching the Order Support Centre," Remmy said. "It should be coming soon."

Davi did as he was told. He watched as people entered the Support Centre with meek expressions, many of them looking beaten and destitute. If he weren't watching closely he would have missed most of them, there were so many successful people milling around in front. They had the cheery faces, spoke amongst themselves, but after watching for a while, it was plain that most of them weren't in line at all. They were part of the window dressing, and they shielded a large portion of the main line leading inside. The queue filled with ragged folks who looked like they were carrying all they owned on their back, or in old shopping bags.

They were refugees from other worlds that had been hit so hard by the Holocaust Virus that there was nothing left to sustain them at home. The thick smell of rotting corpses and the sounds of machines trundling down the streets, cleaning up after the carnage were the norm on those worlds, in those towns and cities. Davi knew the sights, sounds, and smells well. He'd seen two cities just like that since his exile. He wondered how many more ruined places he could stand seeing.

"You keep drifting off," Isabel said to him from behind.

Her slender hand laid on his arm. There was a fry in his hand, half way between the cup and his mouth. He ate that one and put the cup back on the counter. Davi hadn't even realised she was there. "I'm just remembering a few people we lost along the way." He said it before he remembered that she lost someone important too. The report was clear; Clark was dead and there was no neural imprint to rebuild from. "Sorry."

She closed her eyes for a long moment and nodded before speaking. "It's all right. This trip was dangerous, everyone knew. I only hope it's worth it in the end."

"Can it be?" Davi asked.

"It has to be," she said.

A flash of light so bright that all colour seemed to wash away for a moment burst from the Order Support Centre. The lines scattered, people ran frantically away from something inside. Davi caught sight of something glowing for a moment, then, for just an instant, he saw what it was. Emiss, their guide through Trest, stood with arms outstretched. Her face was distorted, it seemed almost enlarged by an expression that was so filled with hate that it outshined the light fighting to burst through her skin. He could see bright red and yellow fluids rushing through her body, burning her clothing away.

Soldiers barely had time to draw their rifles and sidearms before the chemical reaction reached its critical point. Davi wasn't the first to dive over the counter when she exploded, rending hundreds of humans to shreds inside and outside of the Order Support Centre.

Remmy led the charge behind that counter. Crouched down low, he had his ripper out. When the forced silence that followed large explosions was over, he fired at the nearest staff member of the Flipper Boy, half severing his neck in a two second burst. Isabel scrambled past the dying cook and flipped a small access panel open. Remmy continued his rampage, Kipley, and Judge joining in. Mary rolled to the other end of the circular counter and took a watch position.

Davi knew what his job was, and turned his attention to the events outside, over the edge of the counter. The blast and carnage ended less than twenty metres from where he took cover, and soldiers hadn't recovered their senses yet, let alone the hundreds of surviving civilians who were knocked down, stunned still, or just starting to panic.

The floor was scorched in a radiating semicircle pointing away from the Order Support Centre. The dead and dying littered half of the shopping gallery, and having to stand back without offering assistance caused a pang of regret that Davi found difficult to ignore. The transparent ceiling just above the Support Centre had blown out completely. The darkened entrance to the Centre itself was a blackened hole. Emiss had taken revenge for whatever wrongs the Order had brought on her, and then some.

People were starting to move, to moan, and in some cases, scream. Chaos was coming.

CHAPTER 26
PANIC

Davi and Mary both knew their roles. They were charged with watching the crowd, the guards especially. If someone noticed them hiding behind the counters of the Flipper Boy and was about to get aggressive, they would be the first to raise the alarm for everyone else. The recovering crowd wasn't getting immediate support from security or medical personnel. A panic was imminent. There was no crowd control, no members of security were taking the initiative and directing people. Not being able to jump out and start directing the innocent to safety made something inside Davi hurt.

They trained Freeground soldiers as guardians first. He had just witnessed a massacre for the sake of the issyrian race on a world Freegrounders had no business fighting for. The first emergency team emerged from the north exit. There were six of them, flanked by a pair of utility bots. Dozens of stunned people called out to them as they passed, and they were ignored, blocked by the hard, tall steel of the support bots. They may have been on antigravity skids, but they were still the better part of a ton each.

Neither seemed to be armed, and they were causing a fair amount of chaos as they made their best speed towards the Order Support Centre at the opposite end of the shopping gallery. As if spurred by something Davi didn't have time to notice, the crowd began their wailing and screaming as the stunned silence of the immediate aftermath became the bedlam of terror. The able bodied trampled the injured, each other, and crushed towards the exits nearest them. The hard floor rumbled under the pounding of thousands of frantic feet.

The emergency team stunned people who got between them and the Order Support Centre. The few guards and soldiers who were present were swallowed by the maelstrom of panicked people. Their own fault, they should have taken control. If Davi were in their place, he knew he wouldn't have let things get so bad.

When the first of them came towards them, he was waiting for it. A woman rushed towards his section of the counter, and he raised his ripper, shaking his head. "Not here!" he shouted just loudly enough to be heard in the racket.

The woman elbowed the young man at her side hard, then he saw the gun and ran in another direction. A few behind them noticed him brandishing a pistol before he lowered it, and their hesitation directed the people behind to instinctively bound away, towards the next booth. That wouldn't last long.

He looked over his shoulder in time to see Remmy push Isabel away from the access panel, shaking his head.

"Sorry!" she was saying. "I told you you should try to decode this thing, you're the expert."

"But you're shit with a weapon," Remmy replied. "I thought you could pop the inner hatch while I helped sweep the employees out of the way."

"You mean I didn't want to kill these workers," she replied. "These were innocent people."

"There's no such thing here! Everyone around us is a card carrying member of the Order of Eden, they are the enemy as much as any soldier."

"Just get us in," Isabel replied, drawing her pistol. It seemed too big for her, but she brandished it with surprising familiarity. There were lies in the neural report from Clark's head, somehow they'd managed to paint her as an innocent who would turn from combat. What Davi saw then told him otherwise; she was as ready to kill as he was, and she joined him at the counter.

Davi decided to put that aside like so many other things as he focused his attention on what was happening beyond cover. The panicked crowd was getting closer, he readied his weapon. There was no stun setting - anyone who came too close would be shot through with several high velocity blades. Pain and blood would cause more panic.

Several men, all dressed in what looked like the colours of some kind of sports team, pressed by, bending metal stools that were driven into the floor as solidly as any support beam. Davi cringed as he heard bone crack and one of them scream. The crowd was pressing too closely. "Stay back!" he called out as loudly as he could. He couldn't see past the wall of people who tried to shy away from the sturdy booth, and only the first row could see him and Isabel with their weapons in hand. She looked at him nervously.

Davi could see no alternative but to set the velocity of his weapon as high as he could, hoping that the projectiles would break the sound barrier and frighten the crowd away. He fired up, and never thought he would be so relieved to be half-deafened by the sounds of weapons' fire.

"Good thinking!" Tamera said as she fell in beside him. She set her firearm to match his.

"Yeah, let's be all loud and obvious for the soldiers who'll probably be here any minute," Kipley added.

"He's saving lives, asshole!" Isabel said before letting loose with her own burst of fire in the air.

The panic of the crowd, and the randomness of their flight were reinforced as a beaten up armoured shuttle came out of the clear blue sky, thundering towards the opening in the gallery ceiling. The doors along the sides slid open as it slowed, firing emergency deceleration thrusters until it was within a few metres of the shredded metal roof.

Doctor Marcelles, in the dark amber armour Davi had seen in the last moments of Clark's neural report, was the first person he saw leaning out the side of the ship. A dozen other issyrian soldiers leaned out with him. The pilot barely gave the fleeing public enough time to get out of the way before touching down, shaking the ground hard enough to rattle Davi's teeth.

The crowd was even more frenzied before as more gunfire - not theirs - pierced the air. Their reinforcements had arrived, and so had some of the Order's. The civilians were caught in between.

Davi looked around quickly and didn't see soldiers, so he jumped up on the counter. "Take the tram exit!" he shouted. He pointed to the exit behind the crowd in front of him, and after yelling the same thing several times while watching for soldiers the crowd started turning. He knew he was living what could be his last moments very foolishly, but he would rather die knowing he tried to save people from the impending crossfire than sitting idly by.

It was working. The people nearest to the subway exit were rushing down the steps, and the access ramp. To his horror he saw the strobing light of weapons' fire coming from the tram entrance to which he was directing people. More soldiers were on their way, and they weren't afraid to cut their way through the people they should be protecting.

Davi was yanked off the counter by Judge. "You're going to get killed!"

He started to reply, but the words got caught in his throat. Instead he managed to say, "More soldiers are coming from below." At a glance he could see that Remmy had cracked the access panel in the middle of the counter island floor and was opening the hatch that led to the environmental regulation systems. They were moments away from breaking through into the planetary environment systems.

The frenzied crowd split under the pressure of gunfire from two sides. Some ran over the counter and right between everyone hiding behind it, rushing to the other side, over the opposite counter and beyond. Many went around, bumping the fixtures hard, but after less than a minute, Davi could see the open firefight between the issyrians led by Doctor Marcelles, who brandished a heavy double barrelled rifle in either hand, and the Order of Eden soldiers who struggled to make entry from exits all around them.

Davi was relieved to have an enemy to aim for. Kipley was gleeful; there was a glint in his eye that didn't belong to a sane man. It was his favourite type of situation - a shooting gallery from good cover.

Using shields made from old ship plating, several issyrians rushed from the shuttle and started to cross the twenty five metre distance between them and the counter. Two issyrians were trying to cross carrying gas canisters the size of a man's head. Even with the makeshift cover carried by their fellows, they couldn't quite make the distance thanks to the enemy's suppressive fire. There weren't many soldiers firing, but they all seemed to know that keeping the issyrians pinned down in and around the shuttle would be better than letting them progress.

Enemy soldiers were breaking through the thinning civilian mob that retreated from the tram steps. It was chaos there more than anywhere else, with people trying to get to the subway and as many trying to retreat from the soldiers forcing their way up. Davi saw a few soldiers break through and caught his first target full in the face. He watched with relish as blood, bone, and flesh sprayed out the back of his helmet. Their armour wasn't made to resist the hardened blades of a ripper.

Judge and Kipley focused their fire on the same exit, and they did not go wanting for targets. The soldiers broke through the civilians blocking the way and surged up in teams too large to count. Their relentless push paid off. For every soldier Davi and his team managed to kill or immobilize before they reached the top, another made it to the gallery proper, where they retreated to the nearest cover so they could dig in for a firmer counter-offensive.

The counter strike was coming from the far end of the gallery behind them as well. By the time the issyrian team was halfway to them, their cover was taking fire. Sparks and bits of white hot metal were flung into the air as a heavier shot struck the deck in front of the stand. "A few of those hit us and we won't have much cover left!" Davi shouted.

"Where do you want me, boss?" Kipley shouted between bursts.

Davi looked in every direction, trying to get a good read on the situation. There were a few soldiers taking cover wherever he looked. Their hold was getting shakier by the moment. "Are you ready for the canister, Remmy?" he asked.

"I'll be ready in twenty seconds! We're just breaking into the pipeline now."

"All right, I need two volunteers to make the distance between us and those issyrians!" Davi said.

Tamera thumped him on the shoulder with her fist and nodded. Davi couldn't help but be surprised but nodded after a moment.

Kipley laughed loud enough to break through the cacophony. "Have I ever turned you down?"

Davi looked towards the issyrians, who were bracing behind their heavy portable cover, trying to inch the armour plating they carried along to create more cover between the shuttle and the counter island, where they were trying to open a main terraforming pipe. "All right,you're going to have to get a canister from the issyrians and rush back. Go on three!" Tamera and Kipley positioned themselves, ready to spring over the sturdy counter top and across the distance as fast as they could. As Davi signalled his count with his fingers, he couldn't help but think that he had never seen twelve metres look so long in all his life. When he flashed three fingers, the pair were off.

Kipley and Tamera sprinted as hard and as fast as Davi had ever seen, and after five steps one was struck fully in the chest by a broad pulse beam. Kipley didn't pay any notice to Tamera as an entire section of her upper torso was vaporized. Davi didn't watch long enough to see if Kipley made it all the way, but turned towards the origin point of the beam burst.

The soldier bearing the heavy cannon was under thick plated metal. The blades from Davi's ripper sparked against the surface, showing no sign of penetrating. It was the heaviest armour Davi had ever seen, partially mechanized, but definitely built onto a soldier, or something shaped like one. He took careful aim at the slowly marching, dark green plated combatant and tried to fire on the horizontal lights running down the front of his helmet. The blades from his ripper sent sparks in all directions, but he didn't see any real damage. "What the hell is that?" Davi asked.

"That's the kind of armour we thought all Order Knights wore before we saw one slumming it the other day!" Remmy shouted over the din. "Aim for the power cable!"

"Isn't an Order Knight some kind of framework?" asked Judge.

"It'll disarm his main weapon, so he'll have to come after us with coarse language and fisticuffs!" Remmy answered. "And, yeah, some of them might be frameworks, I've never seen one go down."

Davi, Judge, Remmy, and Isabel all aimed for the cables leading to the soldier's weapon. Most shots missed, their broken blade ammunition turning into high speed flack that caught the soldiers around him by fortuitous chance. Another beam flashed from the muzzle of their target's weapon, burning into the floor close to Kipley as he ran back with the canister of toxins in a grinning frenzy.

Davi couldn't help but notice that the container was of a Freeground design. It was another sign to him that he was fighting alongside Freegrounders who had turned their back on their people entirely, to the point of assisting another people with the construction of terrible weaponry. It was a breach, but he wasn't innocent of that himself. Getting involved with the politics on Uumen was an unrecoverable deviation from the mission. He returned his full attention to the Order Knight and took a moment to sigh in relief as one of the armoured cables showed some evidence of damage and fraying. The Knight twitched as a hail of blade rounds ripped at his weaponry. There was no telling why exactly, but something - perhaps a busted control or power system - forced him to detach the harness that supported his large weapon and let it drop. Without drawing another weapon, he leapt over thirty metres, landing with a skid towards the issyrians who tried to hold their makeshift shield wall halfway between Davi and the shuttle.

"Focus fire on the rest of the soldiers! Ignore the Knight!" Remmy ordered as he took the canister from Kipley, who was all too eager to surrender it and get back to the fight.

Davi turned his attention back to the tram entrance. "What about the knight? Can't we slow him down?" he asked.

"Don't worry!" Remmy shouted back as he stomped the canister firmly into the terraforming pipe that led outside.

Davi watched as the Order Knight leapt into the air again, only to collide with Doctor Marcelles in mid-air. The doctor landed atop the armoured soldier and dug into him with bare claws. The scream of metal being torn apart pierced the air. Marcelles pried the top half of the Knight's helmet open and reached inside. With a motion as casual as peeling half an orange out of its shell, the human-issyrian hybrid ripped most of the soldier's head free of its metal carapace. A personal shield repelled most of the bolts of energy the other soldiers fired at him.

A beam weapon caught Marcelles in the shoulder, severing his arm, and before Davi's eyes, another grew in its place. It took less than two seconds for the arm to fully form. Marcelles leapt back towards the shuttle, signalling in mid air to Remmy, who peeked over the counter behind him and shook his head. "Two more Order Knights just arrived." He dropped the canister into the hatch they had come to secure. "But we're done here."

"Retreat!" Davi called out.

Kipley was over the bar, shooting and running before Davi finished giving the order. "Come get me, you mother-fuckers!" he screeched with a wild laugh.

"I think he's starting to think he's charmed," Davi told Judge as he got ready to make the leap.

"We've all got our time," Judge replied.

Davi turned to signal everyone else to follow, and when he looked back towards the shuttle he saw what was left of Judge fall over the other side of the bar. He didn't even hear his best friend die. He was alive one moment and gone the next. Gretch bumped his shoulder, "Nothing you could do, come on!" he said.

Press on. It was what Judge was good at, and Davi followed his example, rushing across the no man's land between the counter tops and the shuttle. The issyrians dropped their makeshift cover as they passed, joining their flight.

By the time Davi was aboard and the shuttle was taking off, they were down to two issyrians, Isabel, Remmy, Mary, and Kipley.

CHAPTER 27
THE DEAL

Through the rear view of the armoured shuttle, Davi watched the products of the canister pour out of the old environmental terraforming systems' pipes. A brown tinged font of air filled the sky and spread faster than anything he'd ever seen. "A package of viruses targeting the Order's terraforming crap carried by trillions of nanobot crop dusters." Remmy said. "That should do it."

Davi sat quietly, trying not to think about Judge, the best right hand man he'd ever had, and Tamera, who he just met. She might have been a pain in the ass, but she had the kind of dedication to duty that he couldn't help but respect. Under other circumstances they could have been close friends, but there was always a tendency to glorify the dead.

"Fuck, I can't believe I'm alive," Kipley said with a chuckle. He drew several sour stares from human and issyrian alike. "I was sure that big fucker Judge would outlive me."

"Shut it down, Kip," Davi growled.

"Shut 'er down!" Kipley shouted, pumping his fist in the air.

Before anyone could stop him, Davi leaned back and kicked Kipley in the face as hard as he would the Order soldier who killed Judge. He sat back with his hands up, watching Kipley reel from the blow, holding the right side of his face as he leaned across Isabel's lap.

"Mother fucker! You trying to kill me?" Kipley said.

There wouldn't be any retribution from the irritating grunt, he knew better. Davi sat back and crossed his arms, breathing deeply, trying to take control of the rage he felt towards the only survivor of his unit. "This one cut deep," Davi growled finally. "So shut your hole before I have it wired shut, hear me?"

"Yes, Sir," Kipley barked with a salute. The whole right side of his face was red; the bruises would start coming out soon.

Davi let his gaze drift to the transparent metal beside Kipley, and he watched as the Regent Galactic forest began to discolour, turning a sickly shade of green and brown. The heavy branches already seemed to wilt, but that could have been a trick of the eye. Doctor Marcelles entered the rear of the shuttle and sat in one of the many empty seats. "Congratulations, ladies and gentlemen," he offered quietly. "The mission was successful, the toxins are spreading better than expected thanks to an eastern wind. The Order will not be able to prevent a full ecological shift on this planet."

"Thank God," Remmy said. "There's no way I'll take that ride again."

That was met with momentary, timid chuckles and weak smiles.

Davi let silence settle over the occupants before asking, "So that's it, we take you back to the Sunspire. We held up our end."

Doctor Marcelles regarded him, obviously ill at ease and nodded after narrowing his solid yellow eyes. He was looking less human all the time.

They crossed under some trees and into shadow, into some tunnel that led through a lake that had emptied and begun to rot. It was a former clutch, where thousands of issyrians once lived underwater. The darkness outside seemed to bring silence to the shuttle occupants, who passed bottled water around in the dim cab light.

Davi had never participated in a mission where he didn't know their exit details, how they were going to get off world once their work was done, and he took it as a bad sign. Being left with one squad member, Jack Kipley of all people, didn't make anything better. At a glance he could see that Kipley had fallen asleep, and Davi envied him.

The shuttle landed so softly he could only tell by the easing of the engines under his feet. Remmy handed him a water bottle and nodded. "We're on our way back, Jack. We're just transferring to another ship."

The hatch opened, and with no other options, Davi shook Kipley. "Switching transport. Almost home," he said.

Kipley roused as though from a deep sleep and repeated; "almost home." He drew deeply from a bottle Remmy handed him on his way through the hatch and said; "Almost home, Dad."

The ground was soft underfoot, and the smell reminded him of the garden pods on Freeground, after the artificial rain had soaked everything in its path. The landing lights of over a dozen shuttles were the only source of illumination. He followed Remmy and Doctor Marcelles to one at the rear, and Isabel was already climbing into the cockpit. "These are loaded with issyrians," Davi said to Remmy as he caught up.

"Yup. Everyone who had anything to do with Trest, the whole ghetto," Remmy replied.

"You and I both know that's not the deal," Davi said.

"C'mon, Lieutenant," Kipley interjected, sounding sincerely desperate. "I thought about what you said, my luck's runnin' out. There's just the two of us, and where we're going after this mission is through can't be better than where we've been."

Davi disregarded him and continued to press Remmy. "I don't know that this will work, it's not like we're dealing with Freeground, it's up to an Oversight Officer, and you know what she's like."

"No, Sam," Remmy said with a smile that was visible even in the dim light. "It's your call. You're the commander on the ground, you tell us if this goes. We'll deal with the rest once we're in the hangar." Remmy paused a moment, watching Davi closely. "So are we on, or are you pulling the plug on us?"

Davi looked at the silhouettes of issyrians hurrying between the shuttles. Emergency lights didn't let him see much. The people who would be marooned, left to the mercy of the Order of Eden if they didn't escape, looked skeletal, or as if whole pieces were missing. They were in no shape to fight a force like the Order, especially since they'd be seeking nothing more than retribution on a global scale. "We're on."

CHAPTER 28
THOSE DAMNED REFUGEES

"The scans are in and confirmed, Sir," reported the flight officer. "Seven hundred and eighty nine issyrians, many smaller signals who are most likely children, and nine humans."

Captain McPatrick tapped his finger against the bridge rail, watching the shuttles on the holoprojector with a furrowed brow. "And there's no sign that they're being pursued."

"Nothing for eight point four million kilometres. All signs say they're clear," the flight officer replied.

"Should we signal them, Sir?" asked the lead comms officer. She was an impatient one at the best of times, and her tone offered more advice than Captain McPatrick was interested in hearing. It told him that they should leave the shuttles be, offer no navnet instructions, and leave the solar system, call it a lost cause. That would irritate Freeground Intelligence, which would be gratifying for a while, but he didn't know if Anderson was ready for that kind of move.

"Put the ship on full alert, and get a full squad to the bridge. Send four squads to the main hangar. Any other ready teams should report to adjacent compartments," Captain McPatrick ordered calmly. Alarms went off across the ship, waking anyone at rest and prompting all hands to report to battle stations. "Now you can signal them." He took a deep breath and shook his head before activating his comm and entering Doctor Anderson's ident. "We've got returns and refugees coming in. I'll meet you in Forward Observation."

"And I was just falling asleep," Doctor Anderson replied. "See you there."

"Should I inform Oversight?" Captain McPatrick asked.

"She's Oversight, she should already know, shouldn't she?" Anderson asked with a smirk.

Two soldiers in full combat gear followed Captain McPatrick off the bridge. He knew that two more cloaked soldiers joined them the moment he stepped into the lift. He was never alone. Something he liked about serving on a ship like the Sunspire. What he didn't like was the amount of pointless reporting and record keeping he had to do for Oversight.

He was beginning to understand why his nephew defected. It took every scrap of effort Captain McPatrick had to remain in control of his own ship. If he stopped jumping through hoops that were presented as elective, he would start losing his command. It was what Freeground Intelligence Oversight wanted, to take control with a captain aboard so he could take the fall if anything went wrong.

He accessed the latest program to hit his comm - an elective memory test. That morning the program had read several different expressions to him, and he was to recite them if prompted. "Expression," he said.

"A bird in the hand?" asked his comm.

"Is worth two in the bush," he answered. "Next."

"Friend?" it asked.

He thought a moment, not recalling what the computer was talking about. He could guess the expression, but it was a memory test, and guessing wrong could be worse than not guessing at all.

"Friend?" it repeated.

Then he remembered. "One old friend is better than two new ones." The door opened as he said it, and Wheeler stepped inside.

"That's good, never heard it before," Wheeler said. "Where's it from?"

"These God damned tests Oversight has me taking. I don't know the original context of the saying," Captain McPatrick said. "Sorry."

"Electives," Wheeler said. "I've been doing them ever since I came aboard. Trying to get that crap out of the way so they can check me back into service the moment I deliver."

"I don't think you have a shot, doesn't matter what you're offering. Freeground won't take you back, they're exiling, not recruiting. But that's just my thoughts on it."

"Want to put your credits where your opinion is?" Wheeler replied, smiling. It was impossible to put the smug man off. McPatrick liked him less with every passing moment. "If you bet a thousand I'll tell you what I'm trading."

"Testing me," Captain McPatrick scoffed. "Presenting me with a decision that Oversight will review - whether or not I take the opportunity to pay an informant for information."

"What's the right decision according to the regulations, old horse?"

"Commander's choice if it doesn't directly pertain to the mission, essential if it does," Captain McPatrick looked Wheeler in the eye with a stare that normally made seasoned officers' palms sweat. The aggravating traitor didn't flinch. "I'll take your bet. What are you trading?"

"Information straight from Order of Eden Command," Wheeler replied.

"What about Regent Galactic?" asked McPatrick.

"Regent Galactic was completely taken over by the Order a month ago, when a freak called Meunez got himself jacked into their primary network. It's all one incestuous organization now, most call it a religion."

"I can't say that was worth the bet," Captain McPatrick said.

"Oh, that's not all," Wheeler said. "As a sign that I'm really dedicated to rejoining the upper ranks of Freeground Intelligence, I've signed my claim on the Triton over to Fleet Command."

"Jacob Valent's ship?" Captain McPatrick said, knowing that it would get a rise out of the other man. The guards behind him were loving the exchange, but kept quiet. "I heard about that. Don't believe you'll go through with it though."

"My ship," Wheeler snapped. "Taken directly from Sol Defence about thirty years ago. They let it go then, that makes it mine."

"I'm sure if we had a Sol Defence officer aboard, they would have something to say about that."

"That's the thing, isn't it?" Wheeler replied. "Sol Defence has been out of the picture for centuries, keeping to their own small part of the galaxy. I'd say that makes anything taken across their boarders free and clear. When the Carthans fail to get in touch with anyone there, and realize that they have a token that will earn them an ally in Freeground thanks to yours truly."

"The Carthans, or you, or Valent, someone will derail that deal," Captain McPatrick said. "It'll never happen."

"Ah, it's Valance now, Valent is dead and his replacement is rotting on a moon a couple of sectors over. You really should try to keep up, your age is showing," Wheeler said. "Getting back to the point, it doesn't matter if the deal doesn't go through because it's all Freeground Intelligence's problem now. I've signed on the dotted line, as they used to say."

Captain McPatrick decided that the conversation had gone on long enough. If Wheeler was tethered to Freeground Intelligence, then McPatrick had to weigh everything he said around him carefully.

"Cat got your tongue?" Wheeler pressed.

To the Captain's relief, the lift doors opened. "Damn thing's running too slow," he muttered as he exited. Observation One was only a few metres down the broad, polished silver and grey hallway. The double doors opened to the largest leisure space on the ship. He had ordered it turned into a galley. The bar had been split in half. One part was converted into a matter recycling station, the other was rebuilt as a row of ration dispensers. The attached lounges had been turned into Officer's Mess compartments. He couldn't abide the playground mentality of the previous design, and the new version of the observation section still pleased him to no end. It said something about the Sunspire: this is not the ship Jonas Valent abandoned. This is a ship of duty and honour. There was no more important message, as far as Captain McPatrick was concerned, especially since they were forced to ferry traitors and exiles around.

It had been a short trip, and Captain McPatrick only had four months with the new crew of the Sunspire, but they had shown him their dedication and a high level of competence. That's why, when a squad of soldiers escorted Omira, the thing that Doctor Marcelles had become, Remmy, Isabel, Mary, Davi, and Kipley into the main Observation Deck shortly after he arrived there, his mood soured even more.

As Captain McPatrick wordlessly followed the large group into one of the two dimmer, more well furnished Officer's Messes, he looked them up and down. It looked like they had just been in a fire fight. They were all battered and ragged, even Isabel, who he guessed only found herself on the front lines by bad luck or force. He tried not to stare at Doctor Marcelles; his dark amber armour and dark skin gave him a sleek appearance, but he still looked like an error in genetics to McPatrick. He was a walking mess of a hybrid, a freak with no business being alive.

"It is good to finally meet you, Captain," Doctor Marcelles said, starting to approach from across the room.

Captain McPatrick only held up his hand in response, and two of his soldiers stepped between him and the doctor as though they were an extension of his arm. "We're waiting for someone."

"Ah," replied Doctor Marcelles. "It's like that, then."

Wheeler didn't waste time. He walked around the soldiers and offered his hand. "Welcome, Doctor Marcelles."

"Thank you, mister Wheeler," Marcelles said, shaking the man's hand with a smile.

Obviously surprised, Wheeler took a step back, looked Doctor Marcelles up and down, then nodded to himself and rejoined Captain McPatrick. Doctor Anderson entered and nodded at Remmy first, then took everyone else in. "Lieutenant Davi, report," he ordered.

Davi stepped towards Doctor Anderson and snapped to attention. "In brief, Doctor Marcelles would not return with us unless we assisted him in contaminating the planet's atmosphere with a compound that would destroy the Order of Eden's ecosystem transforming forests. Since our orders were to retrieve the target using any means necessary, we proceeded. After the mission was complete, the doctor would not return with us unless we brought the rest of his people with him. I was sure the Order of Eden were looking for us, and I did not have much time to debate the finer points of the target's extraction, so I decided more was better than none at all, and have brought the issyrian refugees aboard with Doctor Marcelles."

Captain McPatrick watched Davi as he rendered his report and, without the assistance of a comm unit scan, decided the lieutenant was telling the truth. Davi had a habit of delivering, of completing objectives, and it was good to see he didn't disappoint.

"I'm not sure you've brought us Doctor Marcelles, Lieutenant," Wheeler said with a grin that Captain McPatrick would love to wipe off his face. "The first time I met Doctor Marcelles, I had him practically dissected alive aboard the Triton." He looked around the room for a moment before going on. "How did it happen, Clark? And where is the good doctor?"

For a moment Captain McPatrick couldn't believe what Wheeler was saying, but a glance at Remmy, who was turning deep red, and Mary, whose hand was in search of a sidearm that was taken from her when she boarded told him that Wheeler's judgement was spot on. While it was useful to have someone there who was so astute, it was frustrating that it was Wheeler, the ultimate traitor. "Out with it," Captain McPatrick said. "I need to hear this."

"Marcelles was found dead aboard the Fallen Star," the human-issyrian thing replied. His face slowly shifted, the features becoming that of Clark Patterson as he spoke. "When we entered the vault the ship tried to connect with the framework circuitry Intelligence put in my head, and if it weren't for Omira, the neural circuit would have killed me. She used technology in the ship's lab to implant the last version of the framework technology. It took days, but the upgrades stuck, and I came out feeling like myself again."

"But not looking like yourself," Captain McPatrick added.

"I looked perfectly human at first. After we returned to Trest, I swam in the spawning pool as an initiation into the issyrian House there, and the framework technology adapted so I could communicate with them." To Captain McPatrick's surprise, Clark Patterson seemed almost overcome with emotion, and found it difficult to continue. There was something going on that could change the course of the future forever if they let it. How things would shift would be up to whoever was allowed to leave that room alive.

Clark finally went on. "The sadness I found there was as deep as my own for the murder of my sister. The difference between us was simply that they didn't feel the outrage I did. That was, until they were exposed to me. I didn't know it at first, but issyrians don't feel what we call anger often. Persistant disruptive emotions are enough to get you exiled from your House, sent out of the clutch. So, even in the worst cases, there are normally limits to how far an issyrian will take revenge, if they bother at all. Their instincts are to rebuild, reinvent themselves. When they felt my anger towards Freeground Intelligence for killing my sister, and for what the Order of Eden were doing to their world, at how trapped I felt in our missions, they began to learn what it was to be furious."

"That is why I didn't tell you what would happen when you entered the pool," Omira said. "The aggression and other negative emotions that normally lead to disharmony in a clutch are too mild to affect the change you've brought to the issyrian people here. Normally, exposing them to human anger would be a tragedy, but not here, not where they are dying and defenceless. They needed that outrage to survive."

"The youngest became almost feral," Clark went on. "The elders in the spawning pool were able to calm them, but the fighting instinct will always be there. As for the rest, well, they became warriors, and more issyrians joined me over the next week. I learned from them too, and since I have full control over this version of the framework tech, I was able to adapt, to create a warrior class of issyrian. For the first time in thousands of years, the issyrians have a warrior caste, and from the ashes of Trest they will rise and found a Great House."

"Ashes?" Wheeler asked, alarmed for the first time. "I thought you were looking to restore Uumen so issyrians could rebuild their colonies."

"The Order of Eden will enact a scorched earth policy, reducing Uumen to barren rock, but not before they have analyzed the canister used to deliver the toxins into their atmosphere. It's of Freeground design," Clark said. "It's time for Freeground to get involved with the war, whether they like it or not."

"You son of a bitch!" screamed one of the soldiers. Captain McPatrick gestured towards the lunging soldier and two more held him back. If he gave the order to blast Clark Patterson to pieces, Captain McPatrick was sure it would be followed without hesitation. That wasn't the wise course, but it was the one he'd rather see followed.

"Freeground has been on the galactic sidelines for too long," Clark said. "It's time for the Freeground Nation to wake up and see everything humanity and the other races have done out here, the good and the bad. If they don't open their borders and their minds, Freeground will descend from stagnation to extinction. Whatever good we have to offer the universe will simply disappear. Freeground will be just one of a hundred lost civilizations that are a minor footnote in history."

"This isn't about progress, it's about revenge," Doctor Anderson said.

"No, leading the Order of Eden to this ship was about revenge. The Sunspire, and everything it's come to represent under the oversight of the Puritan Party is an insult to the legacy of this vessel. A legacy your nephew was an important part of," Clark said to Captain McPatrick, who bristled at being singled out. "Terry Ozark McPatrick won't welcome you with open arms if you survive to see him, not after discovering that you're letting Freeground Intelligence Oversight tell you how to run your ship. A trap he didn't let himself wither in."

Captain McPatrick had heard enough. "Take him and everyone else into custody. Signal the helm to execute a retreat course."

With inhuman speed and power, Clark Patterson struck the guards nearest to him, driving them back into the soldiers holding position at their rear. Isabel, Mary, and Remmy were ready. They sprinted for the lifts just down the hall. Captain McPatrick stepped over a recovering soldier and drew his sidearm.

"Stun!" Doctor Anderson shouted.

With Remmy dead in his sights, he flipped his weapon's switch from kill to stun and downed the former Intelligence Officer. He took a shot at Mary, but she made it into the lift just in time.

"Disable the lifts," Captain McPatrick ordered.

"Too late, the express lift has already activated. They're already in the launch bay," replied an officer from the bridge. "And we're-"

"Then vent the atmosphere, lock the ships and emergency vacsuit stations down," McPatrick replied.

"Yes, Sir. There's something else, Sir; we're picking up incoming signals. At least four squadrons of fighters and several gunships. They're blocking our retreat course."

"Here we go," Captain McPatrick said to himself. "Launch alert fighters from the aft bay, and send security down to the auxiliary launch bay. I want those traitors taken, dead or alive."

"Tell your bridge staff not to vent the launch bay. I need that next generation framework, and the others will be important to Intelligence," Wheeler countered.

"You can have that one," Captain McPatrick said, gesturing to Remmy as soldiers rolled him onto a collapsable gurney.

"He has nothing to do with framework tech," Wheeler replied. He tapped his comm unit several times as he strode out of the observation deck. "I'll just have to do this myself."

"Sir, someone has taken control of the environmental and launch controls of the auxiliary bay," announced a bridge officer in Captain McPatrick's ear. He watched as the door closed behind Wheeler. He gestured towards it, commanding it to open and there was no response.

"Let him go," Doctor Anderson said. "We follow him, and we keep ourselves tangled in whatever he's cooking with Oversight. I bet he's headed off the ship."

"I hope you're right," Captain McPatrick replied. "Today is getting worse by the second."

CHAPTER 29
FULL CIRCLE

They were being allowed to leave. That was the only conclusion Clark could come to as they emerged from the express tube and didn't see any soldiers. That would change quickly.

As they ran between the hastily landed shuttles they'd come in, Clark could feel the collective relief of the issyrians who had followed him. The hatches were open, the sounds of their footfalls echoed in the cavernous landing bay. The shuttles were already half empty.

When Clark completed the transformation from human to advanced framework, he inherited all the research Doctor Marcelles had been doing on the physiology of issyrians. How framework technology and their vastly different race crossed over was remarkable, and as soon as they returned to Trest, he followed through with an experiment that Doctor Marcelles himself was afraid to conduct. He waded into the issyrian home spawning pool and allowed his framework body to begin a cycle of assimilation and transformation.

The issyrians welcomed him, and after a painless transformation he gained the ability to communicate with them chemically. In trade for the secrets of their race and the ability to incorporate enough of the issyrian physiology to become something far more than human or framework, he gave them his rage, his need for revenge, and the desire to fight. With Omira's assistance, Clark and the issyrians formulated a plan.

The plan, eventually perfected by Remmy who made a few devious changes, would firmly implicate Freeground Intelligence, and would violently transform the wild life of Uumen so it could become much more like a primordial version of the issyrian home world. It would also deliver them to the Sunspire, so they could take advantage of one of the greatest secrets held by the issyrian race.

They could disappear. Only focused scans would be able to detect them once they began to shift the pigment of their skin to redirect light and lowered their body temperatures to match their environment. An issyrian doesn't even have to breathe for hours, even days if they are carrying the right liquid nutrients. As Clark ran towards the lift holding the Sunspire's compliment of new high speed cloak ships, he knew he was surrounded by issyrians.

"We don't have Remmy," Isabel said. "How are we going to take three ships without him? We need a third operator."

"We'll have to take two instead," Clark replied. "There won't be much breathing room."

"It's doable," Mary replied. "We're not moving in anyway."

Clark watched for any indication that the Sunspire crew realized that they weren't headed to their own shuttles but to the rare high speed cloak ships. An invisible issyrian pressed a ripper into his hand, and by the time he looked up, the lighting in the bay went out.

"They're about to flood this deck with soldiers," Mary announced. "Everyone got their eyes on?"

"One sec," Isabel said, stopping.

Clark collided with her, and picked her up in his arms instead of stopping. He had no problem seeing in near complete darkness. "Get the rest of the issyrians out of the shuttles and moving to the new ships."

"Yes, Sir," replied one of the invisible issyrians behind him.

"What about Remmy?" Isabel asked him quietly. She had her environmental mask on, and could see his face in the sparse light.

He made an effort to make his face look as much like it did when he was human as he could. "He's on his own. You know him, he'll weasel his way through," he answered.

"You're probably right," she replied dubiously.

Clark put Isabel down at the rear of the shuttle. An instant after her feet touched the deck, the Sunspire soldiers began their incursion. It wasn't a blind assault, but well directed and fierce. Hatches opened in all directions and several squads descended from the ceiling. Dozens of ill issyrians were caught in the open and cut down in the first seconds. Clark found it difficult to adjust to the strobing white light of their weapons, but focused on the points of flashing light even as he caught a round in the side. The framework technology regenerated the skin over the wound, and his issyrian biology fortified the new flesh. The side of the high speed cloak ship was strafed several times by intense fire as they got the hatch open and he marvelled at his luck. The barrage of heavy rounds missed him, and missed Mary, who moved inside the shuttle fleetly.

Then he looked down and saw Isabel's legs. Before he could stop himself he reached down for the rest of her, and touched what remained. Too little to save. Several rounds tore into him from behind, nearly cutting him in half despite the density of his flesh. During the seconds it took to regenerate he almost lost himself in the outrage he felt at losing her, but a voice drew his attention away.

"Clark! We need you in here!" Mary shouted. "We have to go now or it'll never happen."

He looked towards the ragtag shuttles that they'd arrived in and watched as two out of three issyrians were blasted to pieces by the Sunspire soldiers. They had their orders - to kill these traitors, deal with this situation so it could be resolved before the Order of Eden ships arrived. Clark tore himself away, knowing that he would have given the same order during his old life, the life in which he'd known Isabel and Remmy.

Instead of climbing aboard the cloak ship, he let his instincts lead him to the fight. From one hand he grew predatory claws, with the other he set his ripper on high. In a few swift leaps he was amongst the soldiers firing at the issyrian civilians, and he fired his ripper at point blank, weakening armour. His claws plunged into human bodies while the ripper tore into soldier after soldier.

Humans were shadows compared to issyrians. He pretended like Mary, Isabel, and even Remmy mattered as much as they did when he was simply human, but, in truth, they didn't. Limited by verbal communication, humans were less important than any issyrian, who he could feel, taste, and smell even metres away. The soldiers he slashed, eviscerated, and ultimately obliterated were shadows in the dusk - insubstantial and immaterial. He leapt away from them before the last two lost their feet.

Human medicine would save most, but they would never forget how it felt to have his claws tear through their bellies, across their backs or throats. Just like he would never forget Isabel, and how she reminded him of what he was before his transformation.

CHAPTER 30
THE EXILE

Remmy opened his eyes and sat up hurriedly. It took him seconds to get a read on the situation. He was in a one man cell in the brig. It was one of the nicer ones, thankfully, with a padded cot, blankets, a sink and toilet. There weren't many classy units aboard the Sunspire, and the full length transparent steel door told him that he'd been dropped into one. The question was, why?

"Welcome back," said the voice of Lieutenant Davi.

Remmy stood and walked to the door so he could see across the hall, where Davi sat up on his cot. "My head doesn't hurt," Remmy said. "I'm not even fuzzy-brained. I'd think that after a stun like that-"

"You'd have a roaring headache under these lights? Maybe get stun sick?" Davi asked. "We both got the royal treatment when we were checked in."

"What did you do?" Remmy asked.

"I tracked Wheeler down as he was leaving, tried to detain him. Guess that's not what the commanders here had in mind."

"Why chase after him at all?"

Davi leaned back in his bunk and rubbed his face before answering. He looked tired, worn thin. "You know, after watching most of my team get wiped out, one get checked into psych, and not knowing what comes next, I just wanted some answers. Wheeler seemed like the guy who has 'em. I mean, he picked Clark out in ten seconds, and I couldn't do it in three days."

"Not like we let you anywhere near him unless we had to," Remmy said. "Don't put yourself down, man."

"I just wish I was the guy with all the answers for once. I've been following orders for as long as I can remember," Davi said. "I don't know how, but Wheeler knew exactly when to be here, and he made sure he was gone by the time the Sunspire had to make a break for it." Davi shook his head. "At least he took Kipley with him. He was my last man, but having him around was worse than being alone."

"Why'd he take your broken wheel?" Remmy asked, surprised and still trying to get a whole picture of what was going on.

"The last thing he told me was, 'you still owe me an officer' and Kipley was stupid enough to go along."

"Well, better off ship than on your back," Remmy said. "The Order are after the Sunspire?"

"Affirmative," Davi replied. "Your people got off clean and free. Went straight into that magnetic storm and disappeared. Wheeler was right behind, though. Shannon and two of her Intelligence lackeys just finished my interrogation and exit interview. I'm in Captain McPatrick's hands now."

"I bet you're in for a nice, short stay in the brig," Remmy said. "You followed orders, brought someone you thought was Marcelles back. I'm pretty sure the Captain will set you up aboard somewhere if he's not being mind-controlled by Intelligence. Did you happen to overhear their plans for me?"

"I didn't hear a thing," Davi said. "But if you ask me, you're either in for some serious interrogating or Anderson has an assignment in mind for you. If there weren't plans-"

"Then they wouldn't have gone to the trouble of treating my stun-aches and taking a little tender care putting me in here," Remmy finished. "I feel better than I have in weeks."

They sat silently for several minutes, and Remmy found himself taking comfort in the knowledge that Clark, Mary, Isabel, and the rest of the issyrians most likely made it to the Fallen Star.

"Remmy," Davi said.

"No one else here, is there?" Remmy replied.

"Actually, there are a few others from other squads like ours," Davi replied. "But they're way down the block."

"Oh, so insubordination isn't as uncommon as I thought."

"Apparently Clark's squad and mine were two of the best," Davi said. "But I've got to ask, what really happened on the Fallen Star the first time you boarded?"

"Most of the record is dead on," Remmy replied. He looked up at the flat, beige ceiling. "I hope someone's recording this, because I hate repeating myself." He turned his attention back to Davi and continued. "Things get sketchy once the lab computers in the Fallen Star managed to deactivate the implants Intelligence put in Mary, Isabel, and me. They put something different in Clark, and it reacted badly, started to shut Clark down, or put him into a coma or something. Omira stepped in. We managed to kill a bunch of those big bugs and seal up a part of the lab while she got a framework seed ready. The thing looks like a pill, but it's got enough nanobots and crazy techno mojo in it to turn someone into a framework in a few seconds. I don't understand it, but it looked like Clark was being torn up on the inside. I've never heard anyone scream like that."

"Omira did it while he was awake?" Davi asked.

"There was no time to put him out," Remmy said. "I wish there was, though. There are some things you don't want to see, to hear, and that's one."

"What about the body you delivered?"

"Just a construct. That's a walk in the park for someone like Marcelles," Remmy replied.

"So you did find Doctor Marcelles on the Fallen Star," Davi concluded.

"Right, that's another thing I had to alter a bit in the record. Omira is Doctor Marcelles. He made a lot of changes when he decided it was time to change his appearance," Remmy replied. "Or should I say, when she changed her appearance. Where is she now?"

The cell block hatch opened and Doctor Anderson entered with two security guards. "She's missing. We think she's using a cloak suit, but there's no way to be certain. Do you think she returned to the Fallen Star, Remmy?"

"No, she got what she wanted there. Her research is more important than the ship," Remmy replied. "Even more important than the issyrians, now that the Order have been set back a few decades."

"What did she want from the Fallen Star?" Anderson asked as the security guards opened Davi's cell door.

"Just a copy of all the data in the vault," Remmy replied.

213

"Do you think you could get a channel open to the Fallen Star?" Anderson asked. "Get a link open so we could get the information?"

"Why?" Remmy asked.

Anderson seemed surprised by the question. "You know how valuable that technology is."

"To whom?" Remmy retorted, suppressing a little giddiness. "Is this ship still working for Freeground Intelligence?"

"It doesn't make much of a difference from where you're sitting," Anderson replied.

"Sure it does," Remmy said. "Just by asking me for something you've given me more power than I had a minute ago. Now I want to bargain."

"Before I know whether or not you can make a connection to the Fallen Star?" Doctor Anderson asked. "You have to give me something better."

"Sure," Remmy replied. "I can get you all the research data from that ship, no problem."

"All right, what are your terms?"

"Let me go free on a world where I have half a chance of starting over," Remmy replied. "I'm thinking I could go pretty far if I get involved with organized crime somewhere, so find me a big city, and I'll need start-up money, in local currency. Tell Freeground I'm dead. Oh, and sooner rather than later. I hear this ship is marked by the Order."

"We'll be pulling into a port in about two weeks," Doctor Anderson said. "There are a couple hundred cities that should be ripe for a crime wave."

"Speaking of ripe, I think that data you're looking for is ready," Remmy said. He let a smirk creep out. "I can connect to the Fallen Star, but there's no way I can hack into the vault computers." He held up his hand in a reassuring gesture as Doctor Anderson crossed his arms. "So it's a good thing that I made a copy of Marcelles' data collection chip, then put it in a little scan resistant pouch."

"Where did you hide it?" Anderson asked.

"Give me about five minutes with that toilet and I'll get it for you," Remmy replied. "Might be ten though, those provision bars are pretty dense."

CHAPTER 31
THE BEAST

The cloak ship in which Lucius Wheeler approached the Fallen Star was perfectly visible on sensors thanks to the storm of magnetic fields in the asteroid belt. Mary and Clark stood on the landing deck, watching the sleek ship approach through the energy barrier keeping the atmosphere stable.

"I'm leaving after we deal with this," Mary said. She waited for his response, trying to read him all the while. He'd dropped the armour he carried since he emerged from the issyrian pools for the last time. He looked almost human again, but was hairless. The bone structure of Clark's skull was off; there were inhuman spines and ridges just under the skin. She could even see them through the Freeground style vacsuit he found in their stolen shuttle. She could get used to all of it. What she couldn't accept was how impossible it had become to read him.

"I'll miss you," Clark replied flatly. "But I saw it coming."

"Did you?" She turned towards him, letting some of the anger she had been holding for days, weeks, seep through the cracks. "From what I've seen recently it doesn't even look like you're interested. We just lost Izzie and I didn't see you so much as flinch."

"I took revenge," Clark replied. "She was the only thing that kept me connected to humanity."

"Really?" Mary retorted hotly. "Then why the fuck did you let her believe that everything you felt for her ended when Omira erased the Freeground programming?"

"That's not what-"

"Not what you told her?" Mary shouted. "I know, you told her you still loved her, but you kept drifting away. She was in my arms crying at night when she should have been in yours."

"I didn't know," Clark replied calmly. "I'm sorry."

"I'm still not making a dent here, am I?" Mary looked to the nearest issyrian soldier. "Next time you're in the pool with him, make sure you say goodbye for me. I don't think human speech even computes anymore. Excrete it for me." Mary returned her attention to Clark. "So this is me, saying goodbye. I can't wait for this wanker to land, I'm sure you can take care of it." She stared at him for a moment longer before turning away and striding towards a slip ship. "Why the hell do I have to remember you like this? It's worse than seeing you in a casket."

* * *

Clark didn't let her see how her last jab injured him. It was the only thing in her rant that did. He remembered his friend Mary as if it were a fading dream, the person who was standing beside him the moment before was a shade. Anything that had to rely on speech to communicate seemed so distant, humans were the worst. Mary could never live up to the memories he had of her, and he would never feel close to a human again.

One of the issyrians near him had a gift for understanding human emotion, for recognizing their moods, and the emotions she translated from Mary in the air between them spoke of pain, anger, and sadness. 'Stop' Clark requested in return, using instinct and scent. The issyrian felt the command and obeyed. There was a point, she was trying to tell him that Mary was leaving and would never return.

He didn't bother telling the pair of issyrians behind him why he wanted that to happen. Humans would never matter to him the way they should. He would put any issyrian's life before anyone else's because they understood family better than any other race. They were chemically bonded and everyone knew their place in their House. He was starting a new House of his own, it was a clan of warriors. Humans allies would be nothing more than cannon fodder. Mary would do better on her own.

As the hatch to Mary's slip ship closed, Wheeler's ship landed. The main hatch opened as soon as the ship settled in position and Wheeler was at the forefront, walking towards him with a smile on his face. "You know, when I see a prediction come true with no deviations or complications, it still amazes me. It's like there's a tutorial running in my brain for days at a time."

"What are you talking about?" Kipley asked from his right hand side. He carried a thick-bodied pulse rifle with two secondary solid ammunition clips jutting from the top.

"I've got a few extra memories," Wheeler said, poking at his temple. "Some of them haven't happened yet."

Kipley fixed him with a look of frustrated confusion before shaking his head. "Never mind. The longer I back you up, the closer I am to giving up on straight answers."

"And you've only been working for me a few hours," Wheeler laughed. He finished crossing the distance between himself and Clark then offered his hand. "Good to see you again. Clark, wasn't it?"

"What do you mean, you have memories of the future?" Clark asked.

"Someone looked into a very old machine and saw this meeting. Then a maniac killed him, and someone gave me his memories as part of a trade," Wheeler said. "It took me a while to unlock all of it, especially the visions of the future, but I've got the key, and this moment right here is on the record." Wheeler looked over his shoulder to watch Mary's slip ship lift off and begin reversing out of the landing bay. "I saw her, and you know what? Collins, the former owner of my extra memories, was worried about where she'd end up because he thought she could be trouble." Wheeler looked at Clark and nodded. "I know within a pretty high certainty where she ends up. I'll tell you if you hear me out."

"How can you know that?" Clark asked, irritation boiling to the surface. "There's no such thing as fate."

"Dead on, no such thing as fate," Wheeler agreed. "But there is certainty, and I know for certain that she's so fed up with pulling the trigger that her sword is about to be bent into a plow. Within the year she'll sign up with an organic farming colony and will probably have dirt under her nails for the next thirty years."

"Then?" Clark asked.

"Who knows? I'm impressed that Collins checked her out that far into the future. She must have made one hell of an impression."

He still didn't believe Wheeler, but the prospect of never seeing Mary again caused a momentary pang. However, Clark found it easy to re-focus on the task at hand. "Thank you."

"You're welcome," Wheeler said. "Now, I have a proposal for you and your crew."

"Tell him to sling that rifle and I'll hear it," Clark said.

"Like hell," Kipley replied. "With all these fucking freaks?"

"You'll do it," Wheeler said. "We're surrounded anyway. I bet there are a dozen issyrians we can't see. They're shape shifters. For all you know you're standing on one."

Kipley looked around nervously, sidestepped, then slung the rifle. "Right."

"I'll keep this short," Wheeler said. "You have this ship, the knowledge of who knows how many researchers, the best framework lab in the galaxy, and you're a fresh model yourself. I can get you in touch with the top people in the Order of Eden. I know the Order needs some of what you've got, and it'll be enough to save several issyrian worlds from forced human re-colonization. I can even save Uumen from getting nuked to bare rock."

The issyrians behind him and others hidden around the landing bay all signalled one sentiment at hearing Wheeler's offer. It was a pure, unrestrained 'yes' so powerful it nearly knocked him to his knees. "You can do this?" Clark asked. He tried to use what he learned, to train his senses on Wheeler so he could feel a lie if it came. It was difficult to focus.

"Gladly. I'll gain favour with the Order, and you'll save millions, maybe billions, of your new people."

YES, said the pheromonal sentiment of every issyrian in range. Clark forced himself to breathe, their demands weighing on him. "Order the humans to start evacuating Uumen and leave the solar system. If Uumen is safe in seven days, and all the Order of Eden is gone, then you can set our course. You stay aboard the Fallen Star all the way there and until the deal is finished."

"With these squidies? No way!" Kipley burst.

"Shut it," Wheeler hissed. He turned to Clark. "You have a deal."

"How are you going to get this heap out of here? It's buried in rock," Kipley asked, probably looking for a way - any way - for him to leave the Fallen Star.

"The hull can repel everything attracted to it," replied Shillae, the sensitive issyrian. "We will rise from these stones as though they were as insubstantial as pod silt. What will our destination be once Uumen is safe?"

"Pandem," Wheeler replied. "The throne of the Order of Eden."

EPILOGUE

The blue light streaming in from the transparent wall at the fore of the main observation area faded away as they emerged from hyperspace. Remmy barely took notice of the half dozen slip ships launching from the front of the Sunspire as he poured himself a glass of outlawed scotch.

He raised the glass to the ten inch tall hologram of Isabel hovering over a small comm button. He was issued the new comm unit, a simple chip that was small enough to be housed in anything from jewelry to a vacsuit, when everyone else got theirs. He didn't know why. His name had been wiped from all duty rosters and he was listed in the general manifest as Able Crewman.

"I didn't get to know her," Davi said as he took a seat at the table across from him with a Naganto ale in hand.

Remmy waited until the point in the recording when Isabel realized she was being recorded and laughed, putting her hands up, then he downed the contents of his shot glass. It was real alcohol, contraband Scotch. Why his ancestors drank the stuff after other inebriant drinks became legal, he'd never know, but Isabel deserved a traditional toast. He casually took Davi's ale and washed the scotch down. "To people who deserved to outlive me," Remmy said as he put the half-emptied pint down.

Davi didn't even bother complaining about his stolen ale, gesturing at a passing ensign for him to fetch another. The ensign smiled and nodded as he passed. "I think you've got that in the wrong order," Davi told Remmy. "You raise a glass, toast, and then drink."

Remmy stood, regarded the off-duty crewmen filling the forward observation area and raised the mug he'd stolen. "To everyone who should have outlived me!" he shouted so loudly that, despite a crack in his voice, it was startling. As all eyes turned in his direction, he was about to take refuge in his mug. That's when they began raising their cups. Whether they contained water, juice, or something more potent, it didn't matter.

Somber nods and faces that seemed to know how he felt regarded him as the toast was quietly repeated throughout the room. "To everyone who should have outlived us!" Davi repeated as he accepted a full mug from the ensign. Without hesitation he drank to the toast and sat down. Everyone in the observation deck followed his example, even Remmy. "You're not alone," Davi said. "I lost a lot of people, a few friends."

Remmy didn't know what to say, so he made due with muttering, "thank you."

They sat quietly for several minutes before Davi stood and announced he would get them something to eat. Before he was a few steps away from the table he was stopped by a pair of soldiers. "We're under orders to escort you to the Captain's ready room, Lieutenant," the taller of the two said. "Is that Remmy Sands?"

"Nope, no Remmy here," Remmy said into his almost empty mug.

"Would you please come with us quietly, Crewman?" the soldier said.

"Well, you said please, so I guess I will just this once," Remmy replied. "I'm a little drunk, though," he warned, popping the top back on the bottle of scotch he'd traded copies of contraband news feeds for. "It might take a few drinks for the Captain to catch up." He smiled at the nearby snickers as he followed the soldiers.

The ready room was well decorated, but it didn't look like Captain McPatrick was the one who moved in, at least, not the stern Captain McPatrick who stood behind his desk. Pictures of the First Light crew and of the ship when she was doing that tour were on the wall behind the desk. This was still Terry Ozark McPatrick's office, as far as appearances were concerned. The decision to play the fool as he faced the current Captain McPatrick and Doctor Anderson seemed to come naturally.

Remmy placed his bottle of scotch right in the middle of the captain's desk then let himself fall into the most comfortable seat in range, a lounger occupying the corner nearest to the entrance.

Doctor Anderson cocked his head at the bottle, smiling a little. "Thank you, Remmy."

Remmy casually saluted and nodded in response. "Just hoping you'll join me in celebrating my exit from the service."

"I might, at that," said Captain McPatrick, whose tone carried no levity. "You are the only member of your team who hasn't been declared dead or missing in action."

That got Remmy sitting straight. "But Mary and Clark are out there. Isn't the Sunspire chasing them right now?"

"While I'd like to clean up Clark Patterson personally, as a matter of family pride, that would take this ship into dangerous territory," Captain McPatrick replied.

"Family pride?" Remmy said.

"He's a younger cousin, distant enough to be off the books, thank the stars," McPatrick said. "The last thing my family needs is another disgrace. I was hoping Clark would actually do the opposite, maybe bring some honour back to my line, but you know what happened instead better than anyone."

"We're not here to mourn your family honour, Captain," Doctor Anderson said. "I'm sure if Remmy could have done anything to turn events in another direction he would have."

"Damn straight," Remmy replied. "Clark may have been stiff, but he was a good guy, and didn't deserve what happened."

"On that, we agree," Captain McPatrick said.

"We're here," Doctor Anderson said. "To tell you both why you're going into isolation in secure quarters for the next two weeks."

"You're giving us a time out to think about what we've done?" Remmy asked.

"It's for your own protection," Captain McPatrick said through clenched teeth. "Idiot."

"We just set course for the Rega Gain system, where you'll be released," Doctor Anderson said.

"We're going to pay Tamber a visit," Remmy said, brightening at the notion. It was a truly free world, and where the remnants of the First Light crew officers were last known to be.

"We're not making a social call," Captain McPatrick said. "We are going because Freeground Intelligence has withdrawn their officers, disavowed the Sunspire and her crew. The Rega Gain system is one of the only places we know of that will welcome us."

"Because we already have people on Tamber," Remmy said.

"We can't even trust that," Captain McPatrick said. "We're answering a call from the Carthans. They're looking for any able fighting vessels to sign up, and we're going to investigate the opportunity to engage."

"If I may ask, Sir," Davi said. "Why are we being placed in protective isolation?"

"Because there is a chance that the crew will blame your teams for giving Intelligence a reason to write off this ship," Captain McPatrick said.

"Give them more credit," Remmy said. "They're going to realize that it was their plan from the start. The Puritan Party gave this mission a go ahead because it allowed them to put all their political enemies in the same boat then send them adrift. Even if we were successful, Intelligence would have found a way to make it look like a failure."

"Maybe," Captain McPatrick said, cutting off Doctor Anderson just as he was about to speak. "But over the last nine years this ship and her crew have failed in their mission or been defeated in the field every time she's left space dock. Some of the crew are starting to call her cursed, so I might just put the notion that everything that's happened is your fault as a lesser evil."

"With senior officers like you, who needs enemies?" Remmy asked casually. "I'm surprised you don't just let me run around the ship as a sacrificial lamb. Anything to prevent a mutiny, right?"

"I won't have it on my ship," Captain McPatrick said. "Intelligence Oversight is gone, so now this boat runs by my book. That book says crewmen don't shoot each other in the back, so you're both going into isolation in secure quarters until we can dump your asses off on Tamber. I don't like what happened to your teams, and I don't trust you enough to reassign you. We'll give you some money, a gun, some supplies, and you are on your own. Now, go with the security officers outside. They'll escort you to the bunks you'll call home for the next twelve days."

Davi snapped to attention and saluted. Remmy got to his feet, reclaimed his bottle, and headed for the door. Doctor Anderson caught up to him just as the guards on the other side started walking him and Davi to their new quarters. "Remmy, hold a moment."

"Can I interest you in a drink, Doctor?" Remmy asked.

"Maybe later," he replied. "But in case I don't get a chance to visit before we drop you off on the Tamber Moon, I have some information that could help." Davi stepped in close at Doctor Anderson's urging gesture. "I'll make sure they drop you off in Port Rush, where you can get in contact with Ayan Rice. If you want to join her crew, all you have to tell her is Doctor Anderson sent you, and if she has any doubts, play this for her." He sent a music file to Remmy and Davi's comm units - Vivaldi's Four Seasons.

"I'd rather listen to Stonemark, but to each their own," Remmy said.

"Trust me, she'll know that music is from me, especially the first Concerto."

"Thank you, Doc," Remmy said. "Any other advice?"

Doctor Anderson regarded them both and, after a moment's thought spoke. "Never forget that you did the best you could to help strangers when most of us would have run."

"Even you, Doc?" Remmy asked.

"I'll be finding out soon enough," Doctor Anderson replied.

www.ingramcontent.com/pod-product-compliance
Lightning Source LLC
Chambersburg PA
CBHW060918250626
47159CB00008B/3069